Amy Maxwell's 2nd Chance

Heather Balog

Amy Maxwell's 2nd Chance
Heather Balog

Cover design by: Blurbs and Baubles
ISBN: 979-8-9899382-0-9

Published 2024 by Bad Mommy Books
Published in the United States of America

To my family...the ones who love me unconditionally...and the friends who are like family. Thanks for not having me committed when I tell you about my latest book idea.

PROLOGUE

Okay Amy, you need to focus. Close your eyes.

Now, imagine a meadow. A green, lush meadow with long blades of grass. Imagine you're lying in the meadow on your back. No, don't worry about the grass stains, just relax. You see the white fluffy clouds overhead? Look at those clouds and inhale and exhale slowly. Watch the clouds pass overhead. As they drift by, you will feel yourself getting calmer and calmer with each passing cloud.

Repeat until calm. Repeat until calm. Repeat until calm! Why aren't you calm? This is supposed to make your heart rate slow. Supposed to ease your stress. Stop your spiraling panic.

Why the hell isn't it working?

Stop.

You can do this. You've done this more times than any normal person should ever have to. You've gotten out of more jams than a traffic helicopter. Which is exactly why you're in this situation to begin with. It's your uncanny knack for getting in and out of snafus that's led you down this path—trapped in the basement of the library. I mean, the library, Amy! There's no place more benign on earth, and somehow, you've managed to make this the place you'll meet your maker! How do you do it?

No.

I refuse to believe this is the end. There is some way out of this, and I will find it. But um, God, I could use a little help here. Could you maybe show me the way? And I don't mean to *you. I definitely don't want to see you in person right now, no offense. I need a way out of this mess.*

I will, in fact, vow to become a nun and join a convent if I get out of this one. Seriously, God...I will not let myself get sucked into murder and mayhem ever again. I will be the best damn nun you've ever seen, God.

Oh wait. I don't think nuns can curse. Not that damn *is really a curse per se, but I doubt it's something they're supposed to be saying. Wait...do they have to take a vow of silence? I don't think I can take a vow of silence. In fact, I* know *I can't take a vow of silence.*

No, wait. I'm wrong.

It's monks who take a vow of silence. I'd be okay talking as a nun. But they probably don't want me. I mean, why would they? I'll probably bring a plague of locusts upon their parish or something with the luck I have. Is it a parish? Is that what you call a church that nuns work at? I probably should have this information figured out before I apply to the nunnery.

Although, I couldn't apply until all the kids are grown. There's no way Roger can get those demon seeds out of the house in the morning without having a stroke. Ugh. I don't think I can become a nun. Sorry, God. I'll have to make another deal with you.

Ooo! How about I give up technology? Specifically,

listening to podcasts? That would have been a good thing to give up say, a month ago. If I hadn't become a podcast-listening junky, I would not be in this predicament. Although, one hardly knows where one's decisions will ultimately lead them. Life is just a series of decisions. We can't foresee where we will end up because of those choices. Some regrets are inevitable. It's just a fact of life. We often don't realize we've made the wrong decision until it's too late.

Like the choice to go to my high school reunion. If I could just go back to that day in February when I decided to go, I wouldn't be here right now. I know that *for sure.*

CHAPTER ONE

The door opens and I glance up from my ledger. It's a guy, a lot older than I am. He has really dark, slicked-back hair, and he's wearing a leather jacket. It's slightly unzipped and I can see a white tee shirt peeking out underneath. He has his hands stuffed in his pockets like a tough guy, but I can tell by the way that he's standing that he's nervous. Really nervous.

"Are you the girl who solves the mysteries?" he asks me.

I point to the placard on my desk that reads, Lexie Maxwell, Ace Detective. *"That's me," I confirm.*

"Good. I'm Joe Mack. I called earlier. I've got a mystery for you," he tells me.

"I remember," I say as he unzips his leather jacket all the way before reaching inside. I jerk back for a second, thinking it's a gun, but he pulls out a manila envelope from the inside pocket. He places the envelope on my desk and slides it toward me.

"This is her," he says. "She's been missing since last week."

I open the envelope and pull the glossy sheets out, handling them with care, making sure I only touch the edges and don't leave fingerprints. I stare at the colored photographs, admiring her hair shining in the sun.

"She's beautiful." I tell him. And I mean it. I've never seen a dog with such a shiny coat.

"Thanks," he says gruffly. "She was stolen out of my front yard on Thursday."

**

As I vacuum the crumbs that one of my boys has managed to mash into the low pile rug we have in the den, I am rereading the first book in the Lexie Maxwell series, the one I wrote with Lexie last year. Writing the first and second book in the series was a cakewalk, but now that I've gotten the hang of writing a children's series, I've seemed to have forgotten how to actually do it.

This morning when I sat down to write, I spent an hour staring at the screen until it occurred to me: *Maybe if I reread the first two books, an idea will come to me.* Hence why I am in the process of running the vacuum cleaner over the same spot repeatedly and staring into the pages of a book, much like my teenage self used to when I was forced to do chores and all I really wanted to do was read.

The front door slams and I'm shaken out of my stupor by the sound of feet thundering up the stairs.

"I'm home!"

Shaking the fog out of my head, I glance at the clock. It's three o'clock, so school must be out, and Lexie is home.

"Thank god," I mutter to myself, switching off the vacuum and trotting up the stairs to the kitchen to grab my laptop. Jeter, our golden retriever, is sleeping under a kitchen chair and is startled by my sudden movement, which he seems to think indicates that I am going to start dropping treats all around. He is hot on my heels faster than you can say *gravy train*, almost tripping me up as I head toward the stairs in search of Lexie.

"For heaven's sake, Jeter," I chastise, steadying myself by grabbing the banister. "Go lie down before you kill me with your antics."

He plops his fluffy rear end down on the floor at the bottom of the stairs and gazes up at me plaintively. He stays put while I climb the stairs, but whines softly, as if this whole scenario has broken his heart.

I roll my eyes at his drama, heading toward Lexie's room. The door is wide open—a surprising plot twist when living with teenagers.

"Hey, how was sc—" I start to say as I walk into her room, but then stop when I see Lexie lying flat on the floor, one hand and part of her head underneath the bed, her body sticking out and wiggling like a snake. "What are you doing?"

"Looking for my library book," comes her muffled response. "It's due today and I can't find it. I swear I left it on my desk this morning. It was *The Art of Racing in the Rain*." She pulls her head out from under the bed and looks up at me. "Have you seen it?"

I cringe as I recall the remains of a book that I found in my rose bushes this morning. Jeter had torn the cover off and chewed ninety percent of the pages, so I couldn't even tell what it was, but now that I think about it, it looked a lot like a library book. And it is totally my fault he had it because I left Lexie's door open after I was in there looking for my flip-flops that I thought she might have taken. Turns out that was Jeter as well—he is obsessed with my left flip flops. This is the second library book of Lexie's that Jeter has chewed, and if she finds out, she may have a nervous breakdown like last time, when she thought her library privileges would be revoked.

"Um, yeah, I saw that it was due today, so I brought it back to the library for you when I went earlier."

Okay, a little white lie. I have to remember to stop in there tomorrow and pay to replace the book, so she doesn't find out. And also so Roger doesn't find out. He didn't want Jeter to begin with and loses his mind whenever the dog does anything remotely unpleasant—like pee in his shoes. I swear he only did that once, but we can't seem to get the smell out of the closet.

"Oh, thanks," Lexie says, getting to her feet in the nimble way one can when you're seventeen and don't need supplements so that your bones don't creak before a rainstorm. She begins to sort through a stack of colored folders on her desk, frowning in the process. When she opens the green folder, she grins and grabs a sheet from the inside, slamming it closed and then heading back toward the open doorway where I am still standing.

She looks up as she almost walks directly into me. "Oh. I didn't know you were still there," she says as if

I'm a background character in her life. Which, I guess, I am.

"Um, yeah. Hey, can I talk to you for a second?" I ask as I step into her room and sit down on the edge of her bed without even waiting for her response.

"I guess," Lexie says, following me back into the room. "Everything okay?" She doesn't join me on the bed. Instead, she remains standing and crosses her arms over her chest, regarding me warily.

"Oh, yes, of course." I lightly pat the bed next to me, hoping she'll get the hint and sit down, but she just gives me an odd look and I end up pretending that I was smoothing out the comforter. I open my laptop and click on the document that I've been working on. "I just need your opinion on this scene I've been writing—"

Lexie interrupts me with a groan. "Geez, Mom, is that it?" She smacks her forehead. "The way you were acting I thought you were going to tell me someone was dead or something."

"Well, no, this is a children's series, Lex. No dead bodies."

She stares at me with an open mouth before recognition dawns.

"Not with the book!" She groans. "Listen, I don't have time for this. I'm meeting Kiara so we can study for midterms."

"Oh, of course. Well, later then?"

She holds up a hand. "No, not tonight. I have to work on the article about the winter dance for the paper."

Oh.

"Tomorrow then?" I ask hopefully.

"Can't," Lexie says, leaving the room. "I'm working tomorrow. And then I have a date after work."

"A date?" I widen my eyes. "Who do you have a date with?" *Don't say Robbie, don't say Robbie.*

"Or whatever. Not a date. I don't know. I'm just going to the coffeehouse with Robbie. It's open mic night and he thinks he's a poet or something this week." She rolls her eyes. Her on-again-off-again relationship with Robbie, a guy she met at robotics camp, is a little weird to say the least. He reminds me of George McFly from *Back to the Future* and not in a cute geeky way.

"Oh," I can barely get the words out as I watch her retreat down the stairs and back out the front door.

With a sigh, I flop on my side and sink onto Lexie's pillow, gazing at the ceiling, hoping inspiration will come. When I got the idea to write a children's series after the conference I attended where a woman was murdered back in October, I told the Roger and the kids about it…with trepidation. I figured they'd most likely make fun of me, but to my surprise, they all backed the idea wholeheartedly, especially Lexie.

The night after I brought up the idea, Lexie knocked on my bedroom door while I was reading. She hopped on my bed with a notebook, and when I asked her what it was for, she flipped it open and showed me an outline for a series she had been considering writing herself, one about a girl detective. I think my mouth dropped so low it hit the comforter.

Lexie and I went through her ideas together and I

was blown away by how good they were. This was the perfect series for *us* to write together. She was a little reluctant at first, saying she didn't really want to write the series, she didn't have time. She wanted me to take the idea and make it my own.

So initially I started writing the first book without her. But it felt weird and wrong, so soon I started asking her for her input. Could she read these pages I wrote and what did she think should happen with this plot hole I found?

As the days went on, the more I could see she actually did want to write it with me. She seemed to enjoy sitting down and working on it, coming up with new ideas and characters. She and I were both thrilled when my agent said she wanted to publish a three-book series after reading the first book we wrote together. We ended up writing the second book in less than a week, over Christmas break, and they are both set to be released before the summer.

But now it's time to write the third book in the series and I have hit a brick wall. The daughter who was so excited to write with me, has all but ghosted me in the last few weeks. Every time I think I have a chance to sit down with her and go over the plans for this last book, she has something to do. Yeah, yeah, I get it, it's her senior year and everything, and I don't want her to waste it with me, but she doesn't need to fill up every second of the day with "stuff." I'm starting to feel like she's avoiding me on purpose.

As I struggle to sit up and get off Lexie's bed,

hoping that the answer to my writing woes will fall into my lap, the answer *does* fall into my lap. Well, sort of. I jostle the bookshelf next to the bed—the one Lexie put together herself while swatting off Roger's offers of assistance because, and I quote, "I don't need a patriarchal figure to do my manual labor for me"—and it collapses under the weight of her books.

"Damn it, Lexie," I mumble, leaping to my feet, surprisingly more agilely than I thought possible, and survey the damage created by the collapsed bookshelf. A tsunami of books is sliding across the floor, creeping toward my feet like a wave on the shoreline. As I jump back to get out of the way, one title catches my eye. *How to Plot Your Children's Book.* When we decided to write this series together, Lexie ran out to buy books on how to write a book. Judging by the state of her bookshelf, it's something she does when she gets excited about anything—her form of therapy if you will. Even though she showed me the book, we never ended up reading it or even flipping through it.

I reach down and rescue the book before leaving the room, making sure to close the door this time. Lexie can deal with that mess when she gets home. I've got a book to read and a problem to solve.

CHAPTER TWO

I'm in the zone, fingers clacking away on my keyboard, when I hear my phone buzzing. I pat the pockets of my yoga pants and realize I don't have my phone with me. *Where the heck did it go?*

It buzzes again, and my eyes scan the room, trying to figure out where the sound is coming from. *Buzz, buzz, buzz*—my phone is dancing across the kitchen island.

Groaning, I lumber to my feet, my back protesting the sudden change of position . I've been stationary for all of twenty minutes, so of course my body has decided to stiffen up quicker than a corpse. After reading the first chapter of the writing book last night, I am attempting to do this crazy thing called "plotting" for the next book in the Lexie Maxwell series. I am deep in the throes of this plotting right now. Writing hopefully will come easier afterward. Well, at least that's what the book tells me.

I grab the phone off the island and flip it over in my hand, frowning when I see that it's not a text message or a phone call that's setting off all the alerts, it's a social media app notification.

"Are you frickin' kidding me? I got up for this?" I rub my lower back, trying to prevent it from seizing up on me. I have half a mind to fling my phone across the room.

But still, I've already gotten up and now I'm curious

to see what is causing such a massive influx of notifications. It has to be juicy because my phone has buzzed at least three times since I've picked it up.

I squint at the screen—another bonus of middle age has been going blind as a bat practically overnight. I've enlarged the font on the screen of my phone so many times it's like I'm reading texts one letter at a time.

I try to open the app but of course, my phone immediately retaliates against me for not updating my phone, and shuts down like a teenage girl who has been told she can't go see an R-rated movie with friends and has decided to give you the silent treatment by slamming the door in your face. Not that I know from experience or anything.

I attempt to open the app again with the same result.

Maybe I should update my phone.

I reluctantly open my phone settings and press the button to update to whatever number it is this time. So annoying. Every time I get it updated, a new update comes out twelve hours later. Which is why I started refusing to do the updates. I figured I would just wait for the next three or four updates down the line.

I am immediately rejected.

Your phone does not have enough space for this update.

Since my phone is a model from about six years ago, I'm not surprised.

"This is just a ploy to get me to buy a new phone," I mutter angrily into the phone as I close it and stomp back over to my laptop. I have a cardinal rule that I'm about to break—I do not do anything on my laptop except write or work on my blog. No Facebook, no Clock app, no Amazon. Once I am on that computer, I am only allowed to use it for work. Otherwise, I seriously wouldn't ever get anything done. I'll end up ordering seasonal dish towels or blinking-light Christmas sweaters for Jeter.

I'm going to have to break that rule now. The need to know what those Facebook messages are is literally eating me alive. Okay, maybe not *literally*, but it'll drive me bonkers if I can't find out what's going on until later. I need to know *now*.

I won't be able to concentrate on work, I reason with myself as I log into Facebook on the sacred laptop and click on the messenger icon at the top of the screen.

This is better in the long run. Otherwise I'll be so distracted. And what if there's some kind of emergency? Like an inmate broke out of prison and is running around the neighborhood peeking in windows looking for—

My jaw drops when I see the reason for the massive blowup.

Hey y'all! It's Suzie Sunshine! You know, Suzie Radner from high school? Uh, huh, I actually married a guy whose last name was Sunshine...perfect for me, don't y'all think? Anyhoo...just wanted to give y'all a shout-out and invite you to THE event of the year. Guys...it's our high school reunion. Twenty-five years! And I am on the committee. Scratch that, guys. I AM the committee.

I can't even finish the message without my mind

starting to reel. First of all, *Suzie Radner.* That girl was cringe before cringe was even a word the kids were using. Her high-pitched peppy voice filled the PA airwaves every morning for four years of high school. She was on the morning announcements committee, the newspaper club, the prom committee, captain of the cheerleading squad, the drama club advisor, and the class president for four years straight. You couldn't spell school spirit without Suzie Radner. If there was a school-sponsored event or a committee to be part of, Suzie Radner was there. And she was in charge. Every. Single. Time. Mostly because people didn't want to evoke the wrath of Suzie if she didn't get her way. Or listen to her nails-on-a-chalkboard screech if she got pissed off. If she's organizing this reunion, then we're in trouble. It's going to reek of Tiger's pride.

I need something to drink if I'm going to stomach the rest of this invite.

I glance at the clock and realize it's only eleven-thirty in the morning. Wine is out of the question…drat.

I make myself some tea while simultaneously wishing it were something stronger and wondering how we are having a twenty-fifth reunion already. If I do the math then...*shit.* We've been out of school for *more* than twenty-five years. It's actually been twenty-six years. The realization that I am that old is like a sucker punch to my gut. I mean, I knew I was old. I have a kid in college for heaven's sake. But the idea that I'm old enough to be celebrating a twenty-five-year high school reunion blows my mind. I remember when my mother went to her twenty-year high school reunion.

Twentieth! That would have made her five years *younger* than I am now! And I remember looking at the pictures she had developed from the event and thinking that she and her classmates looked so old and frumpy. They had dress suits with shoulder pads and puffed sleeves. Blue eyeshadow and hair sprayed to the heavens. There's no way I could be that old and frumpy.

I glance down at my gray yoga pants with the stain near the crotch and the hole along the seam. The ones that Lexie has forbidden me to wear out in public. I'm not old and frumpy at all. I'm young and slobby. I'm not sure which is worse.

Ignoring my attire, I continue to read Suzie's message, noticing before I do, that it has seventy-one responses to it—scratch that—seventy-two now. This reunion is one hot topic. I guess I can see why. After more than two years of various stages of lockdown, we're all starved for human connection outside our families who we have seen more than enough of. At least we think we are. We're starving for human connection until about ten minutes into the "connection" and then we realize we want to throttle the person we're "connecting" with.

We would have had the reunion last year, but helloooooo, like Covid! And also, no one volunteered to help out either. Like I said, I AM the committee, but please, please reach out to me, my sweets. I would love if y'all would help me out in planning this event. I want it to be the best gosh darn tootin' reunion that this town has ever seen!

Way better than the class of '95...they had their reunion at an amusement park! Can y'all believe that?

I have to stop reading because Suzie's attitude is so sickeningly sweet it's making me want to hurl. And what the heck is with all the southern colloquialisms? Suzie was raised in Jersey with the rest of us.

I click on Suzie's profile, thinking that it'll give me some insight into her ridiculous accent—yes, I realize that I can't actually hear it in her writing, but somehow a southern accent is screaming at me through her words.

Suzie's Facebook profile looks about as carefully curated as one can possibly get. Suzie's husband is a dentist in Atlanta. She runs an art gallery. She has one daughter and one son—they look to be in their early teens—and picture after picture shows them together, all blonde and tanned with perfect, straight and white teeth.

In a pumpkin patch (#fallfun), on vacation in the Caribbean (#vacavibes), eating pizza at a pizzeria (#eatlocal), at the beach with her daughter (#girlsday), and after her son's football game (#Fridaynightlights)

Seriously, they look like the family you get when you buy photo frames. There are no pictures of her son shaving fur off the dog's tail or her daughter slamming her bedroom door so hard that it comes off the hinges. There are no pictures of her husband falling asleep in his armchair while watching reality TV, hand down his pants, potato chip crumbs dotting his beer belly, snoring like a freight train. It makes me want to vomit. Partly because I feel like it's fake, and partly because I'm worried it's not. This really is Suzie Sunshine's life. I had to know that she would eventually end up in a perfect situation—perfect husband, perfect kids, perfect life. Suzie was never in danger of becoming like me in high school.

I flip back to the original message, the one where Suzie is practically begging for help with this reunion. I can't *imagine* why no one has stepped up to help her. *Insert sarcasm here*. I never worked with her on a committee, but my friends Kelly and Brenda had, and they told me she was a nightmare control freak with a Napoleon complex. Kelly quit the prom committee because Suzie had her single-handedly crafting all the paper flowers for the tables and her hands were gnarled by the end of the first week. She had to go to physical therapy to get them to straighten out again.

Anyhoo y'all, I've taken the liberty of booking The Wine Bistro at the Stables for our reunion. It's the perfect venue—it overlooks the river and has the best food. Seriously, it is to DIE for! I had the pleasure of hosting my parents' fiftieth anniversary there and it is the BOMB! The venue can accommodate up to 300 guests as well.

Three hundred guests? What the heck is Suzie thinking? We don't need a venue that accommodates three hundred people! Our class was only 150 or 160 or something like that to begin with.

Because of the backlog from weddings being postponed, the only date that the venue was able to give me is April 1. We need a minimum of 100 guests and it will be $100 a head, for food only, cash bar. So if you decide to bring a guest, it's $200 a couple (for those of you who didn't do so well in math...LOL! J/K!)

I almost spit the tea across the table. *Two hundred dollars a couple? Is she smoking crack? And it's a cash bar to boot? Holy crap!* That's more expensive than that time Roger and I went out for our anniversary and got appetizers *and* dessert. Going to this reunion would be unnecessarily expensive.

That settles it.

I will not be going. It's too much of an expense. Besides, I'd need to lose at least twenty pounds to even show my face at this thing. Can you imagine showing up and people don't recognize you because you look like your face has been inflated with a bicycle pump? I mean, that would have to be even more embarrassing than the fact that I've done nothing with my life. And what if Libby is there? Libby Farrington was my arch nemesis in high school, and I can't even begin to fathom facing her again even under the best of circumstances, let alone looking like I do and being a loser like I am.

My finger hovers over the RSVP button. I want to hit "no," but I'm afraid. I'm afraid it looks like I'm running away or I have something to hide. Well, I do have something to hide. I'm forty-plus years old and my life is nothing like I thought it would be at this point in time. I always thought by the time my high school reunion came around, I'd *be* more, and I'd have something awesome to brag about.

I mean, yes, I have a great life. I'm not trying to sound ungrateful or anything, but some days, especially days like I've had lately when I'm struggling to come up with a plot to the book, keep my kids from going off the rails, and preventing the washing machine to go off balance yet again for the third time today—why does it always do that when I'm washing sheets?—I always wonder if there is more to my life, or this is just it.

I mean, I don't have a real job and I didn't even finish college because I couldn't hack it. When I was in high school and visualized myself going to my reunion, I'm sure there was a limo that delivered me, a gorgeous guy on my arm, a fit body in an enviable dress, and business cards to be handed out with my name embossed at the top and CEO or something at the bottom. I can only imagine how lame I would look to Libby Farrington and all her friends. I can't go to this reunion. I haven't done anything exciting with my life and it would be an embarrassment to show up, twenty pounds overweight as well.

Speaking of twenty pounds overweight, what am I going to make for dinner? I muse as I close the laptop and head over to the fridge to ponder my choices. Pulling open the fridge doors I am shocked to discover nearly barren shelves. A groan escapes my lips as I recall the shopping list I made last night and how it still sits on my nightstand because I got sidetracked by the book on how to plot. I jumped out of bed this morning and immediately started working, which is quite unlike me. I have been on a roll…and I would still be on a roll if it were not for that stupid reunion invite.

In fact, I realize as I gaze down at my slipper-clad feet, I never even changed out of my pajamas today. I mean, it's difficult to discern my pajamas from my regular clothing, considering it's all just yoga pants and hoodies, but still, I like to at least make an effort to not wear the same pajamas for more than one whole day. I usually change before lunch, but with nothing in the fridge, there's no lunch to eat. I could always have something delivered, though. I hate to do it, but I know Allie's Uber Eats log-in and she gets free delivery.

No wait, that doesn't work.

Even if I order lunch and we get takeout for dinner tonight, there isn't enough food in this fridge to get Colt through an entire night of snacking, and there definitely isn't anything for breakfast tomorrow.

Off to the grocery store I go—after I change into my going-out yoga pants and hoodie, of course.

**

"Amy? Amy Maxwell is that you?"

I am enjoying a fantasy in the middle of the produce aisle, considering the cucumbers in front of me (hey, Laura listens to smut romance novels while she's shopping, why can't I indulge in a little fantasy myself?) when I hear a voice calling my name.

I don't recognize the voice and it's pretty nondescript, aside from being decidedly female. Other than that, I have no idea who is calling my name and whether it's someone I want to talk to or someone I can't stand altogether. PTA mom or a neighbor? One of Allie or Lexie's friend's moms or someone I was in a playgroup with once? Colt's teacher or that therapist I saw briefly after being kidnapped in the Caribbean?

I don't think I really want to talk to *any* of those people, to be honest. I *could* pull my hoodie over my head and pretend I don't hear them. Or pretend I don't speak English. It's too late to make a run for it because I feel a hand on my arm.

I turn slowly to face this unknown assailant and am immediately taken aback by the fact that I truly *don't* know them.

Plan Pretend to Speak Spanish can still work, Amy!

I open my mouth to no hablo ingles when I realize I no hablo Espanol either. There's no way I can get away with that plan.

Ooo, maybe sign language? I know the alphabet and chances are this woman will have no idea what I'm fingerspelling if I move my fingers fast enough.

I have no chance to do anything though because the woman clasps her hands together and beams at me. "It *is* you!" She uses her bright blue coupon organizer to fan herself. "Imagine running into you in the produce aisle of my local grocery store! I'm so sorry I'm gushing, but I'm your biggest fan!"

This woman is a fan? A fan of what?

"Your website!" she says, answering my unspoken question. "Your post last week was spot on! I have a college-age daughter and I read it to her all the time. It is the funniest stuff, for real! I can totally relate to everything you're going through."

It takes me a minute to slide the puzzle pieces together in my head.

Your blog, dummy! She reads your blog!

"Oh well, thank you," I reply, my face turning a similar shade to the selection of apples in the bin next to me. I've gotten a lot of positive comments on my blog over the years and even a smattering of fan mail, but I've never encountered a fan out in public before. At least not one that was a virtual stranger. A few of Joey's friends and a couple of moms at the school have told me they enjoyed reading my work, but never a total stranger. I'm pretty sure I have no idea what the proper protocol is in this situation.

Do I offer to give her an autograph? Like sign the cantaloupe she has in her cart or something? Take a picture with her? Oh gosh, I hope not. I look terrible today. Oh who are you kidding, Amy...you look terrible every day.

"My sister will never believe I met you! She's going to be super jealous! She loves your blog as well. In fact, she claims *she's* your biggest fan."

"She does?"

Two random stranger fans in the same family? What

are the odds? Maybe I should play the lottery today.

"Well she isn't because I am," the woman gushes. "You're just the best! Anyway, I hate to bother you and I know you must want to get on with your shopping," the woman says as she shoves a piece of paper toward me. "but would you mind signing my grocery list?" She laughs nervously. "I wish I had a blank piece of paper."

"Um, no that's fine. Do you, um, have a pen?"

The woman frowns and pats at her pockets. "No, actually, I don't. Oh man! I can't believe this! I'm so close to getting my hero's autograph and like a dummy, I don't even have a pen!" She palms her forehead. "My sister's never going to believe me now."

"No, no, it's alright," I stammer as I dig through my own purse. "I have a pen. I always have a pen on me." I laugh nervously.

I don't look at her as I uncap the pen and quickly scribble my name at the bottom of a list of various grocery items including chocolate, Depends, evening primrose oil, and jumbo tampons. This woman must be perimenopausal as well.

She leans forward to look at it and says with a smile. "That's great. Can you put my name at the top?"

Right. Her name. Part two of autographs 101. Or probably part one. I'm such a dolt. No wonder no one ever asks me for my autograph. No, no one ever asks you for your autograph because you're not famous. This woman is probably on some sort of medication. Or in need of medication.

"Sure, what's your name?"

"Paula," she says. And she quickly adds, "I know, it's awful, but my cousin was a huge fan of *The Magic Garden* and my parents made the mistake of letting her name me."

"Oh, no it's—"

"I mean, who lets a four-year-old name a baby?" I write Paula on the top in my swirly script as she tells me this. "I guess I should be grateful she didn't name me *The Chuckle Patch*."

I nearly spit my gum at the woman as I hand the paper and pen to her. "Yes, I guess that's fortunate."

Paula holds the paper up and smiles. "Thanks so much, Amy!" She tucks the list and the pen into her purse. "It was a pleasure meeting you." She pivots on her heel and before I know it, she's disappeared into the bakery section.

It's not until I'm carrying my bags of groceries into the house later on that I realize she kept my pen. And I don't have a picture of myself on my website.

CHAPTER THREE

I have managed to put the reunion out of my mind by the end of the week. How, you ask? Well, it's simple. My children have completely upended my life with projects they don't tell me about until the night before (Colt), play practices they forgot about (Evan), a case of "mono" that warrants me driving three hours to pick up them up only to find out it's just a cold (Allie), and avoiding me altogether as I struggle to write the final book in our children's series and could use their input (Lexie).

For the first time in almost a week, I am working on the book when I'm alerted to a message on the computer. I stare at the lower right-hand corner of my laptop, wondering how the heck I'm getting a Facebook message on the laptop when I have specifically turned off the alerts on the laptop.

Oh wait, I think I must have turned them back on when I was reading through the thread for the reunion.

And then I remember the reason I turned off the alerts in the first place. Yup, I have no willpower. I click the alert. It's telling me that a Facebook group has been created for the reunion and before I know what I'm doing, I click on the link that leads me to the page.

Amy! You are supposed to be working! Close out the tab! Go back to work!

There are probably a hundred messages on the page,

and I am immediately overwhelmed.

See, Amy? This is exactly why you should close this page out and go back to work. You already decided you're not going to the reunion, you even RSVP'd no…wait, you didn't RSVP, but you're going to RSVP no. Why look at these messages? They're just a waste of time and maybe they'll even get you aggravated.

My finger hovers over the X button at the top of the page, but then my curiosity wins out in the end and I find myself quickly scrolling through the entire message thread. Mostly it's ramblings about how everyone adores Suzie and they're *soooo* grateful to her for taking on this task (I notice that not one person actually volunteers to help; there are lots of "Oh I'd love to help, but…"). There are some compliments on Suzie's "beautiful" family (I guess they internet stalked her as I did) and a few people sending their regrets that they won't be able to attend the reunion.

I read some of the names of those who will not be able to attend the reunion for a variety of reasons—family vacation, working, kid's hockey tournament, having a baby (who's having a baby at our age?), back surgery (that's more believable), and the generic, one-size-fits-all "prior engagement." For once I wish that people would just be honest and say, "I don't want to come." Why do they always have to make up an excuse?

Of course, my brain whirls to come up with an excuse for why *I'm* not coming to the reunion.

What can I say? Colt has a soccer game? Ugh, he doesn't play soccer anymore. Um, Evan's playing

Dorothy in the school play? That's not until May. Lexie's getting an award? If she is, she probably won't tell me about it in case I actually show up to see it. Allie's got mono and needs her mommy to nurse her back to health? Lies.

My eyes trail back across the screen and I see several people chattering back and forth about who is coming and who they didn't think they'd ever see in a million years. I glimpse my own name, causing my eyes to nearly bug out of their sockets.

What in God's name could they possibly be saying about me? Have they not stopped their relentless bullying and gossip yet?

My eyes linger a bit longer before I shake my head. *Let it go, Amy,* I warn myself. *You have a ton of work to do before the boys get home. No good can come from dwelling on the past.*

Do I listen to myself? No. Of course I don't.

My blood pressure rises as I start reading—I'm expecting to see some shit talked about me. But instead I stop in my tracks. I blink several times, trying to figure out if I'm seeing things. Maybe it's time to change my contacts?

But no. There it is in black and white, from a Penny Whitaker.

Hey, did you send the invite to Amy Maxwell? I hope she's coming...I love her blog! Have you heard about some of the adventures she's had lately? That woman is a rockstar! I would love to see her!

My face is bright red as I realize this girl… this

woman…is talking about me. She's a…fan? I had no idea I even had fans! Well, except for that wacko in the grocery store last week. *Damn it, that was my favorite pen.*

I sit back and take a deep breath, in awe that within a week I've discovered not one, but two people that love me…or at least they love my blog.

Maybe…I'm not in such a rut after all? Maybe I have something to be proud of? Maybe I can go to this reunion and hold my head high?

With a click of the mouse, I check off the RSVP—*I'll be there.*

**

"Are you kidding, Amy?" Roger frowns at me over the rim of his reading glasses. He reminds me of my father when he does this and it's quite unnerving. The only difference is my dad would peer at us over the top of his newspaper and Roger is peering at me over the top of his phone. We don't get a newspaper anymore—we used to, when we first got married, but then the paper became sparser and sparser with each passing year. Who reads newspapers anymore? Oh wait, my dad does.

I shudder to think of all things that have gone by the wayside in my lifetime. Newspapers, tape players, CD players—although record players seem to be making a comeback—

"Amy!"

Roger startles me from my reverie, still peering at me like the ghost of my father of yesteryear. "What were you thinking?" he asks agitatedly.

"Honestly? That you look like my father peering at me over your readers."

Roger scowls. "Very funny. I meant what were you thinking saying yes to the reunion? What possessed you to respond yes?"

Do you mean what possessed me? Like was I actually possessed by a demon that took over the body that originally swore I would never attend a high school reunion and made me RSVP yes? And Venmo the full amount for two guests to Suzie Sunshine even before discussing it with Roger?

"I really have no idea," I mutter, even though I have an inkling of an idea. It was that moment of fandom from Penny Whitaker, that small, infinitesimal second that I thought someone liked me and really wanted to see me.

I leave the table to grab a bowl out of the cabinet and dump a package of meatball mix into it.

"Well, I can't go on April first," Roger tells me.

I scowl at him. "You mean, you don't want to go. Geez, Roger, I never ask you for anything."

"That's the Mets home opener, Amy," Roger says with a scoff. He waves his hand toward the calendar on the kitchen wall as if the day were not months from now and I could see the shiny words "Opening Day," written in bright red ink. As if I'm supposed to know the Mets opening day schedule months in advance. It's pathetic enough that Roger does.

I grate some Parmesan cheese into the bowl and sprinkle in breadcrumbs before answering. "Roger." I knead the meatloaf mix with my hands while not rolling my eyes in an amazing feat of willpower and restraint. "Isn't opening day usually in the early afternoon? The reunion is at seven o'clock. The game will be over by then."

"But I won't be home by then. It'll take at least an hour to get out of the parking lot. And the traffic to get home could be several hours. Plus, what if we want to tailgate after the game?"

I stare at him as if he is speaking a foreign language.

"What are you talking about? Why would you need to get out of the parking lot? Traffic? Tailgate?" Every word I utter makes even less sense coming out of my mouth than it did coming out of Roger's mouth.

"Since when do you tailgate when you watch the game? Are you having people over?"

The guy who can't even make his own dentist appointment can make plans to have people over two months in advance?

Roger frowns at me. "I told you Greg from work scored some primo seats for the game. His wife does PR for Citi Bank so he—"

"Primo seats?" I'm immediately suspicious. "How much do primo seats cost?" I'm mentally running up a tally in my head. Nosebleed seats at a baseball game run in the fifty-dollar range nowadays. I can only imagine how much "primo" seats cost.

"Nothing. They cost nothing. Did you hear the part

about how his wife works for the PR department?" Roger scowls at me.

"Oh."

"Yeah, and these seats come with butler service and an open bar."

"What? For free?" The reunion wasn't even coming with an open bar and it was going to cost me several hundreds of dollars. Suddenly going to an opening day game with Roger sounds much more enticing than going to this stupid reunion. Even if Penny Whitaker (which one was she again?) is looking forward to seeing me and chatting with me about my blog.

"Does he have any extra tickets?"

Roger looks aghast as if the idea of me horning in on his "boys' day out" is akin to a colonoscopy.

"Forget it," I say, waving my hand dismissively. Roger's entire face immediately relaxes.

"Sorry. Next time," he says, visibly relieved.

"I paid for two people for the reunion though," I say, hearing my voice dissolve into whininess.

"Can you get your money back?" Roger asks, always worrying about the finances. Even though that is not what's worrying me. What's worrying me is going to the reunion without someone by my side. Someone that I can whisper to and who can burst out into laughter as if I've said the most hilarious thing ever. You know, to make other people jealous they're not in my immediate circle. I haven't discussed this with Roger yet, but he was going to be that person. Okay, maybe it's a bit juvenile, but so was most of high school.

"I don't know," I mutter, turning the oven on to preheat. As I shape the meatloaf into the pan, I stare at the pathetic lump of meat, knowing that the kids are going to turn up their noses at this meal. They hate meatloaf, but I've run out of ideas to please everyone at mealtimes. I've decided to either just please myself or make the simplest meal imaginable. That would be meatloaf.

"Well can someone else use your extra ticket? You know, someone who wants to go to the reunion but hasn't bought a ticket yet?" Roger asks, coming up from behind me to peer at the meatloaf. Out of the corner of my eye I see him wrinkle up his nose in disgust. He hates meatloaf as well. Oh well, maybe someone else will step up to the plate to choose a meal or cook a meal around here if I make enough food that they don't want to eat.

"I don't know," I grumble, knocking him with my hip so that I can shove the meatloaf into the oven.

How would I possibly know that, Roger? I don't keep in touch with anyone I graduated with. Well, aside from liking the pictures of them and their families on vacation and their kids' back-to-school pictures, I don't really *know* anyone I graduated with. Or rather, I don't know them anymore. I don't know who purchased tickets already and who would want to.

Plus, how do I admit that I can't even get my husband to go to a reunion with me? People will think I made him up—just like I made up the "boyfriend from camp" my sophomore year because I was the only one in my friend group who didn't have a boyfriend at the time.

"Well maybe see if one of your sisters can go with you. They both went to that high school. They'll know more people than I would at any rate."

I whirl around after slamming the oven door with the meatloaf safely ensconced inside. "That's not a bad idea," I say, my mouth hanging slightly agape. Roger beams. "But I'd have to ask Joey. There's no way I can spend four hours watching Beth shmooze with my former classmates."

"Whatever," Roger says with obvious disinterest. He's off the hook and that's all he cares about.

He leaves the room to go pass out in front of the TV before dinner, and I head up to the bedroom. I click on the lamp next to my bed and dig through my closet until I come across a red wrap dress that I think I look pretty good in. Making sure the bedroom door is locked—Roger has a sixth sense about when I'm naked—I slip out of my yoga pants and hoodie.

"Okay, well that's not going to work," I say a few minutes later as I attempt to pull on the wrap dress. The dress is stuck halfway up my body and completely twisted around my middle. Either this dress has shrunk, or I've grown. And considering that I just watched an expose on how America collectively went up two pants sizes during the pandemic (while eating ice cream), I'm inclined to think it's the latter.

I struggle out of the dress and let it fall to my feet in a heap. Lifting my foot to kick it across the room, I catch a glimpse of myself in the mirror. For a second, I think I'm looking at my mother. No, I think I'm looking at my *grandmother*. My mother was never this out of shape.

My boobs are blobby messes barely being held up by a bra that's seen better days. In fact, it's so threadbare that I think dental floss might be a better option to contain the girls. My gut pooches over my equally threadbare granny panties, and if I tilt my thighs outward, I can make out burn marks from my thighs rubbing together. And lumps. My whole body is so…*lumpy*. And puffy. Even my face is puffy, which makes no sense because it's sagging at the same time.

I step closer to the mirror, evidently to torture myself. The fine lines and wrinkles that showed up on my face a few years ago are not so "fine" anymore. In fact, the ones that run east to west across my forehead are starting to look more like craters than "fine lines."

Damn. Why didn't I start using anti-aging face cream in my twenties?

My mother and Beth both warned me that the wrinkles would come out of nowhere, completely marring my unlined babyface, but of course since it was my mother and Beth warning me, I completely disregarded their advice. I'm ashamed to admit they were one hundred percent correct. It's like someone shrink-wrapped my face and then released it.

I purse my lips together—even they're starting to wrinkle. I rarely wear lipstick, but I recently attended the funeral of one of my dad's friends and I swear my lip wrinkles completely sucked up the lipstick. I was so horrified that I rubbed the lipstick completely from my lips and opted for a double layer of ChapStick.

I push my cheeks back with my hands, imagining how I would look if I got a facelift. "Don't be ridiculous, Amy," I chastise myself. I can't afford a facelift. But Botox. That's a possibility. Maybe that so-called baby Botox. My friend Laura just had her forehead done and she looks great. It can't be that expensive because Laura has a billion kids and is a stay-at-home mom. If she can afford it, maybe I can save up some of my book money and use that for Botox?

I shake my head. Spending money on frivolous things is not a good idea right now. We have one kid in college and another starting college next fall. And truth be told, she's a lot more ambitious about colleges than her sister was. Translation: she's looking at much more expensive, out-of-state colleges that will require taking out loans to finance. She's smart, but not smart enough to get a free ride at those institutions.

I shake my head and catch another glimpse of my perimenopausal, midlife crisis, post-pandemic body. Averting my eyes, I pull on a pair of pajamas—over-sized roomy ones that hide my gluttonous, gelatinous body. I immediately feel better. But it won't do just to hide in over-sized clothing. This body isn't a healthy one. Forget the fact that it's definitely not an attractive one (seriously, what does Roger see in me?), but my health is paramount. Especially now when I'm facing my 25th high school reunion head-on. I need to do something about it.

I sink down onto the bed and reach for my phone on the nightstand. I pull up the calendar app and count down the weeks until the reunion in April. According to my calculations, I've got about eight weeks to get myself in shape. I don't have to show up to the reunion in this unhealthy body. I can fix it. I still have time.

Before I know what hits me, I find myself on a popular weight-loss app, one that touts itself as a "Lifestyle change" app rather than a weight loss one. I quickly enter my stats and my desired goal, a twenty-pound weight loss. I figure that's doable. And even if I only get halfway there, that should get rid of a chin or two, right?

The app spits out the number of calories I can consume and how long I need to exercise each day in order to achieve my goal. My mouth falls open in disbelief. Basically, I'd need to subsist on about 800 calories a day and/or exercise for four hours a day to burn any excess off.

"That's impossible," I mutter to myself, clutching my chest and feeling so utterly hopeless. How did I let myself go this much? I should have cracked down on this years ago—way before this dumb reunion was staring me in the face.

"What's impossible?" Roger asks. "The fact I'm a magician?"

My head snaps up and I see him standing directly in front of me, waggling his eyebrows. I have no idea what he's talking about until I see him hold up a bobby pin. Roger has picked the lock to our bedroom door. I can't even have a breakdown in peace.

"Roger…" I start to sigh when the sound of the

smoke alarm starts blaring.

"Shit!"

I run out of the run and pound down the stairs, smoke wafting into view before I even hit the ground floor. Dashing into the kitchen, I can see the smoke pouring out of the oven.

"Shit, shit, shit!"

"You have to put money in the swear jar, Mama," Evan says matter-of-factly as he trails into the kitchen right behind me.

"Thanks for reminding me!" I dash over to the oven to shut it off, while trying to remember if we ever got a new fire extinguisher after I needed to use the old one last month. I left brownies in the oven and fell asleep on the couch. In my defense, I had been seriously sleep-deprived between working on the new book series and all the Christmas preparation and execution.

I grab a dishtowel and wave it uselessly in the air, trying to get the smoke to dissipate.

"You have to open the windows," Roger grumbles as he storms over to the sink and throws open the window.

No kidding, I want to say, but I hold my tongue as I drag a stool over to the smoke alarm and remove the batteries.

"Don't forget to put those back," Roger says in a patronizing tone.

"I always do," I reply sweetly. Ugh, the fact that I just said *always* is depressing. Is there anyone on the planet that burns more meals than I do?

"What's for dinner?" Evan asks.

I open the oven door. Well, there *was* meatloaf in there. It's now a charred brick of coal.

"Who wants to order pizza?"

Hell, the diet can start tomorrow.

CHAPTER FOUR

"Amy? Is that you?"

I hear a woman's voice in my left ear and my spine straightens. I'd know that menacing voice anywhere! It's Libby Farrington.

I spin around gracefully, my periwinkle blue dress—the one that brings out my eyes—swirls around my kneecaps, my martini not sloshing over the sides of the glass at all. I am the picture of beauty and grace.

"Libby?" My voice raises an octave as I watch my high school nemesis waddle over to me. And I do mean waddle. Her entire body is as squishy as a stress ball. Her ankle-length muumuu slaps against her puffy ankles which push over the tops of her orthopedic sandals that she wears with compression socks. Her once gorgeous auburn curls form a frizzy halo around her head, and I can see patches where she is going bald. As she gets closer, the crop of acne on her forehead is so noticeable that I avert my eyes out of pity.

"Amy, you look amazing," Libby gushes, her rotten teeth giving way to a stench that almost knocks me over.

"Um, gee thanks, Libby," I mutter, covering my nose discreetly.

"Tell me," Libby says as she grabs my hands and squeezes them, her skin damp and clammy. "What have you been up to? I mean, obviously your blog...which is

amazing, by the way. I never miss it."

"Um, thanks," I mutter again, my eyes roaming the room, desperate for someone to save me. Twenty-five years ago I would have chopped off my left arm to have this kind of positive attention from Libby Farrington, homecoming queen, head cheerleader, and all-around most popular girl in our grade. But now...I just want to escape from her.

As an answer to my prayers, Penny Whitaker swoops in and grabs my arm. "Sorry, Libby but Amy is coming with me. I'm the president of her fan club and she's doing a book signing over here." She sweeps her arm toward the middle of the room where a podium has been erected, next to a table piled high with my book! The memoir I haven't even written yet is completely finished!

"You're just going to have to wait in line like everyone else, Karen," Penny says with a jerk of her head toward the line that appears to have no end.

"Her name is Libby," I whisper to Penny. "Remember?"

Penny rolls her eyes. "Nope. She's a total Karen."

Ah, I see what she did there. "Bye Karen!" Penny cries out as she whisks me away toward the podium. "You look like shit, by the way!"

Libby bursts out into tears, "I've fallen apart since my husband left me for a younger woman and my kids refuse to talk to me and I've gone bankrupt!"

"Couldn't have happened to a nicer person," Penny mutters under her breath as she gives me a wink and propels me toward the podium. "Now, are you ready to

greet your adoring public?"

"Um, I guess so," I stammer. Penny whirls me around and I'm greeted by a giant crowd shouting, "Amy, Amy, Amy!"

"Are they all here for me?" I stare open-mouthed at Penny.

"Yup!" she says with a nod. "They love you!"

**

"I love you Amy, but this is definitely outside of the scope of sisterly love."

"Huh?" Joey has shaken me from my daydream.

"Spending four hours with the losers you graduated high school with?" Joey sounds like I just asked her to donate a kidney to me. Which, considering all I've done for her in the past few years, would barely repay her debt.

"Come on, Joey. It'll be fun. There's going to be a DJ and I looked at the menu. It looks delish."

"I'd rather have a pap smear."

"I don't think you're supposed to get pap smears when you're pregnant," I inform her, recalling what my midwife told me when I was pregnant with Evan and became a slight hypochondriac because it seemed everyone I knew at the time was being diagnosed with a terminal illness.

"Funny, Amy," Joey scoffs. "You really should consider a future in comedy," she adds, with sarcasm that is unlike her usual way-too-peppy self. I swear ever since she announced this third pregnancy she's been quite the grouch. I mean, granted, I'd be a witch too if I had two little kids running around and I was over forty and pregnant, but Joey has not been taking this in as much stride as she did the first two pregnancies which were also complete surprises. I guess it's the whole "being forty" thing that's getting to her. I didn't take turning forty too well either.

"Ladies and gentlemen, I'm here all week," I deadpan.

I hear a harumph on the other end of the phone, but no other response from Joey. I try to switch tack.

"Seriously, though, it'll be fun for you to get out of the house."

"I get out of the house, Amy."

"To go to work," I scoff. "You get out of the house to go to work. How much fun is that?"

"I like my job. Remember, I design my own clothes? And when I get out of the house to work, I have long conversations with adults where I'm not interrupted to wipe anyone's butt or cut their food."

"That would be quite awkward. I think HR would have to get involved if you were fielding those requests all day."

"Again with the comedy. But seriously. I enjoy going to work when I get to. It's nice to be able to put together a sentence without being—"

Right on cue my niece starts howling in the background.

"—interrupted," Joey finishes with a defeated sigh.

"Exactly why you could use a night out with me," I

say in a sing-song voice.

There's a moment of silence on the other end and Joey lets out another sigh. "I can't say it sounds like fun."

"Oh come on, Joey. You'll be with me." I pause for a beat and then add, "Don't make me evoke the clause."

"What clause?" I can almost see my sister's eyebrows furrowing.

"The *I've saved your life on multiple occasions and you owe me one* clause."

Another harumph on the other end of the phone before Joey says, "First off, Jason saved my life on both of those occasions, and I wouldn't have been in a life-or-death situation to begin with if it were not for you and your inability to stay out of trouble."

"For the record, this last time was 99% Beth's fault."

"True." Silence. "Okay, fine. I'll go. But on two conditions. One, you get me a root beer float on the way there. And two, we leave when I say I'm tired. I can't stay out very late."

I clap my hands together. Not only is she going to come with me, she's going to give me the perfect excuse to leave. Who's going to argue with a pregnant woman?

Not me, that's for sure.

"You've got yourself a deal."

Great. I have a date for this thing! Now I just need to lose twenty pounds.

**

I rub my hands together and take a deep breath. The treadmill looms in front of me in all its glory. After relieving it of its laundry, it is ready to be used. Which is nearly a first for the treadmill. We got it three years ago when I had this burst of reality that I was soon to be hitting the magic age of forty and I was in the worst shape of my life (that is until my current shape). I used it exactly three times before it became the unofficial closet for laundered clothes that haven't made their way up to the bedroom closet yet. But that's all about to change right now.

I climb on the treadmill and hit the start button. The belt hums and jerks a bit—probably because it hasn't been used in forever—but then starts moving at a slow pace. I look at the emergency strap that I'm supposed to clip to my shirt in case I fall and need to stop the treadmill, but I can't imagine needing to use it since I'm going so slow.

I study the programs mapped out on the display screen. *Hmmmm, Intervals. That sounds like something I should be doing. Didn't I read somewhere that interval training is the best way to lose weight?*

I press the button for *Interval* and the pace picks up a tiny bit. I look down at the screen—I'm going at 2.5 miles an hour. *I can walk faster than that can't I?* I bump it up to three miles an hour and settle into a comfortable pace. It's much easier than I had imagined it would be. I must be in much better shape than I thought!

I can almost feel the fat melting off my thighs already. And that feeling...is that adrenaline? Wow! This is great! Why did I stop doing this?

I crank up the music in my Air pods and pump my arms. I almost feel like dancing. I attempt to do a little shuffle on the treadmill, but I quickly lose my footing. I clutch the side rails, saving myself from catapulting off.

No, no. Don't fall.

I regain my balance and pump the arms again, feeling great. As easy as this seems, I decide that I'm only going to go a mile and then call it a day. Baby steps. Then tomorrow I can go two miles and then three…

You've got this, I tell myself. And I do.

Until about thirty seconds later when the belt makes a whirling noise and starts to speed up.

What the actual…

I drop my pumping arms and grab onto the sides. My fingers grip the rails and my arms become stone-like as my legs whip around on the treadmill belt like an octopus on roller skates. I frantically search for the stop button while realizing that even if I could *find* the stop button, there is no way I can *press* the stop button without lifting a hand off the rails, and that would result in road rash on my face.

Damn it, why didn't I clip that emergency stop key to my shirt like the directions said to do?

As my pulse quickens, my breath comes out in spurts, and before I know it, I'm full-on panting. I try to check the mph window to see just how fast I'm actually going, but I'm bouncing up and down so rapidly that my vision is a bit blurry.

Is that 7 miles per hour or 9? There's no way I'm

going 9 miles an hour. Heck, there's no way I'm going 7 miles an hour either. Is that the stop button? Oh, maybe I can hit it with my nose.

Then, as quickly as the treadmill sped up, it slows down, causing me to stop short and almost smack my face on the display screen. Oh, that would have been great.

How did your first day of exercising go, Amy? Well, I have a chipped tooth, a fat lip, and I think I dislocated my shoulder. Any other questions?

Since the treadmill has returned to a snail's pace, I am now able to extract my gripped fingers from the rails. I wiggle them for a second to get the blood flowing again before I hit the stop button. That is enough for today. I'm sure I've gone a mile. Heck, I was running so fast I probably went two miles.

The treadmill grinds to a halt and I once again almost hit my face on the screen, but this time it's from shock. I am forced to confront the fact that I have only been walking, erm, running at a high rate of speed, for three minutes. And I've gone…0.25 miles. And burnt 33 calories. *How is that even possible?*

Annoyed, I step off the treadmill, wondering how I can be so damn sweaty without even going a mile. I pull up the app on my phone and enter in the big deal 33 calories into the spot for exercise. Excellent. If I continue at this pace, I'll hit my goal weight by the year 2177.

I head upstairs and grab a paper towel to blot myself with. As I pat my face down, I wander into the living room peek out the window. It's sunny and not too cold today. Maybe I'll just walk Jeter later. That'll certainly be safer than using the treadmill. Unless he sees a squirrel and pulls me across Main Street like he did a few weeks ago. I'll have to bring the air horn to scare him into behaving on this walk.

But first, I have to decide what to cook for dinner. The macaroni and cheese with hot dogs I was planning to make is certainly not going to cut it if I want to lose weight before the reunion. I need to find something that will be healthy and keep me below my remaining allotted—I check the app on my phone—five hundred calories for the day.

I open up my laptop and immediately break my own rule by going on Pinterest. As much as I want to sit down and work on the book (okay, I'm totally lying, I don't want to sit down and work on it at all), I have to get *Operation Reunion Bod* underway now that I know I've got someone to go with me.

I type "healthy recipes" in the search bar and am immediately assaulted by hundreds of pictures. As I scroll through them, I must admit, they look yummy. And as I delve into the directions, I discover that most of them are simple, requiring only a few ingredients.

Why haven't we tried eating healthily before? All these recipes look delicious, simple, and easy. You like simple and easy, Amy. Heck, simple and easy is difficult to mess up. Even you can make these recipes. And that'll cut down on the need to order take out, which not only will help save money, it'll save calories as well.

I head over to the pantry and peer inside. This is

when I realize why I haven't made any healthy recipes yet. It doesn't appear that I have the ingredients for such recipes.

Sighing, I glance at my watch. It's Wednesday and nearly noon, which means the grocery store is safe for another hour or so. The senior bus goes to the grocery store every Wednesday at 1:10 pm. Not 1:00 or 1:30, 1:10 pm precisely. There would be anarchy if the bus came at any other time, I'm sure. The seniors in this town are very particular about their outings. If I'm going to get in and out before the bus comes, I won't have time to shower.

I lumber up the stairs to pee quickly and dab some deodorant under my arms, hoping I don't run into any rabid fans at the grocery store today.

CHAPTER FIVE

"Amy, I just finished the new book and I'm floored. How did you write it in a week?"

My agent is gushing at me over Zoom as I lean toward the computer screen to apply a stroke of eyeshadow to my lid, seamlessly transforming myself into a woman who is ten years younger than I actually am. "Oh it was easy. It came to me when I was jogging last week."

"Jogging? I didn't know you jogged."

"Of course I jog! How else would I have lost twenty pounds in one month?" I reply with a laugh.

"That is true," my agent says, peering at me through the screen of the computer. "I must say you do look marvelous. And now I know how you did it."

"Yes, jogging and eating healthy were the keys to my success," I tell her as I sweep eyeshadow across my other lid. Is it just me or do I look twenty-five?

"Who knew!" my agent exclaims. "I'll have to try it sometime."

I laugh. "Well, it's not for the faint of heart, that's for sure."

My agent cocks her head to the side. "Oh, was it difficult?"

I nod. "Oh yes. In fact, it was so hard the first time I walked on the treadmill that I nearly gave up." I smile at her. "But I didn't. I persevered. And now look how amazing I look!" I sweep my hand over my body.

"You do look incredible. And that's what I admire about you, Amy. You never give up."

"She doesn't," the deep voice behind me confirms.

I glance over my shoulder to see Raul, the neighbor's pool boy, step into the room. He snakes an arm around my waist and pulls me closer, purring in my ear as he does.

"You look so sexy, Mamita."

I giggle as his breath tickles my neck, sending delightful shivers down my spine and then settling in my groin.

"Amy has to go," Raul tells my agent in his delightful accent. "We have plans." He winks at me as he ends the Zoom call with a press of his miraculous fingers. Those fingers trail across my exposed shoulder and I—

**

We are sitting down for dinner the next night and Lexie groans.

"What?" I snap. I must admit, I've been a bit snappish since I've been cutting back on the calories.

"It's Thursday, Mom," Lexie whines. She points to the plate I've set down in front of her, piled high with shredded Brussels sprouts and grilled chicken in a wrap.

"We always have tacos on Thursday."

"These *are* tacos, Lex," I tell her with all the energy I can muster.

Lexie lifts the wrap up and examines it with a sniff. "These are *not* tacos. Tacos have meat and cheese and lettuce and sour cream. These have none of that."

"Chicken is meat."

"We don't need cheese and sour cream," Roger points out before taking a bite. I see his face crumple as he swallows, but he quickly tries to cover his disappointment by making sounds of approval. "So good," he says in an unbelievable voice.

"Ugh," Lexie groans while taking a bite of the "taco." She frowns and makes horrifying faces as she eats, but I don't hear another word out of her mouth.

Colt however…

"I'm not eating this," Colt says with a scowl. He pushes the plate away and gets up from the table.

"Just where do you think you're going?" I snap.

"Making a peanut butter and jelly sandwich," he says as he opens the cabinet to take out the bread.

"I'd like something else, too," Evan informs me, pushing his own plate away. "We've had nothing but gross food for the last two days."

"That's not true," Roger says, shooting me a sympathetic look. "We had those really delicious stuffed peppers last night."

"Yup! Really gross food!" Evan says.

"They were yummy," Roger argues.

"If they were so yummy, why did you go out to the store when Mom was in the shower and get

McDonald's?" Lexie asks, pointing a finger at Roger.

I turn and glare at Roger. "You got McDonald's last night?

"I, well, I…" Roger stammers, his face getting red.

"Jesus, Roger. How can I expect the kids to support me in my quest to change our eating habits if I can't even get you to support me?"

"I…didn't…well, I…" Roger still can't string a coherent sentence together, and the kids have all crossed their arms over their chests to glare at their father.

"You got McDonald's and you didn't share with us?" Colt asks, insulted. "You know Mom tried to starve us last night! We could have died from malnutrition!"

"You can survive for a week without food," Lexie informs her brother.

"Not if Mom keeps making this stuff," Evan says. "Why can't we order pizza?"

"First off, we eat too much pizza. Secondly, we order out too much. Thirdly, we need to eat healthier. Our eating habits are shit." I tick off all the reasons on my fingers.

"You owe money to the swear jar!" Evan announces, pointing at the jar on the counter that only *I* seem to put money in. Everyone else just curses under their breath in this house.

"This doesn't have anything to do with the reunion coming up?" Roger asks with an arch of his eyebrow.

"This has nothing to do with the reunion," I scoff (lie). "I just want us to eat a little better. What's wrong with that?"

"This stuff is inedible, that's what's wrong with it," Lexie says as she pokes at her food. "I can't wait to go to college next year so I don't need to eat this garbage."

"Okay, that's enough!" I announce as I rise to my feet and start gathering up the plates, starting with Roger's.

"Hey, what are you doing with that?" he protests as he attempts to grab the plate back, but he's too slow in his old age.

"Throwing out the *garbage*," I hiss.

"*I* didn't say it was garbage. Lexie said it was garbage," Roger points to our daughter like he's tattling on her.

"You were thinking it," I retort.

"Amy." Roger tilts his head and peers at me like a specimen in the zoo.

"What?"

"Calm—" I shoot daggers at him and he clamps his mouth shut before he can finish the stupid sentence he was about to utter.

I pick up the kids' plates, piling them all on top of each other. None of them even attempt to stop me. In fact, I see Lexie pull her phone out of her pocket despite the "no phones at the table" rule.

"What are you doing?" I turn my attention on Lexie. My wrath is so immense it's having ADHD right now and doesn't know who to yell at.

"Ordering food," she says without looking up.

"The hell you are." I make a grab for Lexie's phone with my free hand, startling her. Her arm flies out in reaction, and she ends up hitting my other hand, the one that's balancing the "taco" tower. Brussels sprouts and other healthy ingredients go raining down on the table in slow motion and I'm powerless to stop it. I can only stand there with my mouth gaping open, still as a statue.

Roger and the children are also frozen, everyone afraid to move. It's so quiet that I can hear the kitchen clock ticking. After what feels like a century, I see Roger mouthing "get out of here" to Lexie. She doesn't have to be told twice. She leaps to her feet and scrambles out of the kitchen, both boys hot on her heels. I guess no one wants to be around when Mount St. Mommy Monster erupts.

I don't erupt though. Instead, I drop the plates on the table (it's already a mess, so what does it matter?) and sink back into my seat, ignoring the fact I'm sitting on a bed of Brussels sprouts. My desire to fling the plates at the wall has abated, but it's taken over by my urge to cry.

I cover my eyes with the heels of my palms and yelp. *Damn, jalapeno juice.* Now I'm really crying, but these are tears of pain, not sadness.

"What's the matter?" Roger jumps up from his chair and dashes over to me, placing his hand on my shoulder.

"Nothing," I growl, shaking his hand off. "Don't touch me."

He removes his hand, but he doesn't leave my side. Even though my eyes are now closed, I can feel his presence hovering over me. Maybe if I keep them closed tightly enough he will disappear. I've tried it in the past and it hasn't worked, but one can always hope for a miracle.

Okay, I know what you're saying. *Amy Maxwell, you are a selfish bitch.* Your husband is concerned about your welfare, and you can't just appreciate him?

Well, dear reader, I hate to burst your bubble, but I've been married to this guy for twenty-three years and I can assure you that it's not my welfare that he's concerned about, but his own. You see, he has learned a thing or two over those years. He knows if Mama ain't happy, ain't nobody happy. Or something like that. Usually, he opts to ignore my moody outbursts, but this involves food and Roger doesn't want to lose an appendage if he tries to order food like Lexie did. But he is also hungry and wants to eat. He'll need to soothe me before taking care of his hunger so that he doesn't have to to sleep with one eye open.

"I just want you to be happy," he says, treading lightly. *See?*

"Bullshit," I snort. "Go order food." I wave my hand toward the living room. "The kids too." Roger starts to move toward the living room, given permission. "I guess no one cares about their health. Or my health for that matter. I guess we'll all just have heart attacks from all the junk food we eat." I shrug my shoulders.

Roger halts in his tracks, considering whether this is a trap or not. I can almost hear the wheels turning in his brain as he thinks about his response. There are a few different paths he can take, and there's only one that will earn him the husband of the year award.

He opens his mouth, and immediately all hopes of

husband of the year are dashed. "Maybe you need to see Dr. Singh for some medication. You know, something to calm you down a bit—"

My eyes pop wide open and Roger backpedals quickly. "I was just suggesting it because you seem a bit tense. Maybe a massage or more food or…" His voice trails off before he pivots and tries a different tack. "You want pizza or Chinese?"

I throw up my hands and run out of the room, grabbing my laptop in the process. If I can't eat, I might as well get some writing done.

I lock myself in the bedroom and drop the laptop on the bed before fluffing my pillows so I can prop myself up to write. My bed is definitely not my favorite place to write, but it will have to do as my kitchen table looks like a crime scene right now and I am not in the mood to clean it. If my family knows what's good for them, it will be cleaned before I go back downstairs.

I open up my word doc and scan what I wrote this morning, instantly appalled. For some unknown reason, my lovely children's book with my own daughter as the detective is laden with sexual innuendos, referencing the size of another detective's…*brain.* This is followed by a line that says *it's not the size of your brain, it's what you do with it.* I would have normally ignored the obvious misstep and chalked it up to stress, but as I read on, I see I've named a character Raul and have described his undulating *brain*.

For heaven's sakes, Amy! What the hell is wrong with you? This. Is. A. Children's. Book. Why does your mind keep sliding into the gutter? Are you having some sort of breakdown?

For a brief second I wonder if in fact I am currently experiencing a breakdown and my mind has splintered. It is quite unlike me to come up with sexual innuendos in real life, let alone while I'm writing.

And then I recall that I recently started taking these pills that I bought off the internet that swear they're going to balance out your hormones and get rid of your mommy gut.

Hmmm, there must be something in them that makes you horny. Maybe there's some male hormone in it.

I stare down at my mommy belly that is not even a centimeter less bloated than it was when I started taking those pills a week ago. I will be cutting them out of my daily routine for sure. Heaven knows I can barely write to begin with, I certainly don't need the distraction of peppering my children's book with highly inappropriate language because I'm randy. I better not tell Roger about this.

But for now, Amy, let's get back to the book, shall we?

I delete the inappropriate sentences and then my hands hover over the keyboard and…nothing. It's like they're frozen in place.

"Agggrrgh," I yell with anguish. I jump off the bed and terrify Jeter who has been sleeping on the floor. "Oh my God, Jeter! I'm so sorry!" I reach for him and he backs away, whining as he retreats. With a sigh, I open the bedroom door and he bounds out, looking back at me every few seconds to make sure I'm not following him.

"Great." I can't do anything right today. I can't write, I can't lose weight, and I've even managed to find myself on the shit list of the most happy-go-lucky dog on the planet. Maybe I just need to take a break from writing. Yes, that's it. Take a short break, go for a walk or something, and then get right back at it. I close my laptop and head back downstairs.

"Jeter!" I call as I enter the living room. He's lounging practically upside down on the couch, legs akimbo in the air and his dopey head lolling off the cushion. How that's comfortable is beyond me, but it's Jeter's preferred sleeping position. He eyes me warily, but still does not move. I guess his memory is longer than that dumb dog trainer said it was.

I reach for his leash on the rack by the door and he instantly bounds to his feet and leaps from the couch in one swift movement.

"That's a good boy," I tell him as I clip his leash to his collar. His tail wags enthusiastically and I am forgiven for my earlier transgression.

"I'm going for a walk! With Jeter!" I yell to nobody in particular. I get grunts of acknowledgment from the kitchen, so I guess their food has arrived. *Ah, food. How I miss you, dear food.*

We're wrapping up our walk about twenty minutes later and I am physically spent. I know that doesn't seem like much of a walk, but trust me, with Jeter's energy that's equivalent to taking a one-hour HIIT class…or wrestling a shark. But now my mind is finally clear. I am ready to get back to work on the book! Sexual innuendos be damned! I have decided...

An idea hits me like a ton of bricks. Porn. Well, not actual porn, but erotica. From what I've seen online, there is a huge market for spicy romance. Yes, spicy romance, that's what it's called now. Not erotica. Maybe I can put these weight-loss pills to good use after all.

CHAPTER SIX

"Hello sexy stranger," the husky voice behind Simone says.

She whirls around and finds herself face-to-face with ~~Jason~~ Raul.

"Well hello to you, too," Simone purrs as she eyes his body up and down. His biceps are straining in the t-shirt that's trying to constrict him; he looks incredibly uncomfortable. Before Simone can say another word, Raul tears his t-shirt from his body and Simone gasps with delight. Raul's tanned chest glistens with sweat from the intense workout he just endured at the gym, his pectoral muscles are almost throbbing from—

I stop typing.

His pectoral muscles are throbbing, Amy?

Seriously, I should just stick to writing children's books. This is going nowhere fast. The next thing I know I'll be looking up all the euphemisms for a certain male body part.

I reread the chapter I've written already and I shake my head, annoyed with myself. Each sentence gets progressively more cringy than the previous one.

Why did I think I should write spicy romance again? I don't even *read* spicy romance. I don't know the first thing about the readers' preferences. There's no reason for me to try to work out my um, sexual frustrations in writing—I should just stop taking those vitamins and my libido will dry up like its usual spongelike self within a day. When that happens, I'm sure I would rather deadlift at the gym than have anything to do with any euphemism for a male part.

I push away from the table. Speaking of the gym, maybe I should just skip this writing session today and go work out. Yes, that's the solution. When in doubt, work it out.

**

I have to admit I'm nearly dying as I pedal away on the stationary bike Roger bought a few weeks ago because Dr. Singh told him to. This is the first time I've been on it and I'm not doing too bad, I don't think. I promised myself I would start off easy—a half an hour for the first time. I found a YouTube video of this instructor who I think might be slightly psychotic because she keeps insisting we "jump" and "run" which is ludicrous on a bike. And I don't like her music at all, so I've got my own music piping into my Air Pods from my phone. It's not always the best tune for the exercise, but it's a heck of a lot better than this psychopath's heavy metal she's got blasting.

Still, I've been doing the best I can. It must nearly be time to stop because I'm as hot as hell, and I have sweat pouring from my body in places I never knew you could sweat. And holy cow, why doesn't anyone warn you how much a stationary bike hurts one's lady bits? I don't think

I'm going to be able to sit for a week.

Needless to say, I am thrilled when the Beyonce song I am listening to on my Air Pods is curtly interrupted by the ringing of my phone. I glance down at the screen and discover it's Joey calling. I've never been so happy to be interrupted in all my life. I nearly lose my balance as I take my hands off the handlebars (forgetting that I'm standing up in the saddle and pedaling at some ungodly speed…seriously…who does this lady think I am? Lance Armstrong?). I can just hear the smug psycho spin instructor going on about bike safety like she did in the beginning of the video that I fast-forwarded through.

"Joey?" I pant, attempting to disentangle myself.

"Amy?" Joey sounds concerned. Aww how sweet, I must sound like I'm in pain…like I am. Sometimes my sisters are the most selfish human beings on the planet and other times they surprise me.

"You sound like you're really far away," she continues. "Do you have me on speakerphone? You know I hate when you put me on speakerphone."

And today is not one of those days where a sister of mine surprises me with their empathy.

"No, Joey, you're not on speakerphone," I sigh. "I have my headphones on, that's all."

"Oh, okay," Joey says.

"Glad to meet your approval," I mutter through clenched teeth. Thankfully, Joey doesn't hear me. Or if she does hear me, she doesn't care because she immediately begins to launch into some diatribe that involves the words "baby," "labor," and "dreaming" all in a row. I can't really understand what she's saying though. I'm probably using up too much oxygen while exercising or something. There's ringing in my ears…maybe that's the problem.

"What are you talking about?" I turn down the resistance on the bike. Maybe that'll help.

"The reunion," Joey says in a tone that indicates to me that this is not the first time she's explained this during our brief conversation.

Ugh, the reunion.

"Amy are you okay? You're breathing kinda funny," Joey says.

I should probably get off the bike. I'm getting dizzy from the workout, and I should probably eat some macros or something. I just have to figure out what they are first.

I slow my legs down until I feel like I can stop without spinning out of control, and then grab a giant swig of water from my ecologically sound water bottle that Lexie insisted that I buy instead of the plastic ones that the boys take three sips of and then leave lying around the house.

I breathe a sigh of relief as I climb off the bike and wipe my face with a towel.

"So what about the reunion?"

I climb the stairs to the kitchen and peek out the window. I let Jeter outside right before I went to work out because it's one of those gorgeous days in March when the sun is shining and it's 60 degrees. It would be criminal to ask him to come in, because I checked the weather for the next ten days and it's going to rain eleven of the ten days. Or so it seems.

Joey sighs that exasperated sigh again. She sounds like Beth did the time Sebastian was at her house and flushed all her tampons down the toilet causing the toilet to overflow all over her newly renovated Roman-style bathroom. "I just told you. Don't you listen?"

"Of course I…" My voice trails off as I spot Jeter in the back by my rose bushes that I've all but given up on since we got him. He took an instant shining to them when he was a puppy and has made it his mission in life to unearth the roots of every single one of them before he turns three. It's not the digging in the ground by the rose bushes that catches my attention, though, but the small furry object that he's tossing up in the air and catching.

Did he take one of his toys outside again? He knows he's not supposed to—wait, is that moving? Oh my god, it's moving! It's not a toy…it looks like a…squirrel?

"Jeter!" I yank open the sliding glass door. "Drop that! No, wait, release that? Let it go?"

My brain scrambles to recall the command they taught us in obedience school. Jeter was valedictorian of his obedience school class and then promptly came home and forgot every single thing he was taught. He might as well have been an obedience school dropout. In his defense, I haven't remembered anything he was taught either.

"Leave it!" I call out, finally remembering the command that's supposed to make the dog drop whatever he's not supposed to have, whether it be a piece of pancake or rat poison. Or in this case, an injured squirrel.

Jeter turns to gawk at me with a confused look on his face that indicates English is not his first language. He ignores the command and tosses the poor rodent up in the air, proceeding to catch it in his teeth. I swear I see a smile of delight on his face.

"Oh God, Jeter!" I step out onto the deck and remember the phone in my hand. "Joey, I'll have to call you back!" I press *End* forcefully and shove the phone into the pocket of my leggings (yes, they have pockets…amazing!) and stomp across the deck while trying to come up with a game plan to get my dog to drop the injured, angry, and possibly rabid squirrel that doesn't include either of us getting bitten or losing an eye. Thank God he's up to date on his rabies shot at least, but I'm not and don't they just shoot you if you get rabies? Or is that just for dogs? Either way, I'm not getting bitten. Which means I'm not going anywhere near the dog or the squirrel.

I grab the snow shovel that's leaning against the deck, thankful for once that Roger is lazy and doesn't put things away. As I storm across the yard, I glance around for something to distract Jeter so that he'll drop the squirrel and it'll either limp off to lick its wounds, or I'll have to hit it over the head with the shovel and scoop it over the fence into Mr. Nelson's yard. He doesn't have a dog, but he has a lovely compost heap that reeks in the summer months so the dead squirrel will fit right in. He won't even notice it, I bet.

The hose is lying on its side, not coiled up as it should be. Colt probably rinsed off his baseball cleats and didn't wrap the hose up even though he's been told to do so a million times. Again I'm grateful for the laziness of my male family members because I don't have to sit here and fiddle with the hose. I just need to grab it, turn it on, and spray it in the general direction of the dog. He hates baths so much that he'll drop the squirrel and run to cower by the back door. At least that's the plan.

And of course, I turn the hose on full blast and the pressure of the water causes the hose to lurch forward and I fall on my rear end, water spraying all around the yard like a geyser.

"Shit!"

I try to get to my feet, but the water is quickly making the grass slippery and muddy, and it takes me much longer than I'd like to admit. Once I'm vertical, I realize I'm completely soaked through, but I have managed to distract Jeter at least. He has dropped his prey and is staring at me…I swear...open-mouthed.

I turn off the hose once I manage to limp my way back over to the spigot and Jeter trots after me with interest. Apparently I'm more of a spectacle than the squirrel, who I am happy to report, seems to be no worse for the wear and is scrambling up the nearest tree.

After letting Jeter in, I dry myself off and go upstairs to the bedroom to change out of my wet and sweaty clothes. You would think I had a hell of a workout the way I look now. Maybe I should shower?

I strip off my clothes in the bathroom, contemplating whether to weigh myself. The scale is challenging me from the other side of the room. I have made a pledge that I will only weigh myself once a week (and thus far, the once a week weigh-ins have only yielded a three pound weight loss, which may or may not be attributed to the fact that I had the touch of a stomach virus last week). But I've been working extra hard the last couple days and truly, I feel thinner. I must have lost another two or three pounds.

Temptation overtakes me as I step onto the scale, stark naked. The numbers blink up on the screen in angry red font and I find myself squinting to read them, leaning forward in the process. My feet are still wet from my socks being soaked with the hose water, which causes me to slip off the scale and fall…*almost*…face first into the sink.

You might say it's thankful that I did not land face first into the sink because I would have bashed my nose or maybe even lost a tooth or something if I had done so. True, that might have been worse than what actually happened, but who knows?

I stick my hand out to stop myself from smacking my face on the sink, but of course, that causes my wrist to bend back as I collapse not-so-gracefully to the floor.

Now I am naked, lying on the bathroom floor, nary a towel in sight, with pain shooting up and down my arm. Using my left hand on the sink for leverage, I clumsily haul myself to my feet, sighing with relief when I am finally erect. With one last final insult, I trip over the blasted scale as I leave the bathroom, sending pain radiating through my pinkie toe. The one I've broken twice already. If my wrist wasn't throbbing I would chuck the damn thing out the bathroom window.

So now I'm limping (naked) to my room with my hand dangling from my mangled wrist like a disembodied limb. I'm gasping for air by the time I manage to get back to the bedroom (geez, you would have thought after several weeks of working out I would be in *slightly* better shape).

I pull open my underwear drawer with my left hand and grab the least stretched out pair that I can find before sitting down on the bed. I dangle the underwear in front of me and push my feet and legs through one at a time, standing to tug them over my hips, a feat that takes me way longer to accomplish than it should have. In the process, my boobs jiggle precariously, and I realize there's no way I'm going to be able to manage a clasp on a bra with one hand. Thankfully, I have some loose camisoles from when I broke my clavicle.

However, as I try to pull one on, I realize that Roger had always been home to help me into the camisoles when I was recovering from that injury. Today I'm by myself and have somehow managed to get myself stuck in this thin piece of material, both arms coming out of one hole.

Now I'm really out of breath. And I'm trapped.

I need to call for help.

My phone is still in the pocket of my leggings on the floor, so I dig it out and stare at it morosely.

Who can I call that isn't going to make fun of me and use this situation to mock me till the end of my days?

My mother? My sister? Roger?

I scroll through my contacts and select one. The phone rings as I put it to my ear and a voice on the other end says hello.

"Laura?"

CHAPTER SEVEN

"Amy, I can't believe you're hurt!"

"Amy, are you going to be okay?"

"Amy, how will you sign my copies of your books?"

"I was here before you! She needs to sign mine first!""

Laura waves her hands in front of the crowd before speaking. "Please step back and allow Mrs. Maxwell some space."

"But I want to give Amy these flowers!" A woman steps forward and I think I know her. Is that Penny Whitaker? The classmate who reads my blog? She waves the flowers in Laura's face and Laura, annoyed, snatches them from her.

"I'm sure Amy will love them," Laura says with a huff, as if I am not standing right there. She's taking her bodyguard duties very seriously.

A well-coiffed woman I vaguely recognize steps toward Laura. "I've been waiting for two months to see Amy and have her sign my copies of her book. They're for my daughter. She loves the Lexie Maxwell series. How can I explain to my child that her hero can't sign the books?"

A tear trickles down her face and I realize where I know her from. This is Suzie Sunshine, the girl I went to high school with. Well, that makes sense since I'm at the high school reunion. Good thing I thought to bring Laura along as a bodyguard.

"My daughter is going to be upset as well!" Another woman says as she pushes forward. For some reason she's in a sparkly blue ball gown. A tad bit overdressed for a high school reunion.

The woman continues, "My husband and I flew all the way in from El Paso when I heard that Amy Maxwell was going to be at the high school reunion and that she could sign copies of my daughter's favorite book. My husband Grant went to school with you, Amy. Don't you remember Grant?"

She pulls a portly, balding man toward her and I gasp. This can't be Grant Westwood! He was one of the hottest guys in my grade! He looks like someone's out-of-shape, beer-loving dad. Kind of like Roger but not nearly as cute and cuddly as Roger is.

"Um, yeah, hi Grant," I manage to stammer, a lot like the way I used to stammer around him when we were in school together and I had to ask him for the simplest thing, like could he grab my pencil that rolled under his foot? He looked at me with the same expression he's looking at me with now...blank and vacant.

"Anyway," the woman says, shoving Grant aside, "I told Grant there was no way we could miss the reunion since you are our sweet, precious Ainsley's favorite writer." She beams at me and then adds as an afterthought, "Ooo, let me show you a picture of Ainsley!" She scrolls through her phone and pulls up a picture of a bucktooth, pimply faced kid who kind of

reminds me of the dentist's niece in Finding Nemo.

I resist the urge to back away and instead I say, "What a lovely child."

The woman places her hands on her hips and frowns at me. "She is *a lovely child. And she's going to be devastated to learn that I came all this way and you couldn't even sign her favorite book for her."*

Laura inserts herself between me and the woman.

"Ma'am, can you step back? Don't you see that Mrs. Maxwell is in a full body cast and can't sign anything?"

"Laura, it's okay," I finally say.

Laura turns to me, eyes wide. "But Amy, you can't possibly..."

I nod solemnly. "I cannot let this child down. I can't let any of the children down. Put the pen in my mouth."

"Put the pen in your mouth?" Laura looks at me like I've lost my marbles.

"Yes, I'm going to write with my teeth."

"Oh, Amy you're a hero!" The woman with the awkward looking child clasps her hands together in prayer as Suzie Sunshine bursts out into happy tears.

**

"Mom!" Lexie shakes me and I wake up with a start.

"Huh?" I sit up, giving myself a headrush, and gaze around. It's dark in the room and the light is pinkish purple outside. I had lain on the couch after the kids came home with the intention of just closing my eyes for a few minutes, but I guess those few minutes got away from me. I reach over to the light on the end table and turn it on. Lexie is eying me with concern.

"Are you okay?" she asks.

"Yeah, why?" I ask, adjusting the ace bandage on my wrist, which got twisted while I slept.

"You were moaning and making a lot of noise while you were sleeping."

My face flames as I try to recall what I was dreaming about. I don't think it was the spicy romance I've been trying to write, but you never know. "Um, just my wrist hurts." I hold up my wrist for Lexie to see as I stand up and head into the kitchen.

"Oh, okay. What's for dinner?" Lexie asks.

I turn and stare at my daughter, open-mouthed. After a minute she shrugs and throws her hands in the air.

"Dad told me to ask. He said he's very hungry."

I do a double take, but I'm not sure why. Typical Roger behavior. He must think I'm Superwoman because even when I have a sprained wrist, he still expects me to sort out dinner. I can't cook…I can barely hold a fork.

I glance at my watch. It's just after six o'clock. I open my mouth to reply, but I shut it before I say something I'll regret. Instead, I reach into the junk drawer and extract a handful of takeout menus. "Tell him to pick," I tell Lexie as I shove them at her.

"Great, takeout again!" Lexie grumbles, not taking the menus.

I glower at her. "You complain when I cook, you

complain when we have take-out. There's no pleasing you." I peer at her. "You could cook, too you know. It doesn't have to be me."

"I don't know how."

"It wouldn't kill you to learn. In fact, today's a great day to learn."

"Really?" Lexie replies with one hand on her hip. "Is someone coming over to teach you?"

I growl at her and she laughs.

"Relax, Mom. It's just a joke."

"There's some leftover quinoa salad and grilled chicken in the fridge," I reply, jerking my head toward the refrigerator.

"Never mind, never mind!" Lexie holds her palms up before taking the menus from my outstretched hand.

"Tell him just order me a salad from wherever he picks."

"Your phone is ringing," Lexie informs me as she leaves the room in search of her starving father.

My phone is, of course, in the living room. I curse silently as I dash into the room and snatch it up without looking at the display screen.

Please don't be Beth, please don't be Beth.

It's not Beth.

"Geez, you're a difficult one to get a hold of," Joey says after I say my hello.

"I'm right here, same number I've had for fifteen years. I'm not hard to find." I run my hand through the hair that I haven't washed in nearly a week now. It's too difficult to do with one hand and when I asked Roger to help me with it yesterday, he thought it was some flimsily veiled invite to sexy time in the shower—he immediately started groping my boobs. I had to shove him out to finish washing up. I really wasn't in the mood after my injury…and the fact that I stopped taking those hormone pills.

"How's your broken wrist?"

"It's just a sprain. I need to rest it for two weeks," I tell her. It turns out, a sprained wrist is a heck of a lot more annoying than a broken wrist. At least when you have a broken wrist you get a cast and everyone is slightly sympathetic. A sprained wrist hurts just as much (at least I think it does) and all you get is an ace bandage and no sympathy from your family who expects you to cook dinner for them.

"Lucky you," Joey says.

"Well, not so lucky. The kids and Jeter aren't really helping me out with resting."

"But at least you're not on bedrest," Joey says.

"Why would I be on bedrest? I have a sprained wrist and I think a broken pinkie toe. But that's happened before..."

"I don't know!" Joey says with a whine before adding, "I'm on bed rest."

I hold the phone away from my face and stare at it with surprise before putting it back to my ear.

"You're on bedrest? Why would you be on bedrest? When did you go on bedrest?"

"That's what I was trying to tell you the other day, Amy," Joey sighs. I grimace. I vaguely remember a phone conversation with Joey on the day I fell, but I don't think I ever discovered why she was calling.

"But…why?" This is Joey's third child. She's never been on bedrest before. In fact, with Amelia, she actually went ice skating a week before she gave birth (much to my mother's utter horror). And now she's telling me she can't even get out of bed?

"*Apparently* I have a prematurely effacing cervix," Joey says in a tone that leads me to believe she doesn't hold much stock in this particular diagnosis.

"A what now?" I've never heard of such a thing, and I had all sorts of fun ailments when I was pregnant with my kids including placenta previa and pre-eclampsia.

"It means my cervix is thinning out too early and I'm at risk of premature delivery. They said the earlier I deliver, the greater the chance that the baby will have…issues. They couldn't really pinpoint what *issues* they were talking about, but they said it's not good to have the baby at this point. Oh and I'm old," she adds bitterly.

"Oh wow." That sounds serious. "So they think bedrest will help?" .Tucking the phone between my chin and shoulder, I pull a pot out of the cabinet and fill it with water. I'll make myself some brown rice and anyone else who wants to eat it can join me.

Joey blows out a loud breath. "There's not much else they can do. I'm only thirty-one weeks so they want me to hold off delivering as long as possible. Especially given my *age*."

She tries to snort but there's a tremor in her voice

and it breaks my heart. Joey's scared. She's not often scared so this is upsetting on many levels. I'm scared for her. This is a high-risk pregnancy and Joey's baby's health and future depend on however the next few weeks go.

There's an uncomfortable silence in the air as I search for something caring and reassuring to say. Instead, I blurt out, "So I'm going to have to go solo to this reunion then, huh?" which is decidedly not caring nor reassuring in the least.

I want to grab the words out of the air and shove them back in my selfish mouth

There's silence on the other end of the phone and then Joey says, "Well, I feel bad about that."

"No, no! I didn't mean it like that. You shouldn't feel bad about it!"

Ugh. I just opened my mouth and stuck my own foot in it. Joey's dealing with a life-and-death situation here and I'm worried about going to a reunion alone. *What the hell is wrong with me?*

"Well you can always ask Beth to go with you—"

"Honestly I'd rather swallow nails."

"She's not that bad, Amy," Joey tells me in a matter-of-fact tone.

"She almost got both of us killed the last time I did something with her, remember?"

"That was partially your fault too," Joey tries to reason with me.

"She was the one who snuck into a crime scene!"

My voice has gotten so high that Roger calls out,

"Everything okay in there?"

"Fine!" I shout back. "Everything is fine!" Even though everything is not fine at all. There are two weeks until the reunion and I'm three pounds heavier than when I started, I'm flying solo at a reunion I didn't even really want to go to, and my sister is on bedrest. What a mess.

"I've got to go, Joey, Let me know if there's anything I can do. Actually, I'll have Roger drop some chicken parm off to you tomorrow so you don't have to worry about cooking anything." Chicken parm is just about the only thing I can make and I have several pans of it frozen in the freezer. My mouth briefly waters for chicken parm, which is a no-no on this low fat, low calorie, low carb, low taste diet I've been doing the past few weeks.

Joey laughs nervously on the other end of the phone. "Oh that's very sweet of you, Amy but Mom is bringing dinner over tomorrow."

"Well I could—"

"And the next day too. So no need to bring me food!" She laughs again and if I didn't know better, I would think my sister was trying to avoid my cooking. Oh, who am I kidding…of course she's trying to avoid my cooking…I'm terrible at it and everyone knows it.

"Okay, then, I guess I'll talk to you tomorrow." I dump a cup of rice into the boiling water and try not to drop my phone.

Joey says, "Well before you go, can I run an idea by you?"

"Yeah, of course."

"What would you say to Jason going to the reunion with you?"

This time, I do drop my phone but thankfully, not in the pot of boiling water. Although there is rice in it so I wonder if that would instantly negate any damage done to my phone.

"Wait, what?" I ask as I tuck the phone safely into the shoulder/chin space again. "Why would Jason come to the reunion with me?"

"Well, because I promised I'd go with you and then I let you down."

"Oh geez, Joey, you didn't let me down." Great, my selfish self managed to make my poor hormonal, on-bedrest sister feel bad about canceling on me. So bad she's offering up her hot husband to take her place. I can't go to the reunion with my sister's hot husband!

"I couldn't possibly take Jason to the reunion, Joey," I say definitively, nodding my head even though she can't see.

"Why not? You have an extra ticket and you don't want to go by yourself. I know you, Amy. You'd rather throw away the money you spent on the ticket than go by yourself. Besides, you can have a few drinks if you go with Jason. Jason's an excellent designated driver."

This is true. My brother-in-law hardly drinks more than a beer or two anymore. He used to drink a lot more, but I guess when you have a bunch of toddlers running around you get too tired to drink.

"That's not fair to Jason. And don't you need him at home to help with the kids anyway?"

Joey is quiet for a minute and then says, "I'll ask Beth to come over and stay with me that night."

I gasp. "Why would you do that?"

"I told you. I feel bad for letting you down."

"You didn't—"

"Fine. I feel bad my body let you down. Is that better?"

"No. You don't have to feel bad about anything, Joey. Really. I won't go to the reunion. It's not that important."

"I want you to go. And Jason has a suit. Plus, he's fine with going."

"You *asked* him if he's okay with it?"

I'm met by a brief beat of silence before Joey lets out a strained giggle. "Of course! Would I commit him to something like that without asking him first?"

Yes, yes, you totally would. Just like you committed to working halfway around the world without asking me if I'd be okay with watching Sebastian first.

I don't say this, of course, and Joey continues. "I'll have him text you to let you know what time he's picking you up."

"Joey, I can't ask you to—"

"Bye, Amy!" Joey calls out cheerfully before disconnecting the call.

I stare at my silent cell phone for a second before laying it down on the table. Am I really going to the reunion with Jason as my date? Oh God, how is Roger going to take the idea of me going out with another man? And not just another man…*Jason Collins*.

CHAPTER EIGHT

"I've been dreaming about you all day," Raul purred as he stepped into the bedroom.

Simone giggled girlishly and flattened the backs of her thighs against the footboard of her bed, Raul running his tongue over his lower lip, Simone's excitement mounting with every step closer toward her that he took.

Raul sauntered toward Simone and her body began to tremble with desire. She ~~bit her lip as~~ gasped audibly as he forcefully grabbed her waist and pulled her toward him, her loins tightening. (Research whether loins can tighten or there's a better word for it.)

"*Simone," he murmured into her ear, tickling her neck with his warm breath.*

"*Raul," she ~~gasped~~ panted.*

"*I've been waiting to get you alone since the day you hired me to clean your pool," Raul whispered.*

Simone looked up at him with her ~~big saucerlike~~ giant blue eyes. "But Raul, that was three years ago. Do you mean to tell me—"

"*Yes, my sweet Simone. I've been waiting for three years to do this." He started licking her neck with that very same tongue that had been licking his lips. Simone shuddered as she imagined that tongue in other places on her body.*

As he ran his tongue all the way down her neck, he

suddenly stopped and flipped her over onto the bed. As her cheek hit the comforter, she remembered the pile of folded laundry that he shoved out of the way in the process and cried out, "No!"

Raul stopped and stared at her back. "What's the matter, my love? Did I hurt you?" he asked in his tantalizing accent.

"No, no," she panted, flipping over onto her back. She propped herself up on her elbows and stared at her lover, trying to remain sexy and calm at the same time. "It's just..." She gestured to the piles of laundry on the bed. "I just spent almost an hour folding that laundry. I don't want it to end up wrinkled."

**

"This is utter horseshit," I mutter to myself before slamming the laptop lid shut. Sure, Simone's a stay-at-home mom having a torrid affair with the hot, twenty-five-year-old pool boy, but for Pete's sakes…who the hell wants to read spicy romance where the heroine is worried about her folded laundry getting wrinkled? I really should completely give up on this writing spicy romance thing. My priorities are too screwed up.

I glance down at my watch. It's nearly four o'clock and Jason is supposed to pick me up at six. I need to stop writing anyway and start getting ready the reunion. With Jason.

Turns out, I didn't have to worry about Roger's

reaction to me *going out with another man* because I didn't tell him.

Okay, okay, yes that is a chicken move, but seriously, I spent endless hours rationalizing with myself that I wasn't truly going on a "date" and that Jason was just accompanying me to a function as my brother-in-law, not as a lover. Ugh, *lover*…I hate that word. It's worse than slacks or moist. And Roger isn't even going to be home when leave for the reunion, so what is the point in getting him all upset about something that he won't even know about?

Okay so once upon a time I had a teensy-weensy crush on Jason…way before he was married to my sister. Heck, it was even before he knew my sister. It was back when I thought he was some shady bad guy living across the street and not an undercover DEA agent. Anyway, after Jason whisked Allie and me away to a secret location on a desolate mountaintop for our safety, Roger turned out to be a little jealous of Jason and the bond that he and I shared due to our near-death experience together. Oh and the fact that Jason is super-hot. Even Roger can see that. Heck, an eyeless potato could see that Jason is hot.

Roger, being a decade older than I am and firmly settled into middle age with a bit of a dad bod, is a tad insecure and gets weirdly jealous wherever Jason is concerned. He has gotten better since Joey and Jason got married, but he often looks like he wants to spar with the guy when they're in the same room. Yes, it's much better not to mention Jason in this instance.

After I agonize for at least an hour about what to wear, change no less than six times (and end up in the very same outfit I started off in), burn the ends of my hair with the curling iron (and then end up having to straighten my hair anyway because the left side of my head absolutely refuses to curl), and do my eye makeup twice because it's been so long since I've put mascara on that it's clumpy and I have to go rooting around in Lexie's room for some clump-less mascara, I am finally ready to go. I am sweating so profusely that I have to put the air on even though it is only fifty-three degrees outside. No wonder I never bother to get dressed up, do my hair, or put makeup on. I feel like I've just participated in a triathlon.

I'm pacing the living room while I wait until I realize that it's not helping my sweating situation. I'm in the process of airing out my armpits in front of the air conditioner vent when I hear Jason pull in the driveway. At least…I think it's Jason. It sounds like there's something wrong with his car. It's really…*loud.*

I peel back the curtains to peek outside and Jeter nearly knocks me to the ground with his enthusiasm. He loves guests, and will undoubtedly lick Jason to death the second he walks in the house. I hope he's not wearing black. I ran out of paper for the lint roller a few days ago and forgot to buy more this morning when I went to the grocery store. No worries, I'm sure I'll be back there again within the next twenty-four hours with the way Colt has been eating lately. In the past day and a half, he's managed to house an entire carton of eggs, two gallons of milk, three boxes of cereal, two packages of chicken breasts, four boxes of pasta, and a partridge in a pear tree. No, just kidding…he hates fruit. No wonder my grocery bill is over a grand every month and I'm there an average of five times a week. If I can only remember to put lint roller refills on the shopping list this time.

I soon discover the reason Jason's car doesn't sound right is because…he doesn't have his car. Instead, he pulls into my driveway on a…Harley?

I blink several times to make sure I'm not seeing things. Nope, my eyesight is fine—that is definitely a motorcycle in the driveway. As he stops the bike, swings his leg over the side and removes his helmet, I see that yes indeed, it is also definitely Jason on that bike. And he's coming toward the house. But the real Jason must have been abducted by aliens because the Jason I know would never ride a motorcycle and does not even own a motorcycle. Also, the Jason I know would not show up to a reunion wearing a leather jacket and…are those leather pants?

Jason (or his imposter) doesn't even make it to the front porch before Jeter starts going nuts.

"Down, Jeter," I command as I grab his collar. I open the door while Jeter yanks me around, attempting to maul Uncle Jason with sloppy doggie kisses. Usually, Jason is all for Jeter's enthusiasm and slobber, but today he backs away slightly. *Hmmmm, I'm really starting to suspect an alien abduction now.*

"Jason?" I wrinkle my brow as I peer at him.

Stop! Don't look suspicious! The alien will know

you're onto him! Wait, can't aliens read your mind? He'll know I'm on to him no matter what...there's no way to hide it.

"Amy," he says drily as he steps into the house.

"Is that a *mustache*?" I ask, pointing to a surprising dark patch above his lip.

Jason's hand reflectively goes to his face and then he scowls at me. "Yes, it's a mustache."

I roll my eyes when he turns around. It certainly doesn't look like a grown man's mustache. It looks more like the scraggly mess of a thirteen-year-old boy who doesn't have enough testosterone to grow an actual mustache. I'm curious how long he's been growing that thing.

"Are you having a mid-life crisis or something?" I ask as I follow him into the house. "What's with the motorcycle?"

He whirls around, a frown etched on his lips. "No, it's not a mid-life crisis! I've wanted a motorcycle for a long time. It's been a dream of mine since I was a kid." He's a tad defensive for someone who isn't having a mid-life crisis.

I put my palms up. "Sorry, sorry. I had no idea." I also had no idea it was dream of his to have a caterpillar growing on the top of his upper lip, but Jason is apparently an enigma to me.

Jason continues to stare at me, and for a second I find myself sucking in my gut, suddenly embarrassed by his attention. I gaze down at the floor and that's when I notice the pink helmet in his hand.

"What's that?" I ask with suspicion.

"It's a motorcycle helmet," he says in a tone laced with sarcasm.

"I know it's a motorcycle helmet," I snap back. "Why do you have it?"

He points in the general direction of the driveway. "For riding the motorcycle."

I narrow my eyes at him. "It's pink. I didn't know you liked pink."

"I don't. Joey likes pink."

"As much as I can see Joey riding a motorcycle, in fact, I can imagine that Joey would be the type of person to actually talk you into getting a motorcycle, there's two problems with that," I say as I point at the helmet.

"What's that?" Jason asks, running his hand through his hair. It looks particularly shaggy. I briefly wonder if he's lost his razor and his brush before I recall he was just wearing a helmet.

"First off, Joey is pregnant. Secondly, she's not here."

"Right," Jason says, shoving the helmet toward me. "That's why the helmet is for you."

I stagger backward, my heel catching on the rug. I know I shouldn't be wearing heels since I'm a walking disaster, but I couldn't go to my high school reunion wearing flats. Not only am I going to be the shortest person in the room—as I was for much of high school—flats make me look completely dowdy and that's definitely not the look I'm going for tonight.

As I fall, Jason's hand shoots out grabs the crook of

my elbow before I can go ass over teakettle. "Maybe you should change into flat shoes."

"I will not," I respond huffily. This is none of his business. "And don't change the subject." I point to the helmet. "You're out of your mind if you think I'm going to the reunion on a motorcycle."

"Why not?" Jason asks, crinkling up his forehead.

Why not? Is he crazy?

First of all…hellooooo, those things are death traps on wheels. Every weekend in the summer there's an article about someone killed on a motorcycle in our town or a nearby town. I'm not kidding…it's like an epidemic. They're just not safe and there's no reason I need to put myself in harm's way for a ride to the reunion. Also, I spent an insane amount time doing my hair and there is no way in hell I'm going to show up to the reunion with half helmet hair, half windblown hair.

"Because I'm not getting on a motorcycle." I cross my arms over my chest. I don't have to explain myself to Jason. True, he's being nice enough to take me to this reunion and I do appreciate that, but it is completely unreasonable for him to show up here with a motorcycle (that I'm pretty sure he didn't have last week) and expect me to hop on it.

"Don't be such a baby, Amy," he says, waving the helmet at me. "It's fun. You're never any fun."

"That's I lie," I snap. "I'm plenty of fun." I can't name a single instance of me being fun in the last twenty-two years, however, that is not the point. "Besides, transportation is not meant to be fun."

Jason laughs. "That's not true. Haven't you ever heard the saying, getting there is half the fun? What do you think they're talking about? Obviously it's transportation."

"They're not talking about—"

"Life's a journey? Again, that one's about transportation."

"No, those are song lyrics."

Jason opens his mouth to speak but I just hold my hand up. "I'm not going on the motorcycle and that's final."

Jason scowls at me. "Well, then I guess we can't go because I only have the motorcycle."

"Good thing I have a car," I reply as I grab the keys from the hook in the hallway and shake them in Jason's direction. "I'll even let you drive."

He snatches them from my hand and turns toward the door. As he opens it and steps out, I swear I hear him mumble, "You're no fun at all, Amy Maxwell."

Oh yeah, Jason Collins? I'll show you fun. You've obviously never been to a high school reunion with me.

CHAPTER NINE

As soon as we pull up to the Wine Bistro, I'm regretting my decision to come to this reunion. The sprawling front lawn in front of the venue is packed with men and women leisurely sipping wine and engaging in casual conversation under strings of fairy lights. Every single one of them looks like they just stepped off the pages of a fashion magazine, perfectly coiffed hair and impeccably dressed, not to mention…*young*. I squint at them as we go by—I don't recognize a single one of them.

I steal a glance at myself in the passenger side mirror and silently gasp at the wrinkles that I thought I hid well with some foundation. These people look at least ten to fifteen years younger than I do. A surge of jealousy courses through me.

Did they stumble upon a fountain of youth or something? Damn it! I knew I should have bought that more expensive wrinkle cream instead of the one in the bargain bin at the supermarket. Maybe one of my social media friends sells some magic anti-wrinkle cream that I can—

"I think the reunion is around the back," Jason says, jolting me from my pity party.

"Huh?" I stare at him and he motions to a sign stuck in the grass. The sign that says *Kensington High Class of*

1997, Around the Back of Building.

Oh. So these people aren't my classmates? Thank God.

We motor along the gravel driveway, kicking up rocks as we go, until we reach the back of the building. A *gigantic* barn the size of a small mansion is spread out in front of us, doors thrown open, music blasting through speakers set up near the exit. I can feel the thump of the bass as Jason pulls into one of the designated parking spots, completely ignoring the line for valet parking.

"You don't want to valet park?" I ask, staring longingly at the much shorter distance to the entrance from the valet stand. If we park, I'll have to walk at least three times as far. In heels.

Jason stares at me as if I suggested he strip naked and go skinny-dipping in the lake behind the barn. While that wouldn't be horrible…*no, Amy! Get your mind out of the gutter!*

"Why would I pay to park the car when I'm perfectly capable of parking the car myself?" He waves his hand around the area in front of him. "And there are plenty of available spaces."

I glance down at my feet, hoping Jason will take the hint but apparently he went to the same school as Roger did when it came to oblivion. If someone doesn't spell it out, it might as well not be real. Which is confounding, considering that Jason is an officer of the law and part of his job is to notice details.

"Plus, you don't have a valet key." Jason pulls the key out of the ignitions and waves my keychain in my face.

"Huh?" I wrinkle up my nose. "What's a valet key?"

Jason gives me that look again. The one that makes me wonder if I have a booger hanging out of my nose or he's considering just how he managed to marry one of my relatives. "You don't know what a valet key is? Where do you live? Under a rock?"

I narrow my eyes at him. "I don't valet park often." In fact, the number of places I've been to in my life that would require me to valet park could probably be counted on one hand. I think the hospital had valet parking when I had Evan, but of course since Roger had insisted we wait till the end of the baseball game to go to the hospital, my contractions were less than two minutes apart by the time we got there, and I couldn't have cared less if Big Bird had parked our car, let alone what kind of key was used.

"It's a key for just the ignition so that they valet drivers can't get into your glove box, or worse, copy your house key, check out your address from the registration in your glove box, and then go rob your house while you're not home."

I stare at him, mouth agape. I would have never thought such nefarious goings-on would have been happening in the valet world, however, Jason has proven that I am as naive as they come. "So we won't be valet parking then?"

Jason ignores me and climbs out of my SUV. I sigh, realizing I have lost this battle, and step out onto the gravel driveway, instantly regretting my choice of fashion over comfort (and quite frankly, safety) as my heels take on the uneven surface. I manage a few steps forward before my ankles wobble. My eyes dart around, searching for something to hold onto as I traverse the seemingly endless path toward the barn door. Jason is several strides ahead before he turns around to stare at me, obviously wondering what is taking me so long. Amusement twitches on his lips when he sees me standing there like a brand-new foal unsure how to use her legs for the first time. The amusement gives way to a full-fledged smirk as he takes a step closer to me.

"Having trouble with your shoe choice?"

I close my eyes and resist the urge to deny it. If I tell him I'm fine, he will walk away from me, even though he knows I'm not fine. But at the same time, the childish side of me does not want to admit he was right and I should have worn the flats.

"If you were a gentleman, you'd take my arm. You know, to help me to the door. After all, you're the one who won't valet park."

Jason's eyes flash with mischief as he reaches my side in three easy strides. "Sure. Blame the parking and not the fact that you wore your f-me shoes," Jason says as he reaches for my arm.

He and I freeze at the same time as we both realize what he's said.

For the first time ever, I see Jason Collins turn a shade of red never seen in nature.

"Um, I meant…" he starts to stammer, but I just grab his arm and start walking. Nope, not going to make this moment even more awkward than it is. I think I hear an audible sigh of relief from Jason as he practically drags me to the door like a caveman.

We step inside the barn and can't help but fall over the long picnic-like table in the entryway. Two women sit at the table—one with a glazed expression on her overly made-up face and the other with immaculate makeup and expertly waved hair. The first gives us a cursory smile while the second greets us with a grin wider than the Panama Canal.

"Hello, y'all!" she calls out, waggling her fingers in the air.

Ah, Suzie.

"Hello, Suzie," I say, plastering a fake smile on my face.

Suzie makes a big show of covering her mouth and squealing with what I assume must be delight.

"Amy Phillips! Well you haven't changed one bit!" she gushes.

I'm not sure whether to take this as a compliment or not, so I just say, "Neither have you, Suzie." Although, to be fair, she had to have work done. Her dress holds up her boobs pretty well, and from what I can see, she isn't wearing a bra. At least not one with straps.

"Aww you're so sweet," she says, swatting at me jokingly. Then her face returns to its normal business-first expression that I recall so well from school. "There are hors d'oeuvres being passed now, and this is for your dinner entree." She hands me a little card with two choices printed on it.

"Check off what you and your guest want and put it

in the mailbox over there." She points toward the other side of the table with her pen. "There's a photobooth at the back of the hall…" points with the pen, "...and yearbooks on that table over there." Again, with the pen. "Joy-Lynn does amazing work with hemp…have you seen her designs on Esty?"

"Huh?" I have no idea why Suzie has suddenly veered off track.

"Esty…you know the online store?" She tilts her chin and gazes at me as if I may be a bit soft in the head.

"Oh yeah, Esty," I mumble, wondering where this is going.

"Well," Suzie clasps the arm of the woman sitting next to her, "she made all the favors! I'm not going to ruin the surprise, but you will just die when you see how absolutely adorable they are!" She presses her finger to her lips like this is the biggest secret she's had to keep since finding out who killed Kennedy.

"Here's your nametag…" Without even pausing for a breath, she hands me a sticky tag with Amy Maxwell (Phillips) written on it, "...and just sign the book…" She nudges the woman next to her. "Joy-Lynn, give Amy the book."

Joy-Lynn. Was she one of Suzie's henchmen in high school? I don't remember her. She obviously didn't know what she was getting into by volunteering to help Suzie out because she appears to be in physical pain as she shoves the book at me.

I disentangle my arm from Jason's and reach for the book that Joy-Lynn is proffering at me. As I lean closer to the table, Suzie winks and me and stage-whispers, "Didn't do too bad for yourself there, Amy."

I have no idea what she's talking about, so I stare at her blankly. She studies my face before jerking her head in Jason's general direction. He is standing a few feet away, arms crossed over his chest, eyes roaming the venue, most likely looking for all exits and possible criminals.

"He is smokin'," she reiterates, waving at Jason.

"Um, yeah…I…thanks," I finally say as I sign my name in the book. "Come on." I grab Jason's arm, leading him away from Suzie and her prying eyes.

"Don't forget to put your nametag on!" Suzie calls after me.

"She's bossy," Jason says with a roll of his eyes as I stop and affix the tag to my dress.

"A tad."

"And you went to school with her? You guys are the same age?" He stares at me for a second and I swear I see his eyes zero in on the wrinkles on my forehead.

I glower at him. "Yes, we're the same age, wiseass."

Jason shrugs. "Oh. She seems older. Probably because she's so bossy."

I narrow my eyes at him. *Nice save, Mr. Collins. Nice save.*

**

I gaze around the inside of the barn and I've got to

hand it to Suzie…the place is stunning. There are so many people here and I barely recognize any of them. Most of my classmates have gotten quite chubby (to my relief) and they all look so much older than I do. At least, I think they look older than I do. I try to sneak a peak of myself in the mirror behind the bar, but it's too far away and too dark for me to tell if I have more or less wrinkles than the woman to the left. I can only see her profile and she looks vaguely familiar, but I can't quite place her. So does the much older looking gentleman she's speaking to in a hushed whisper. There is no way that man graduated with us. He looks at least fifty-five. Still, I feel like I know him too. God, can we really look that old?

As I quickly glance at them, I notice that the man doesn't have a name tag and I can't read the woman's. They both are speaking animatedly and in a heated manner, so I try to listen to their conversation as I pass by without looking at them, hoping for some clue to their identity. I can't make out much of the conversation aside from the woman saying something about going outside.

I turn my head to get a better look at them as they leave and am immediately accosted by the sound of my voice being called.

"Amy? Amy Maxwell?"

I shudder as I recall the dream I had a few weeks ago—the one where I was approached by Libby at the reunion.

I turn my head toward the sound of the voice and find myself face to face with a woman almost as short as I am, and I hate to say this, pretty dowdy. Her hair is in a severe bun (not the stylish messy ones that Lexie and Allie style their hair in) and she's wearing a cardigan and a sweater set, not unlike Mrs. Morris, the secretary at Evan's school who's close to a hundred by now and acts like she's on a first name basis with Satan himself. This woman isn't that old, obviously— she's at the reunion— but I am finding it really hard to imagine that she graduated with us only twenty-five…erm, twenty-six years ago. I glance down at her chest to discover her name sticker has folded over on itself and I can't read what it says. *Drat!*

Obviously, I have no idea who she is, but I can't tell her that. She remembers me…how insulting would it be if I tell her that I can't remember who she is?

"Hello!" I say, smiling as brightly as I can. "So nice to see you again!" *Please tell me your name, please tell me your name.*

"Oh you too!" the woman says as she grips my hands in hers and pumps them enthusiastically. "I'm so glad you could make it! This reunion wouldn't have been any fun if you didn't show up!" She leans in closer to me and says conspiratorially. "This would have been a big waste of a hundred bucks if you hadn't been here. And I'm a librarian, so I don't make much money."

Okay, as flattered as I am that this woman is happy to see me, she's making me feel a million times worse about the fact that I can't recall who she is. I glance around in a panic, praying for someone around me to swoop in and address this woman by name so that I don't have to admit that I don't know who she is.

Okay, there's nobody…except Jason who is practically glued to my side as if he is my personal bodyguard and he certainly wouldn't be able to—

"I'm Jason," he says, extending his hand. "And you are?" He cocks his eyebrow at the woman who practically melts into a puddle when she meets his gaze.

"Oh hello, Jason," she titters. She actually *titters*. I shake my head, aghast at how easily she completely came undone in Jason's presence, until I recall that not too long ago, I would have been similarly undone in the presence of Jason Collins. "I'm Penny Whitaker."

Penny Whitaker? This woman is Penny Whitaker? Geez, she is not what I was picturing at all. Well, honestly, I don't know what I was picturing, mostly because I can't remember Penny Whitaker. The name rings a bell, but her face is a blank to me. At least, her past face is a blank to me. Her present face is well, right in my face at the moment.

"It's lovely to meet you, *Penny*," Jason says in his most sincere hunky voice and then catches my eye. Ah ha, so he realized I had no idea who this woman was and he stepped in to save me…as usual.

Normally I would be annoyed at Jason's presumption, but right now I couldn't be anything but grateful for him butting in. I would have looked like a real ass if I hadn't known who Penny Whitaker was, considering it was her words of praise toward my blog that led me to the reunion in the first place.

"I'm going to go to the bar," Jason says. "You want anything, Amy? Penny?" He smiles at our newfound friend and I swear she swoons. Jesus, I forgot what an effect Jason has on the ladies.

"I'll have a glass of white wine," I tell him, digging through my purse to give him money, which he promptly waves off.

"No, no, I'm good," Penny stammers. "I'm drinking water!" She raises her water bottle with enthusiasm and it sloshes out of the top, landing on Jason's shoe with a plop. Penny stares down at his shoe and then back up at Jason, panic creeping over her face.

"I'm so, so, so sorry!" She takes a step toward him and the water bottle completely slips from her hand, dousing Jason with the remainder of the contents. "Oh my god!"

Jason steps back, the sleeve of his shirt dripping wet. Penny steps even closer—her head swivels from side to side. I have no idea what she's searching for until her eyes light up and she extends an arm out, nearly decapitating the waitress passing by with a tray of mini hotdogs wrapped in buns, and grabs a handful of the napkins on her tray. Stepping even closer to a shrinking Jason, she begins to pat his arm violently with the clutch of napkins.

"I'm good!" he tells her, stepping back as far as he can go without hitting the table behind him.

"Oh just let me…" Penny says as she aggressively dabs.

"Really I'm fine," Jason tells her. "It's just water."

"Yes, thank goodness!" Penny laughs nervously. "Imagine if I had wine?" Her eyes widen and she adds,

"Not that I drink a lot of wine!"

"Water dries!" I say cheerily a few minutes after the fact, and both of them stare at me like I'm the nut.

"Anyway…" Jason says, cocking his eyebrow at me as if he's trying to decide whether I'm crackers or not, "I'll be back in a bit." He turns and practically races off toward the bar.

"Your husband is just the sweetest, Amy," a voice behind me says as I feel a tight grip on my arm.

"Huh?" I turn my head slightly to get a better look at the voice's owner and I nearly swallow the gum I'm feverishly chewing. It's the woman I saw earlier speaking heatedly with the older man. My eyes drift down to the name tag and I immediately realize why I recognized this woman.

Libby Farrington? How the heck did Libby Farrington get here? Didn't she RSVP no? Or was that my imagination? Oh God, I thought she wasn't going to be here.

Frantically I search my brain for its lengthy Rolodex file on Libby Farrington. Divorced from her first husband, two children, but currently married to a…Senator? Or maybe he's a Representative? I'm not sure the difference between the two, I just know he's a politician of some sort running for office in the upcoming election. And no, I don't know this because I've had a conversation with Libby Farrington in the last twenty-five plus years since we've graduated from high school. This is intel that I've gathered solely from social media. Um, no, we're not friends on there either, but some people are quite stupid and don't set their profiles to private. Like Libby Farrington. I can see everything she posts on her Insta and Facebook without even being her friend. Although, considering the fact her husband is a politician and her carefully curated fake life is part of his campaign, I have to wonder if it's not a mistake that I can see everything that goes on in my high school nemesis's life.

Damn it, I felt like some sort of stealth and sanctimonious spy. Now I feel like I've been duped.

But either way, Libby is currently standing right behind me, telling me my husband is the sweetest.

I turn to face her to tell her she's mistaken, and my husband is most likely sitting in a parking lot drinking beers out of the back of one of his friend's pickup trucks, when she continues in a mock whisper, "I mean, that crazy woman spilled water all over him and he was just so *gracious* about it."

She leans even closer, as if Libby Farrington and I are besties sharing a secret. I'm quite convinced I've fallen down a rabbit hole into an alternative universe. "He's also quite delicious." She laughs and then adds, "Not that I'm checking out your husband on purpose, but honestly, it's hard not to notice him." She gives me a friendly little hip-check and a wink. "Good job, Amy."

Now I'm certain I've either encountered an alien life form or I'm somehow tripping acid right now. I cannot for the life of me understand what Libby is saying and why the hell she's leaning so close.

Why is she talking about Roger? Roger isn't even

here? I'm here with...oh...

It suddenly dawns on me (yes, I know, you figured it out three paragraphs ago, don't rub it in) that Libby thinks Jason is my husband. She's not talking about Roger at all, she's talking about *Jason.*

I open my mouth to correct her, but then I snap it closed. Even though I'm privy to her social media, all my social media accounts are private, and Libby Farrington technically knows nothing about me. On my blog, I've never shared a picture of Roger or any of the kids for that matter, all in the interest of privacy (see, I'm smarter than your average Gen X). On my blog, I don't even refer to him as "Roger", but rather "Hubby" or "the Hubs". No one here knows that Jason isn't my husband. Except Jason, that is.

Libby is staring at me with something akin to awe, a look I never thought in my wildest dreams she'd be capable of, much less looking at me with. She made my life a living hell for countless years of school, making fun of me and my chubby arms and chubby face as she waltzed around with her perfect hair and her perfect life and her perfect cheerleader body and her gaggle of friends who hung on her every word and did everything she told them to. So what if she thinks Jason's my husband? It can't hurt…after all, Jason is already here with me, right?

As I consider this, Libby turns to Penny and says, "Don't I know you from somewhere?"

Penny recoils for a second and then clears her throat before sticking out her hand and offering it to Libby.

"Yes, um, I'm Penny. Penny Whitaker? We graduated together."

Libby scrunches up her face as if she is thinking really hard and then says, "Oh yes, hi. Nice to see you again, Penny."

We stand there awkwardly, not saying anything, for what feels like a century, so I open my mouth—probably to make some incoherent and irrelevant comment to break up the silence—when Jason interrupts me by tapping my elbow with a glass.

I whip around and almost knock the wine out of his hand. "Geez, Amy!" He takes a step back and hands me the glass.

After regaling me with the tale of how difficult it was to get a beer at a winery, Jason parks himself at a bourbon barrel table in the corner, a can of beer at hand. Apparently, the bartender had given him a dirty look when he asked what beers they had on tap.

"This is a winery, you know," she had replied with disgust before reaching under the counter and producing a can of very cheap beer that had obviously only been brought in for those without the complex palettes needed to enjoy wine.

Of course, this is all based on Jason's say-so, and she quite possibly didn't say anything of the kind, yet I'm sure Jason couldn't help but cringe when he saw the cheap beer. To his credit, he's drinking it silently, oblivious to the fact the two women standing closest to me are totally ogling him.

I've chugged my wine much faster than I anticipated,

and due to the fact I haven't had as much as a cracker, the alcohol has gone straight to my head and I'm already feeling buzzed.

"How long have you two been together?" Libby asks in a breathy voice as she slowly sips her own wine in a much more dignified manner.

Huh?

It takes my wine-addled brain a moment to realize that she wants to know how long Jason and I have been married.

Oh, this might be tricky.

"Me and my husband?" I'm going for a skillfully evasive tactic, surprising, considering my blood alcohol level has risen faster than Jesus Christ on Easter Sunday. "Oh, nearly twenty-three years now."

Libby's jaw drops. "Really?" She studies Jason with scrutiny. "He doesn't look a day over forty."

I happen to know Jason is many days over forty. Almost as many days over forty as I am, but I don't comment.

"He's just…well preserved," I tell her, causing Penny to nearly choke on her (new) bottle of water and Libby to cackle with delight.

"Oh I'll say," she replies, her eyes raking over Jason's body from a not-so-distant distance. I chew on my lip, hoping Jason can't hear a word of this conversation lest I have a lot of explaining to do. I mean it's improbable due to the noise level, and plus he's staring at his phone with a mixture of amusement and intrigue.

Oh geez, I hope Joey didn't send him an inappropriate selfie or something...if anyone sees Jason looking at some dirty picture, what will they think of him? Wait, Joey's pregnant. Is there any such thing as a dirty selfie when you're pregnant? Oh god, now I really hope no one sees that. They're going to think my "husband" is some crazy pervert with a thing for preggos. Although, to be fair, considering how often Joey has been pregnant, maybe Jason is some crazy pervert with a thing for pregnant chicks.

"What did you say?" a voice interrupts from behind Libby.

I tilt my head to the left to see none other than Isabella Napolitano. I nearly hyperventilate. Isabella Napolitano was not only the most gorgeous and put together girl in our senior class, but her father had connections to a European modeling agency and Isabella was modeling and acting in very front and center places while the rest of us were trying to muddle our way through college. Some of us (I won't name names…okay, it's me) couldn't even make it through our sophomore year in a state school twenty minutes from home, while Isabella was knocking it out of the park on a different continent.

"Oh, just that Amy's husband is well preserved in the finest way," Libby replies with an impish tone.

"Which one is Amy's husband?" Isabella asks with interest. Now this is when I should really interrupt, but honestly, I'm enjoying this. I mean Isabella probably doesn't really care who my husband is and even if she did, it's not like she would be impressed. After all, she's a model and probably dates other models—

"The guy sitting at that table there," Libby replies, nudging Isabella.

"Oh my, he's delectable," Isabella says with a purr. Then she looks at me. "And he's *your* husband? I'm so jealous." She waves her hand toward the bourbon barrel tables on the other side of the bar filled with men who can only be described as grown-up frat boys, if there were such a thing. They all look the same, the only distinguishable difference being the color of the polo shirt each of them is wearing.

"My husband's over there trying to see how many hors d'oeuvres he can fit in his mouth at one time," Isabella says with a sigh.

I open my own mouth, gaping like a fish desperate for air, but I find that no sound comes out. I need to correct her. I definitely need to say, my real husband is currently stuffing *his* face with undercooked hotdogs and overpriced beer at a baseball game. My husband is not the guy sitting in front of you in sexy man attire, sipping a cheap beer but still managing to look, as Isabella said, *delectable*.

But Isabella and Libby, neither of whom would give me the time of day twenty-six years ago unless it was to make fun of me or to make my life a living hell, are not only talking to me with interest, they're jealous of me. Well, they think they're jealous of me because they think Jason's my husband, but let's not trifle over details.

"Ugh, I have to go back to him before he

embarrasses me and I have to divorce him," Isabella says. "I'll catch up with you later." She air kisses Libby before trotting off.

I stare after her until Penny interrupts.

"Hey, your drink is empty!" Penny says cheerfully as she grabs my wine glass. "Let's get a refill!" She reaches over and snatches Libby's glass out of her hand as well.

"I'll get you some too!"

"I'll come with you," I tell her. She places a hand on my arm to stop me. "No, I got this. You stay right there and catch up with Libby." She lets out a nervous titter as she scurries away.

"I'm not…" Libby trails off, staring at her retreating wine glass, her arm outstretched as if to grab it back…and then shrugs her shoulders. "Oh well. Wine is wine, right?" She smiles at me with a glazed expression on her face.

Is Libby Farrington drunk? That's impossible...we just got here.

I almost laugh when I realize that seeing Libby Farrington inebriated would be worth the price of admission. And then I remember the last time I saw Libby Farrington drunk. It was at her house during her sleepover for her thirteenth birthday party.

Oh yeah…by the way, I was at Libby Farrington's thirteenth birthday party. You know, back when we were best friends.

You weren't expecting that were you? The fact that Libby and I were once besties? Oops…maybe I should have opened with that, but sometimes you need to bury the lead to get the optimal reaction.

So yeah…now you know. Libby and I were best friends from the time we were assigned to the Purple table in kindergarten, to that fateful and most unfortunate night at Libby's thirteenth birthday party. The night it all fell apart for our friendship and quite frankly, my life in general.

CHAPTER TEN

Okay, maybe I'm being a tad bit dramatic—you may know by now that I tend to do that—but looking back, the fight Libby and I had that night sent a shit storm of dominoes crashing down for me, and my life at school was never the same.

Maybe Libby is planning to apologize to me? Maybe that's why she sought me out tonight?

I mean, had I known she was here I would have avoided her like the plague. There's no way I would have gone up to her. Tonight is the first time we have spoken, well, *civil* words, in nearly three decades and it could be my second chance. *Maybe my friendship with Libby can be salvaged!*

"So Amy, it's been a long time," Libby says as she slides into the chair at the bourbon barrel table next to me.

So Amy it's been a long time? That's all she has to say after what she did to me thirty years ago?

"Um, yeah, I guess," I reply. I do not sit next to her, even though there are three empty chairs.

Look at you with the sharp-tongued reply. My god they'll be asking you to host the Oscars next with your talent for witty banter and all. Insert eye roll here.

"What have you been up to?" Libby asks before leaning toward me. "Besides shacking up with that hot hunk of a man." She winks at me, and I feel my face burn as I once again pray to God that Jason is so immersed in the game on his phone that he doesn't hear her. I know he wouldn't call me out in front of anyone, but damn, that could make the ride home *awkward.*

But back to the question. Does she really expect me to give her an abridged version of my life that spans three decades? I mean, the episode of "Amy Drops Out of College and Gets Married to a Guy Ten Years Her Senior" is at an entire evening in itself. Not to mention my affinity for falling headfirst into crimes over the past decade. That's a meal we need several courses for.

"Oh this and that," I say breezily, sitting down in the chair next to her. Obviously my body is planning on a long dissertation but my mouth didn't get the memo. "You?" I smile at Libby to encourage her to talk about herself instead, but we are interrupted.

"Hey sweetheart," a male voice purrs and a very well dressed man with salt and pepper hair places his hands on Libby's shoulders. I swear she tenses up before plastering a smile on her face.

"Preston!" Libby says without turning around. "I thought you couldn't make it." Her voice is light, but it sounds accusatory.

"Surprise!" He grins. "My meeting finished up early and I thought I would come join you. You know, like we originally planned." His tone also sounds light…and except for some tension in his face, I would almost think he was happy to be here.

"That's…*great,*" she replies as he rubs her upper

arms with his hands, and now I *definitely* see her tense up.

"Aren't you going to introduce me, love?" he asks her, still grinning. It's then I notice his teeth are unusually white and his fingernails look like he's recently had a manicure. But he's a politician so I guess he has to look good if he's in public all the time. He certainly is dressed for the part of "Senator After Hours" with his mint green button-down polo shirt, navy blazer, khakis, and boat shoes.

Libby's lips stretch into what looks like a pained smile. I quickly glance at the man to make sure he's not actually hurting her with his grip.

"This is Amy Phillips…I went to school with her. Amy, this is my husband…Preston Moore…the third."

"Don't even think about calling me Trey," Preston says with a jokey grin as he shoves his campaign shaking hand at me, his other hand still on Libby's shoulder as if he's afraid he'll lose track of her if he lets go.

I take his hand and it feels like my own hand is in a vice. *Jesus, does he shake all his constituents' hands this way?*

"Um, I wasn't," I stammer, my breathing momentarily halted from the pressure of his handshake.

"Oh that's just a joke," he tells me with a guffaw. Yes, an actual *guffaw*. I've read about guffaws in books before, but I've never actually, up until this moment, heard another human being make that noise.

"So your meeting ended early," Libby says, reaching for her water. She swirls the straw in the glass, glancing around. I bet she can't wait for Penny to return with the wine. She looks like a woman in desperate need of an alcoholic beverage.

"Yes, yes, it did." Preston slides onto the chair next to Libby, arm still draped over her shoulder.

"Wonderful," Libby says in a tone that indicates anything but. She continues to smile, but it doesn't reach her eyes. We sit in awkward silence for a second until she spots Jason behind us. "Oh, we didn't introduce—"

The next few seconds play out in slow motion in my mind as I piece together what she's about to say. She is going to introduce Jason to her husband as *my* husband. And then the gig is definitely going to be up. Like I said before, I don't think Jason will say anything here, but he will certainly look surprised when Libby calls him my husband, and that will be enough to out me.

"Here you go."

Before Libby can finish her sentence, we are blessed interrupted by Penny, who shoves a wine glass at me and then at Libby. I smile when I see she got me a white wine. I can't drink red, as much as I enjoy it. It gives me a hellacious headache. Libby has a glass of red in front of her. She lifts it up as if examining it and frowns.

"I had white wine. I can't drink red wine." With a sigh, she places the wine glass back on the counter.

"Libby," Preston says while grinning, "this nice woman got you wine. Maybe you should be a little more gracious and just drink it. One glass of red wine isn't going to kill you."

I blink rapidly as I stare at him. Does he realize he's

talking to a grown woman…his wife…and not a child?

"But I don't want *red* wine, Preston," Libby says, still smiling as well. "I want *white* wine."

Preston leans in a little closer to Libby and says in a much quieter voice, but one I can still hear all the same, "Drink the wine, Libby."

Without thinking, I grab my glass and proffer it to Libby. "Here, you can have mine. I'll drink the red."

Okay, yes, I don't want to drink the red, and yes, Libby is acting childish about a glass of wine, but something about her husband has made me incredibly uncomfortable and I have a feeling that this would not be the end of this standoff if Libby doesn't drink the wine.

Libby stares at my hand for a second and then up at me, a genuine look of appreciation spreading across her face. I know that look because it's the same look she used to give me when I gave her half of my sandwich almost every day in third grade. That was the year her mom was really into organic foods and most of her lunches looked like something from an upscale Greenwich Village deli—which is great if you're a vegan hipster who likes that sort of thing…not so great if you're a third grader who prefers bologna and peanut butter and jelly on doughy white bread to portobello mushroom and arugula paninis on sourdough bread with bean sprouts.

"Thanks, Amy." She takes my glass and is about to hand me her own glass of wine when Penny leans forward on her stool, her hand flying out, knocking over the glass.

"Christ!" Preston yelps as he leaps to his feet, the red

liquid landing dangerously close to his lap. I recoil, but otherwise am motionless.

"Oh my goodness!" Penny squeals as she grabs for the napkins and starts mopping up the mess as the rest of us sit there stunned and flabbergasted. This is the second beverage she's spilled in less than an hour—I've finally met someone more accident prone than I am.

"I'm so sorry, Amy!" she says, red creeping up her neck. "I'll go get you another one."

"No, it's fine," I say, laying my hand on her arm. "Don't worry about it. I'm not crazy about red wine anyway."

"Then why did you offer to switch?" Libby asks me with a cock of her eyebrow.

"I just…" I glance at Preston who looks completely annoyed by the entire scene unfolding in front of him—Penny mopping up red wine with napkins that are falling apart, Jason observing us from the next table, game on his phone abandoned, and Libby gazing at me with that same look she used to get back when we were friends and I did something nice for her.

Libby was an only child and quite used to getting her own way. She didn't often do nice things for other people, but I didn't mind. It was something that she never understood.

I shrug my shoulders. "I just felt like it."

Libby, for all her faults, seems to understand what I'm saying…she always could read me. And I always could read her. Maybe that's why we didn't make it as friends. Maybe she was too afraid that I would be able to see through her at a time in our lives when no one was comfortable with themselves and didn't want their friends seeing through them and all their bravado. That's one thing Libby had at that time…bravado.

"Thanks," she says, softening and offering me a smile.

"I'll still go get you another one," Penny says. "White this time."

Before I can stop her, she scuttles off to collect the wine. Libby and I sit in uncomfortable silence—if uncomfortable silence consists of the DJ blasting 90s tunes at the top of the decibel register—and both Jason and Preston busy themselves with their cell phones. In fact, while Preston is scrolling through his, it starts to ring and he puts it to his ear, sliding out of his chair and striding toward the exit where there is blessed silence.

Now it's just me and Libby at the table. Maybe I should wave Jason over. He is, after all, my date. *Not your date, Amy. Not your date!*

The next thing I know, Jason standing next to me like I conjured him with my thoughts. I press my hand to my chest. "You scared me."

He doesn't seem to care. "I'm going outside. I gotta make a phone call."

I stare after him with annoyance—he's abandoning me now? When I lose sight of him in the crowd, I turn back to Libby. "So Preston's your husband, huh?"

"Yes, he's a…"

"Senator, I know." I don't really know. I mean, I don't recognize him or anything, but I did Facebook stalk her. "It must be interesting being a senator's wife."

She lets out a laugh that startles the couple at the next table. I don't recognize them, and they look at her as if she's mad. Who knows, she might be. "Well, it isn't exactly what I had on my top ten list when I was a kid, but it has its perks. He takes good care of me and the kids. My ex flaked out and went to find himself when the kids were little. He lives on an ashram somewhere now." She looks thoughtful. "India, I think." She shrugs and takes a sip of her wine. "But being a senator's wife definitely has its pitfalls."

"Oh," I say, surprised by her candidness. "Like what?"

"Oh, like the parties," Libby says. "The clothes I have to wear, being interview-ready all the time."

"You're still talking about the perks?" I smile at her, hoping she realizes I'm joking.

Libby laughs again. "You know, when I think about it, there doesn't seem to be too many of those." Another sip of wine. "Nope, Miss Amy, I'm talking about its pitfalls. Come to think of it, now the kids are in high school, the whole damn thing is a pitfall." She glances over to the doorway where her husband just exited. "Including the man himself."

"Why did you marry him then?" I asks, the words slipping from my mouth before I can even think about what I'm saying. "I'm sorry," I stammer. "That was totally out of line."

"Ha, no, it's alright," Libby says unexpectedly. "Sometimes I wonder the same thing myself." She takes a swig of the dregs of her wine and then stares into the empty glass. "Somehow this conversation seems like it warrants something stronger than wine," she comments with a raised eyebrow. "Too bad they only have wine here."

"And cheap beer," I reply, indicating Jason's beer can that he abandoned, relieved that Libby isn't going to read me the riot act for being so rude.

Libby pulls a face at the mention of cheap beer. I have a feeling Libby hasn't indulged in cheap beer since that night our friendship fell apart. Or at least since college.

"The wine is honestly not bad," Libby says with concession. "And I should know. Preston loves to go on winery tours." She rolls her eyes at the mention of her husband. "He hasn't met a wine he doesn't like. Where I come from, we call that kind of guy an alcoholic." She presses her finger to her lips and giggles. "But don't tell his constituents that. He won't get voted in again if they think he's an alcoholic." She wrinkles her brow and glances around faux conspiratorially. "Then again, maybe you should tell *everyone* that. I don't think I have it in me to do this for another six years."

I am momentarily stunned that this woman, my nemesis for dozens of years, is sharing this soul crushing information with me. She has all but confessed that her marriage is crap and she hates being a senator's wife. I feel like I should confess something as equally devastating to her, like we're playing some adult version of truth or dare.

Before I know what I'm doing, I open my mouth to confess to Libby that Jason is not actually my husband, when Jason himself returns to my side. Speak of the devil.

"Hey, I have to run back home for a minute," he says, jerking his thumb toward the exit.

"What?" I'm sure I'm mishearing him with the DJ being so loud and all. "I thought you said you had to run home for a minute." Home isn't far, but it's at least forty minutes there and back, and Jason is going to miss the meal if he leaves now.

"It's a work thing," Jason explains, an apologetic expression on his face. "I just have to get this file off my computer and I'll be back right away. Seriously, you won't even know I'm gone."

I scowl at him. I didn't want to be at this reunion alone, and now here I am, going to be at the reunion alone. If I had known he was going to bail on me, I just would have eaten the cost of the tickets and chalked it up to a loss.

"I swear," he says leaning closer, "I'll be *right* back." And then he gives me a peck on the cheek before winking, turning around, and waltzing out of there.

My hand involuntarily snakes up to my cheek which feels like it was just branded by a hot poker and not simply kissed by Jason's lips. Now yes, it was honestly nothing more than a chaste kiss on the cheek and since Jason is my brother-in-law, he has kissed me in that manner many times over the past few years. But the way he winked…he *knows* that everyone thinks he's my husband and with that seemingly innocent peck on the cheek, he told me he's willing to play along with the charade. I take a sip of the water on the table and wish Penny would hurry up with my new wine. I could certainly use an alcoholic beverage right now.

"Now that one is a sweetie," Libby says with a playful tone. "I bet he's more fun in bed than Senator Snorasaurus."

I do a spit take with my water, narrowly avoiding the front of Libby's dress. She cocks and eyebrow as I try to swallow the rest of the water in my mouth and it charmingly dribbles from my lips, down my neck, causing me to start choking in the process. I close my eyes as I cough helplessly, looking like the biggest fool in the world in front of Libby.

"Are you okay?"

There's a sudden and intense pounding on my back, so hard that I feel like a rib is going to break and puncture a lung, but the voice accompanying it is not Libby's. When I open my eyes, I see Libby staring at me and Penny at my side, hand poised midair ready to pound me on the back again.

"I'm fine, I'm fine!" I hold up my hands in surrender. *Geez, where did Penny learn to do the Heimlich? Prison?*

"Oh, good," Penny says with an audible sigh of relief. "I was so worried when I came back here and saw your face all red. I thought you were choking to death."

I peer at her with confusion. "Some water went down the wrong pipe. I haven't eaten anything. What would I choke on?" I ask matter-of-factly.

"Oh, right." Penny's face turns bright red and she glances away until her eyes land on the glass of wine she set down on the table when she came back and thought she needed to play hero.

"Here's your wine." She picks it up and thrusts it at me, wine sloshing over the sides in the process.

"Um, thanks," I reply, taking the now sticky glass from her and placing the wine glass back on the table. My bladder is filling rapidly from the drink I had earlier, and after all that coughing and sputtering, I have the weird sensation that some of that might have spilled over, if you catch my drift. "I'm going to go to the bathroom first though."

"Do you want me to come with you?" Penny offers as she pulls her bottle of water from her lips and quickly starts twisting the cap back on.

"No, no, it's fine," I tell her as I stand up. "I'll be back in a minute."

I hurry away quickly, but I can almost feel Penny's disappointment seeping out of her pores and alighting on me as I leave. She feels a bit smothering if I'm honest.

There is, of course, a line at the bathroom—give a bunch of middle-aged women wine. By this time, I have to go even more urgently than I originally thought. I scoot off the line and head to the front of the building, hoping there are bathrooms there.

Of course, Suzie is there with a haggard-looking middle aged man who appears like he has just been listening to her talk about her children's oboe playing or water polo for an hour straight.

"Hi," I say, rushing up to both. "Can you tell me if there's another bathroom available? The line in the woman's room is so incredibly long that I think I'm going to pee my pants." Now my bladder feels like it's going to explode and that definitely does not bode well for the lacy underwear I have on under my dress. Not to mention the fact that my "date" has abandoned me, so if this blows over with a sneeze or laugh or cough, I'm stuck sitting in pissy pants until Jason gets back.

Okay, I see you cringing over there, making a face, thinking it's gross. But please, if you're a mother of a certain age, you know exactly what I'm talking about. Every cough, sneeze, or laugh is like playing Russian Roulette with clean underwear.

Both Suzie and the man turn to look at me with shocked expressions at being interrupted, but the man's expression soon morphs into one of gratitude.

"I have to go!" he says.

"But the dessert bar!" Suzie says, shaking a paper at him.

"So do I!" I shout after him.

Suzie turns and I swear she's hiding a glower underneath her perky exterior. "Amy! You scared him off. I was trying to get him to add some cannoli to our dessert bar."

I am now hopping up and down like a decapitated chicken. "I don't care about cannoli. I only care about finding a bathroom. Do you know where there's another bathroom? One without a line that stretches all the way to

Midtown?"

Suzie sighs and points in the direction of the kitchen. "Don't tell anyone I told you this, but there's a staff bathroom over there. There shouldn't be anyone on line."

"Thanks!" I call as I scramble off as fast as I can possibly go without my bladder brimming over.

CHAPTER ELEVEN

When I return to the table a few minutes later, Isabella is sitting with Penny and Libby. Libby and Isabella are leaning toward each other, laughing merrily while Penny chews on the top of her water bottle, looking like someone kicked her dog.

I pull out the lone chair to sit and all the women look at me with shock. With a racing heart, I try to inconspicuously inspect myself, thinking with horror that I have somehow tucked my underwear into my dress, or I've walked out of the restroom with toilet paper trailing off my shoe. When I find neither of those infractions, I ask, "What?"

Libby takes a sip of her drink and raises an eyebrow before asking, "How did you get in and out of the bathroom so quickly? The line stretches around the building."

"Oh, I—"

"You used the men's room, didn't you?" Isabella says with a knowing nod of her head.

"Oh god, no—"

"I always use the men's room," Libby says matter-of-factly, placing her wine glass down on the table. "Good for you."

"I didn't use the—"

"Believe it or not, it's much cleaner than the

women's room," Isabella says, nodding her head in agreement.

"But what if a man walks in?" Penny asks, gripping her sweater in her hands, face gone pale. If she had pearls, she'd probably be clutching them. "What if you get caught?"

"Oh Jesus," Isabella says with a roll of her eyes. "It's not like they're going to haul you off to jail for using the men's room, Peggy." She and Libby start laughing in that classic mean girl way of theirs…the way that used to drive me absolutely bonkers back in high school.

"Penny," Penny says, but so quietly that I doubt either Isabella or Libby hear her. If they even care.

"Guys, I didn't use the men's room. I just found a different bathroom," I explain, interrupting their laughter. "Suzie showed me a staff bathroom."

Isabella grins and slides off her chair. "Well where is this secret bathroom, because I just happen to have to go powder my nose. And I am certainly not waiting on line with the peons."

I give her directions to the bathroom and she says, "Lib?" waving her hand for Libby to join her. But Libby is on her phone now and completely ignores Isabella. Well, chances are she can't even hear her. I swear I can feel the music in my bones, the bass is pumping so hard. Isabella, who is probably not used to being ignored, storms off in a huff toward the staff bathroom. I watch as she makes a left instead of a right, but it's too loud to call out and correct her. Oh well, I guess she *will* have to wait on line with the rest of the peons.

Libby puts her phone down and leans toward me. "So what's the deal with you and Prince Charming? Tell me everything. Don't leave any details out."

My former bravado and resolve to tell the truth about Jason completely flies out the window as my mouth gets dry and my palms start sweating. I glance around, desperate for some way to untangle myself from this lie that I've let spiral out of control. It's one thing to not correct the misconception that I'm married to Jason—quite another to invent an entire backstory and life for the two of us on demand.

Fortunately, I am saved from answering Libby by the chords of *Ice, Ice Baby.* I slide off my chair, grab both my drink and Penny's hand, and shout, "Let's dance!"

As I get closer to the dance floor, the realization that there is no way in hell that I would have danced in front of these people back in high school, considering I have two left feet, hits me. I didn't even dance at the prom—I spent it cowered in the corner with my date…well, that is when my date wasn't sneaking off to the bathroom to smoke a joint (hey, where is Kevin McDermott anyway? Is he that balding guy there in the corner? Oh, yes, I think I see Kevin's face in those jowls). But it's too late to turn back now. It's either dance like Elaine Benes or admit I'm a liar to Libby.

Penny squeals with delight as we reach the dance floor. There are more than a dozen of our classmates out here pretending to hip-hop dance like they actually can. Unfortunately for them, most of them look like the most "hip" they've got would be the hip in "hip replacement."

But that bodes well for me. If everyone looks like a fool, no one will even care that I can't dance either.

Still, to make this even less painful, I take a big gulp of my wine before getting down to the beat of Vanilla Ice. I'm trying to move all my body parts in some sort of rhythmic fashion (without spilling my drink) when Penny literally starts dancing like she's on stage at a concert as a backup dancer. I halt in my tracks as she busts out moves that would make MC Hammer jealous, my mouth agape.

It takes a second for the rest of the semi-inebriated crowd to catch on to the fact that we have a prodigy in our midst, but once they do, the crowd parts and Penny is front and center getting jiggy with it. Her eyes are almost closed, like she's half concentrating, half taken in by the music. No…consumed by the music is more like it.

When the song is over, Penny's eyes snap open and she stops dancing, met by applause and hoots and hollers. A blush quickly spreads over her face and before I can even identify the next song (I lie…I get it in three notes…it's *Come Baby Come*…I mean really, an amateur could get that one), Penny has whisked me off the dance floor and is dragging me back to our table where Libby sits, Preston next to her, obliviously tapping away on his phone.

"Oh my God, Penny," I gasp as we weave back to our table, people clapping Penny on the back. She has beads of sweat dotted across her hairline and flushed cheeks. Geez, she was really working hard out there. "When did you learn to dance like that?" I ask as we sit down.

A clouded expression crosses over Penny's face, but then she shakes her head quickly and smiles.

"I've always been a dancer, silly!" She beams even brighter. "Fifteen years of dance lessons. I started when I was three years old."

"Wow," I had no idea you could dance like that. You were amazing out there."

A brief flash of that stormy expression and then a broad grin spreads over her entire face. "Not many people do. Or did, anyway. But I've loved to dance since I was a wee bitty thing. I took hours and hours of dance classes a week. I even took classes before school. The studio owner gave me private lessons in the morning before class."

"That sounds expensive," I blurt out, the mom in me doing calculations in my head.

"My mother worked two jobs to pay for them," Penny tells me with a solemn nod of her head. "She took out a second mortgage on our house when I went into high school. Several professional dance companies were scouting me."

"Really?" Libby says and Penny turns an even deeper shade of red while dropping her gaze down at the table and twisting a napkin between her fingers. She doesn't answer Libby, but nods instead.

"That's…wow…um dedication," I tell her. That's one thing I've never understood…parents killing themselves for their kids' hobbies. Although, from what I just saw, I think Penny's dance obsession might have been more than just a hobby, even though, didn't she say she's a librarian earlier? It doesn't seem like she's using her dance background in her current career. She still has talent, although I don't think there's a big demand for forty-something year old women dancers entering perimenopause.

"Sounds like you were on the road to stardom," Preston says.

We turn in unison to look at him. I've almost forgotten that he's there. He immediately returns to his phone.

"Well, that didn't work out," Penny says meekly.

"What do you do again?" Libby asks as she puts her wine glass down.

"I'm a librarian," Penny says, stiffening, almost seamlessly slipping into the role of stereotypical librarian right before our eyes.

"So what happened?" Preston asks her, one eye on her, one eye on his phone. "Why did you stop dancing? Why didn't you sign with one of those dance companies that were scouting you? It'd be a hell of a lot better than being a librarian." He laughs and it sounds downright mean.

Penny immediately resembles a pomegranate.

What the hell is wrong with him? This is obviously a sore subject for the woman and he's ripping open her wounds like Penny's a gazelle and he's a lion on the Serengeti. Does this man have no couth? How did he get voted into office?

"Preston," Libby says through gritted teeth. "That's not an appropriate question."

He looks up at her, his eyes stony. He opens his mouth to speak, but the sound of his phone ringing interrupts him. It's playing *Hail to the Chief.* Guess he's angling for a White House run sooner rather than later. He frowns at the screen, pokes the accept button, and leaves the table without another word to us.

Libby rolls her eyes. "Sorry about him," she says to Penny.

Penny doesn't answer because she's completely absorbed in her own phone. She scoots back in her chair a little, holding the phone close to her chest as she texts away madly, fingers flying over the screen.

"Penny, you okay?" I elbow her gently after she doesn't answer. She jerks her head toward me, pulling her phone closer to her body, almost like Lexie would when texting a boy.

"Huh?" Her face flushes and for a brief moment, I wonder if she's texting some guy. She's certainly acting squirrelly. I'm about to open my mouth and jokingly tease her like she's one of my kids when I realize, she's a forty-something-year-old woman—there's no need for her to get embarrassed if she's texting a guy.

"Ugh, that bathroom took forever! What did I miss?" Isabella asks breathlessly as she plunks her clutch down on the table and shimmies into the chair that Preston just vacated.

Libby turns and smiles at her sweetly, the smile not reaching her eyes. "Not a thing."

Isabella frowns at her and squints her eyes. "Ah, same old Libby...evasive as ever." From her slurred speech, I can tell she stopped at the bar for refills since she left our table.

Libby's eyes flash, and I think she's going to snap at Isabella, but then she quickly regains her composure and says, "What exactly does that mean, Isabella?"

Isabella laughs and waves her hand. "Oh you know, you were always full of secrets in high school. You loved shutting your friends out." She laughs again and playfully punches Libby's arm.

The uncomfortable silence that follows is the kind I always feel like I need to fill by nattering off some inane little-known factoid or relaying some anecdote about my kids or the dog.

"Did you know that ladybugs—" I start to say.

"I've got to go to the ladies' room," Libby says suddenly, grabbing her purse from the table, interrupting anything I would have just said and probably saving me from being stupid. "Where was that *secret* one again, Amy? You know, considering how much I like secrets."

I start to launch into the directions for the second time, but Isabella jumps up and grabs Libby's arm. "I can show you!"

Libby wrests her arm from Isabella in the most delicate way one can when extracting oneself from your best friend. Well, at least I thought they had left school as best friends, but it doesn't look like they've really kept in touch over the years.

"I can find it myself," Libby says as she storms off. She goes in the right direction at least.

I glance at Isabella whose face is crimson. She folds

her arms over her chest and huffs loudly before storming off, not even saying goodbye to Penny or me, muttering, "Some bitches never change," under her breath.

I stare after her. "I wonder what happened with them," I muse out loud. I glance back at Penny, expecting her to answer me or at least shrug or something because obviously she doesn't know what happened between Isabella and Libby, but Penny isn't even paying attention to Isabella…or me for that matter. She's on her phone again, chewing her bottom lip as she texts with fervor.

I wait till she's done texting and has put her phone back in her pocket to ask if she wants to go back out on the dance floor. The DJ seems to be making his way up the 90s playlist I have on my phone and I'm very inspired to dance, erm, sway my hips and bob my head to the music. I'm not sure if it's the music or the copious amount of wine I've had in the last two hours, but my inhibitions are practically nil. I better hold off on any more wine lest I be using that pole in the middle of the barn as a prop.

"Um, …" Penny pulls her phone back out and stares at it. Is she checking the time? "Maybe another drink instead?"

I shake my head. "I don't think that's a good idea." Then I reiterate, "I mean, for *me* anyway. You're drinking water…you could do that all night. I mean, until you end up peeing every twenty minutes."

"Oh yeah," Penny says with a stilted laugh. "You know what? I really should go to the restroom." She slides off the chair and then looks at me hopefully. "Can you show me where that bathroom was again?"

I resist the urge to sigh. Why couldn't these women all have to go to the bathroom at the same time instead of having me give out directions three times now? Or better yet, why didn't they listen to me the first time I gave the directions to Isabella? Oh who am I kidding…Isabella didn't even pay attention when I gave the directions to Isabella.

"Sure," I tell Penny as I slide off my chair. I lose my balance in the process and put out my hand to brace my fall. It bends back against the table, causing me to wince.

"Are you okay?" Penny asks, rushing to my side, throwing her hands out as if she would catch me if I fell.

That's a laugh…she's about a hundred pounds soaking wet and as meek as a mouse. I would crush her if I landed on her.

"I'm good, thanks," I tell her, smoothing my hands over the back of my dress. I probably have wrinkles galore from sweating and then sitting, but then again, I doubt anyone here is looking at my butt. At least, I hope they aren't.

Penny lets out a nervous chuckle as she follows me to the bathroom. "Wouldn't want you hurting your wrist again."

I laugh as well, not even realizing that I never told anyone but my family about my wrist…not even my blog followers.

CHAPTER TWELVE

We're weaving our way toward the bathroom when Patrice Herman practically leaps in front of me.

"Oh my God, Amy!" she squeals in that soprano voice that apparently, she never grew out of. She still sounds like a thirteen-year-old boy in the throes of puberty. I take a deep breath and pray she stops talking. I had a migraine for a week straight when Patrice was my lab partner in tenth grade bio.

"Patrice, hi. How are you?" I ask in the tone of voice of someone who really doesn't care how she is and just wants her to say she's fine and move on. But Patrice was never one for subtleties.

"Oh my God, Amy, I can't even tell you!" Patrice says, waving her hands and grabbing my arm, pulling me closer to her.

Oh please don't, Patrice, I silently beg.

Patrice does not heed my silent begging. She immediately launches into a story about her daughter becoming a representative for some makeup company. I can't seem to follow the story in its entirety because I think she's mimicking her daughter's voice by speaking in an even higher tone of voice than she usually does. I glance around nervously, wondering if the wine glasses people are holding are going to shatter. After a mind-numbingly long time, she says, "But listen to me, going on about my Marina and her accomplishments and we have an actual celebrity in our midst."

I wrinkle my nose and glance around. "Who?" *Is she talking about Libby's husband Preston?*

Patrice laughs and lightly slaps me on the arm. It hurts more than it should. "Why *you*, silly! Your blog is just the best…the absolute best. Every time it comes out, I make Marina sit there while I read it to her. Now I'm sure it must make her cringe to have me reading aloud to her, but she just has to hear your blog…I mean, it's just perfect!"

Oh, I'm sure your daughter cringes when you read to her, Patrice, I'm sure.

"And you wrote a children's series?" Patrice continues.

She cocks her head at me like she's trying to recall if she actually heard that or imagined it. For a brief second, I wonder if she's stalking me because we haven't announced the series yet, but then I remember, I mentioned it on my blog a few times, trying to drum up readership before it was even released.

"Are you talking about Amy's blog?" Another woman sidles up next to Patrice before I can even answer. I squint to place her. She looks so familiar, kind of like Glory Ann, our class equestrian who married an older man she met on a tour when she was racing horses, but she's a good fifty pounds heavier than Glory Ann. Well, probably more. Glory Ann was so thin she nearly disappeared when she turned sideways. I squint even harder to read the nametag that's being swallowed up in the folds in her shirt.

Oh geez, it *is* Glory Ann. I guess she's not riding horses anymore or they would probably need a chiropractor. Okay, I know it's childish and slightly mean, but I feel strangely satisfied to see I'm not the only one who isn't in the best shape of their life.

"I love your blog, Amy," Glory Ann says. "Did Patrice say you were writing a children's series?"

"Yes!" I say with a smile. "The first two books come out in May."

"That's great! My youngest daughter loves mystery books, but I can never find ones that are appropriate for a nine-year-old, other than Nancy Drew, of course, but she told me she doesn't like the way my old Nancy Drew books smell," Glory tells me with a roll of her eyes.

"I understand completely," I tell her. "I believe my publisher is doing a launch party at the end of this month."

Listen to yourself, Amy...publisher...launch party...you sound like a real douche.

I ignore my inner critic because for once, I'm proud of myself. I worked hard on those books…*we* worked hard on those books…and damn it, I'm going to enjoy the accolades for them. Well, not that Glory Ann is offering me accolades, but you know what I mean.

"A launch party!" Glory Ann claps her hands together like a kid. "My daughter would love that!"

"There's going to be kid-friendly finger foods and a magician…I think." I haven't had much to do with planning the launch party and to be honest, that's a good thing. I'm not good at party planning at all and I tend to get overwhelmed easily. But according to my agent, there is going to be kid-friendly finger foods and a magician, so that's what I'm going to tell anyone who asks. I really hope there's going to be wine for the moms too. Not only does wine make kids' events more palatable, but they're also more likely to buy the books with wine being served. I'll have to remember to remind my agent of that.

"That sounds really great," Glory Ann says. "Hopefully there will be some of this too?" She holds up her wine glass and I silently congratulate myself for being a marketing genius who knows what the public wants. Well, I know what exhausted, harried, and overwhelmed moms want when being dragged to a launch party for a children's book series at least.

I smile at Glory Ann. "I'll be sure of it. If you give me your email address, I'll send you an invite."

Glory Ann beams at me and digs through her purse for her phone. "That would be great. I'll text it to you."

Patrice takes a swig of her wine. "I don't suppose you're having a party for your blog?"

"Um, no not right now," I tell, unable to imagine what kind of party I'd have for the blog.

Patrice hiccups and I wonder how many of those glasses she's had to drink already.

"Pity. I'd like some wine," Patrice says with a shrug.

Glory Ann widens her eyes at me before turning to Patrice. "You've had wine, sweetie."

Patrice turns the glass upside down, a drop rolling out and onto the floor, before bouncing up and splashing on her foot. "But I'm finished." She frowns. "I should get more."

"I don't think that's a good—" Glory Ann reaches out her arm to stop her, but Patrice is lightning fast for someone who is inebriated.

"Geez, she's going to be a delight on the ride home," Glory Ann mumbles.

Glory Ann and I quickly exchange numbers and I see Penny out of the corner of my eye. She's swaying from side to side, sort of like she's dancing. I'm wondering why, considering the DJ has taken a break and there's no music playing, when I remember we were on our way to the bathroom. She probably really has to go.

"Sorry, we were on our way to the bathroom," I say with an apologetic smile as Penny shuffles from foot to foot, glancing from the door and back to me. *Why doesn't she just go to the bathroom without me?*

"You could have gone without me," I point out when I rejoin Penny and we resume our trek to the bathroom. "You didn't have to wait."

"Um, I didn't know where it was. I was waiting for you to show me," Penny says.

I sweep my hand toward the bathroom that is *right* in front of us, trying not to roll my eyes. Penny reaches for the handle and opens the restroom door just as a woman strides out, in a flurry. She has to sidestep out of the way to avoid bumping into me. She quickly drops her head as she passes—I think I vaguely recognize her but she's gone before I can recall her name or even catch another glimpse of her face. Not that it matters. She didn't greet me like she knew me. In fact, I'd say she did the absolute opposite and tried to avoid me like the plague. Maybe another nemesis from high school. I had a few.

The air in the bathroom is heavy with a weird feeling of stickiness in the atmosphere, not unlike the bathroom back in high school where we would be accosted by a cloud of *Aqua Net* and *Charlie* upon entry. *It didn't feel like this before.* I get a sense of deja vu and a chill creeps over me.

I chalk up my unease to the fact that I've had way too much wine tonight, combined with the whole surreal feeling of being reunited with classmates that I haven't seen in decades. Since I'm here, I might as well pee, so I step over to the sink to wash my hands before using the stall. In the mirror I can see Penny enter the stall closest to the door…in this bathroom, there are only two stalls, so I have to use the handicapped one, which I hate to do. I always feel like I'm taking something away from a person who might need it more than I do, even if there is no one else around.

I scroll through my phone while I'm waiting until Penny comes out of the stall, but she's already been in there for longer than it would take a normal person to pee. I start to worry she's pooping and I absolutely hate using a public toilet after someone who pooped, so I reluctantly push on the door to the handicapped stall and immediately discover that it is occupied.

"Oh, I'm so sorry," I stammer, backing out, my eyes zeroing in on the stall's occupant. "I didn't realize—"

Is that a nail file?

And then my mouth freezes, half open.

It takes my brain a second to register the scene in front of me, but when my neurons start firing and the puzzle pieces slide together, I open up my mouth all the way and scream.

CHAPTER THIRTEEN

"Oh my God, oh my God, oh my God."

I lean over the railing in front of the entrance, trying to breathe in deeply, but the railing is pressing right into my diaphragm, making it impossible. I want to sit on the ground, or better yet, curl into a ball, but I'm so afraid that the rising sensation in my throat is indicative of the fact that I am going to throw up. And I do not want to choke on my own vomit in front of my former classmates. Although, that would definitely be the topper to my night.

"What happened?"

"What did you see?"

"Why did you scream?"

My heightened anxiety is not being helped by the crowding of said former classmates around me. In fact, they're adding to my stress by getting too close and seriously, are they consuming all the oxygen? They must be because I suddenly can't breathe at *all.*

"Put your head between your knees," someone tells me.

Is that Penny?

I don't know and I don't care. I do exactly what I'm told.

Someone…Penny again maybe...hands me a bottle of cold water and tells everyone to back the F up. Okay, that could not possibly be Penny. I don't think her meek little mouse self could possibly use the F word if she tried.

People inch away and I can see the voice belongs to Isabella. Of course, that makes much more sense. Isabella always had a potty mouth.

"Are you okay?" she asks, genuine concern on her face. "Can I get you something? More water? Wine?"

I stare at her for a second and then I burst into tears. I have no idea what has come over me, but I cannot stop the river pouring out of my eyes.

I need to go home. I need to get in my bed and pull the covers over my head and pretend none of this happened. Because how could it have happened? What are the chances that I would stumble upon yet another *dead body in my lifetime? Why does this keep happening to me?*

Isabella is eyeing me warily and I realize that I am saying all of this out loud. Okay, more like muttering it incomprehensibly out loud, but out loud all the same.

"We should find your husband, hon," Isabella says to me and I wonder what she's talking about.

My husband isn't here. He's having a good old time with his buddies at a baseball game and isn't stumbling across dead bodies like I am. Oh, wait, she's talking about Jason.

But where *is* Jason? He left hours ago to "run home quickly" and I haven't seen hide or hair of him. And hello, I could definitely use his hide right now. Because apparently after I screamed like a banshee in the bathroom, a waitress went into the stall to see what I was screaming about and called the cops. Who are currently on their way and I'm assuming—considering I was the one to find the body—they'll want to talk to me. And I, of course, will have to talk to them. Because that's the thing about stumbling upon dead bodies…the police *always* want to talk to you. And I never know what to say to them.

Yes, I know, it seems so simple, just tell the truth, tell them what happened. But let me tell you something; when you end up in traumatic situations—like finding dead bodies—your mind tends to play tricks on you and your memory isn't as sharp as you'd think it would be. There have been numerous studies done on this, trust me. And when your memory isn't the best, you end up stammering and saying *um* a lot and it makes you look guilty, even if you have *absolutely nothing to do with the dead body in question.*

Tears well up in my eyes and bile rises in my throat as I stand up straight and lean over the railing again, getting a head rush in the process. My knees buckle and I grab the railing before I drop to the ground, my mouth getting all puckery and watery. *I think I'm going to be—*

"Can someone tell me where I can find Amy Maxwell?"

"Huh?" I lift my head, spittle flying off my lips and hitting my hair. Oh delightful. I sneak a peek around and see what appears to be my entire class looking at me. Along with a plain clothes police officer. Probably a detective. Great.

I bet you're wondering how I know he's a police

officer. Well, first off, he sticks out like a sore thumb among my classmates because he has that *I'm working right now, back off* air about him. Secondly, he's about a decade younger than all these people around me. Thirdly, unless he wandered over from the wedding on the other side of the venue to watch me puke in the bushes and knows my name…he's a police officer.

"That's her," Isabella says, pointing a finger at me. I can't help but feel like it's accusatory.

"Thanks, Isabella," I mutter under my breath, and she looks at me with what appears to be confusion. Or maybe it's indignation. Or maybe it's the fact that her face is as unwrinkled as a baby's butt, so I have no idea how to read her expressions.

"You're welcome?" she says. I guess she doesn't know how to read my sarcasm any more than I know how to read her expressions.

The crowd parts as the police officer makes his way toward me, striding confidently. I have never met a police officer who doesn't walk this way. I wonder if they learn to do it when they go to the police academy. Or maybe anyone who doesn't walk like that gets kicked out before they can even become a police officer.

"Are you Amy Maxwell? I'm Detective Garfield," the officer says, extending his hand to me. I'm not sure if it's to help me stand up straight or to shake, so of course, I don't take it at all. Instead, I pop to my full height like a jack-in-the-box and smooth down my skirt. Again, with the head rush and a stomach lurch. I grab the railing to steady myself, inwardly cursing my stupidity.

"Yes, yes. I'm Amy." After a pause, I add, "Maxwell."

The detective offers me what passes as a smile and then jerks his head back toward the barn. "Can you come with me? I just need to ask you a couple of questions."

I feel like the entire swarm of people around me lean closer as my mouth dries up and I search my brain for a response. But what response can I have other than *Sure, officer*? I don't really have a choice, do I?

"Yes…um, sure," I respond in a raspy voice.

Of course I need to talk to Detective Garfield. After all, I'm the one who found Libby Farrington stabbed to death in a bathroom stall at our high school reunion.

**

"Mrs. Maxwell," Detective Garfield says after we sit down at the very same table where I was sitting with Libby and Penny not even an hour ago. He peers at me with his thick horn-rimmed glasses and runs his hand through his ginger hair. He kind of reminds me of Prince Harry. "It *is* Mrs., right?"

"Um, yeah. I mean, I forgot my ring tonight," I hold up my hand, like Detective Garfield needs proof, "but it's Mrs. And also, my husband's name is Roger." I want to establish that fact right off the bat before Jason comes back and this detective gets confused and thinks Jason is my husband. God, I really wish Jason were here. Maybe he'd stop me babbling so I don't inadvertently condemn myself for a crime I haven't committed.

"Me too," the detective says as he holds up his equally naked ring finger and offers me a sly smile. "My wife would lose it if she knew."

I do a double take and widen my eyes as he winks at me.

Is he flirting with me? No, there's no way this guy is flirting with me. He's just being polite. But why is he being polite? He doesn't have to be polite.

I shift from butt cheek to butt cheek on the chair. It's not easy—I nearly slide off the chair since my dress is soaked with sweat. It's running down my back in rivers and pooling in my body shaper. You would think after being interviewed by countless police officers for crimes I have not committed, I would have figured out how to be more laid back and not to appear so damn guilty all the time. And also, that body shapers are the devil's handiwork and make it nearly impossible to pee without peeling the whole thing off, and oh yeah, they make you sweat more than a serial killer on a witness stand. And why am I even sweating? My teeth are chattering like I'm freezing.

Wait, maybe I'm sick...maybe I have a fever? Oh crap. What if I'm coming down with something? I don't have time to be sick. But what if I have something so dire I have to go to the hospital? That might not be so bad. Kind of a vacation of sorts.

The detective clears his throat and I realize he's asked me a question since I went into this "is he" or "isn't he" debate in my head and somehow ended up down the rabbit hole of having to be hospitalized.

"I'm sorry," I say with what I hope is a smile, but considering my teeth situation, it probably looks like I have lockjaw. "Can you repeat that?"

"Certainly," the detective says without a hint of annoyance. "Mrs. Maxwell, can you tell me what you found when you went into the bathroom at approximately 2100 hours?"

Twenty-one hundred hours? My brain is quickly trying to do the math. *Why couldn't he just say nine o'clock like a normal human being?*

"Libby's body. In a stall. Dead body. Nail file," I reply oh-so-eloquently. Dear god, I hope no one ever asks me to get on a witness stand to testify. They'll need a translator to figure out what I'm trying to say.

My hand starts to vibrate violently, and I gaze down at it, confused. *Am I having a seizure? Is that why my teeth are chattering? Oh god, that makes sense. It's an aura, like when I have a migraine except this is a seizure...*

No, I realize. I am gripping my phone so tightly in my hand that I didn't even realize it was there. And it's vibrating because I have an incoming call. I briefly glance at it, wondering for the millionth time since I found Libby's body where the hell Jason is. Is he calling me?

But it's not Jason calling. It's Roger.

I look back up at the detective who, God bless him, is wearing a very relaxed expression for a guy who is investigating a murder at a wine bar full of sobbing and nosy former classmates of the deceased. I glance at his name badge, because despite the fact he introduced himself no less than five minutes ago, I can't for the life of me remember what his name is. It's Detective Garfield. I can't help but conjure up images of everyone's (including my own) favorite cartoon feline.

"Do you need to get that?" Detective Garfield asks with the patience of a saint.

I shake my head. "No, just my husband."

He cocks his eyebrow but continues.

"Okay, so Ms. Farrington was deceased in a stall, you say?"

I nod, surprised to learn that Libby had never taken her husband's name when they got married. She seems like the type of woman who would marry that type of man for the status. I mean, otherwise there was nothing even remotely likable about the guy.

A strangled sob escapes my lips as I realize I have no idea what type of person Libby Farrington became later in life. And now, even though our personal reunion had been going so well and we might have had a second chance to repair our friendship, that has all been ripped away from us. Oh, and Libby's entire life as well.

Detective Garfield pats my hand. "I know this must be hard for you."

I shake my head, but I can't say anything else.

"I'm sorry I have to ask this question," he says, cringing. "But can you describe what her body looked like?"

I don't gasp like I want to. Instead, my eyes simply widen. Whether it's in reaction to his question or to prevent myself from crying, I don't know. Either way, I do not want to tell Detective Garfield what Libby's body looked like.

Sure, I've come across dead bodies before, some horribly mutilated—our neighbor had had half her chest blown off as she sat on her couch and watched the evening news for heaven's sake—but I have to say, finding the dead body of your former best friend is traumatizing in a way that has no comparison. Especially when I consider the way I found her…stabbed through the neck with a nail file.

Actually, I didn't know for sure that it was a nail file, though it certainly looked like one. When I saw Libby, right before my mouth opened to scream, my vision became blurry around the edges and I found myself homing in on the injury—no, injury isn't the right word for something so violent. Injury implies something that can be cured or fixed with a little bit of medical attention. No, this was not an injury. This was a vile maiming. And I couldn't see Libby or the look of shock on her face or the blood-splattered stall or anything anymore. All I could see was that wretched metal nail file sticking out of Libby's neck.

"Don't *you* know what her body looked like?" I ask, and I can't help but sound accusatory. "Why are you asking me?" I'm practically wailing, causing Detective Garfield's pale eyebrows to shoot up into his hairline.

"Okay, maybe not," Detective Garfield says, sensing my horror. "How about you tell me why you were in that bathroom to begin with?"

"What do you mean?" I cock my head to the side. "I was there to…*pee*," I reply with embarrassment.

"No, that's not what I'm asking," Detective Garfield replies, his own face turning pink.

Oh.

"What I gather from the owner of the establishment, that was not the main bathroom. The owner said that's more of a restroom that the staff uses and most of the guests don't know about it. We have no idea what Ms. Farrington was doing in that restroom since we can't ask her, of course, but perhaps you could tell us what *you* were doing there?"

He cocks his eyebrow again and for the first time since I sat down with this seemingly patient man, I truly feel like I've done something wrong. I open up my mouth to tell him about Suzie giving me the heads up about the bathroom, and how I had shared it with Libby and the other members of my party when I came back from that bathroom trip, but again, my vocal cords are frozen as if I am trying to shout while on a sled dog excursion through subarctic terrain.

He stares at me for a minute and then shakes his head. I must look like a fish sitting here with eyes bulging out of my head, and opening and closing my mouth like I'm gasping for breath. *Close your mouth, Amy!*

"I found it?" I croak out.

"Were you looking for another bathroom for a particular reason? Did the other bathroom have a really long line?"

I stare at him. Doesn't this man know that women's

bathrooms have notoriously long lines and we're *always* looking for the shorter line?

"Never mind," he replies, waving his hand like it's the most inconsequential question. "Can you tell me how you know Ms. Farrington?"

Now my phone starts dancing across the top of the table, Roger's name flashing repeatedly. I grab the phone to silence it.

Detective Garfield eyes me. "You sure you don't need to get that?"

"It's just my husband," I say again, waving the phone screen at him.

The detective cocks his eyebrow. "Well maybe you should get it. Maybe he's found your wedding ring at home and thinks you're out with another man."

He grins at me and I nearly choke on my own spit. Which is difficult to do considering how dry my mouth is right now.

"Um, yeah okay."

Detective Garfield pulls his own phone out of his pocket and begins to tap away on it, perhaps answering emails, perhaps just pretending to be busy to make eavesdropping easier.

I press the *answer call* button and press the phone to my ear.

"Hello?"

"Amy, why is there a motorcycle in front of the house?"

Roger's voice shatters my eardrum and I cringe. Looking at my watch, I see that it's well after ten o'clock and he's just getting home. If Libby hadn't been killed and I hadn't been detained by the police, we would have been home before Roger was and Jason's motorcycle would have been gone by that time.

"I don't have time to explain that to you right now, Roger."

"When will you be home, Amy? It's late and I'm tired and I want to go to bed."

I wrinkle my brow and pull the phone away from my ear, staring at it. Yes, I know it's late, but firstly, Roger usually falls asleep in his chair in front of the TV, oblivious to anyone else in the house. And secondly, what does my being out have anything to do with him going to sleep?

"Um, I don't know, Roger. It's kind of a tricky situation right now."

There's silence on the other end of the phone for a moment before Roger sighs and says, "Are you drunk? Do you need me to come get you?"

Annoyance bubbles in my chest. "Do I sound drunk, Roger?"

"I don't know!" Roger sputters. "You're being all squirrely and invasive."

"I am not being squirrely and invasive, Roger. You mean *evasive*, anyway."

"Don't change the subject. You still haven't told me why there's a motorcycle in the driveway."

"I told you, I don't have time to explain that right now."

"So you say, but had you just told me to begin with,

this conversation would be over, but instead, we're still talking."

He does have a point there.

"Well, um, it's Jason's," I say, biting the bullet.

Silence.

When Roger is silent it is either because he's not listening to me, or he is seething. And since he's the one who called me and wanted the answer to whose motorcycle was in the driveway, my guess is for the latter.

Sweat starts to run down my back again. *Say something, Roger!*

"Is he storing it at the house or something?" Roger finally asks.

"Yeah, or something," I practically whisper. I am keenly aware of Detective Garfield's gaze on me. I guess he ran out of things to pretend to stare at on his phone.

"Amy…are you having an affair with Jason?" Roger's voice cracks at this statement and for a second, I almost feel sorry for him. He sounds like he's about to cry. I've never heard him so distraught in all my life. Well, except when the Mets and Yankees played each other in the World Series in 2000 and the Mets went down like a hooker on the strip.

"God no!" I spit out with a laugh that I hope sounds genuine. "Geez, Roger! How could you even ask something like that? Why would you think I'd have an affair with Jason?"

"Well…"

Do not answer that question, Roger.

I cut him off. "It's nothing like that at all. In fact, I'm not even with Jason right now. I'm with Detective Garfield."

The words are out of my mouth before I can even think about what I'm saying.

Holy crap, Amy! That's even more damning than the idea that you're having an affair with Jason! He might think you're having an affair with Detective Garfield!

My face turns bright red as I recall Detective Garfield's banter at the beginning of the interview that vaguely resembled flirting. Geez, they could call me Mrs. Robinson…this guy is like in his early thirties. What would he want with me? He was probably born when I was in high school! I actually shudder at the thought. I have grossed myself out.

"Amy…" Roger's voice has a warning edge to it. Great. He thinks I'm having an affair with this…*child.*

"Are you in some kind of trouble…again?"

Oh wow. It's more feasible to my husband that I am in trouble with the law than it is that I am having an affair. That's…rude.

It's also true.

I sigh.

"Well the police are here and I need to talk to them."

"Oh, Amy," is all Roger can manage to say before he hangs up.

CHAPTER FOURTEEN

Exactly twenty minutes later, I am back out in front of the building, most of my classmates milling about aimlessly.

As I search for Jason—seriously, where the hell is that man?—Penny catches my eye and waves. I groan inwardly as she practically jogs over to me.

"Amy!" she calls out, still waving feverishly.

I pull my phone out and send Jason an angry text message as Penny sidles up next to me.

Me: *Where are you?????????????*

"Everything okay?" she asks me, a high-pitched lilt to her voice.

I eye her warily, wondering if she's pumping me for information. Oh, who am I kidding? I found the dead body of our classmate and just left the detective on the case. Of course she's pumping me for information. I mean, I'd be pumping me for information.

"Everything's fine," I tell her with a tight smile. "Just waiting for…Jason."

Penny thankfully has almost zero interest in my "husband" right now and asks, "Do you need a ride home?"

My phone buzzes in my hand just then with a reply

from Jason.

Jason: *On my way. I'll be there in five. SORRY!*

Oh, he has no idea how sorry he's going to be. Jason is going to be *very* sorry when he discovers the party he left is now a crime scene.

I shake my head at Penny.

"No, Jason said he'll be back in a few minutes." I offer her a tight smile as I slip my phone back in my bag. I cross my arms over my chest and peer down the long driveway in front of the venue, hoping to see my SUV's headlights.

"Everything go okay with the detective?" Penny asks, leaning against the railing.

I shrug. "I guess as okay as it could be."

A look of concern crosses Penny's face and she glances from side to side before leaning in toward me.

"Do they think you did it?" she asks in a hushed whisper.

If I were a cartoon version of myself, my eyes would have bugged out of my head just then.

"No!" I snap, and Penny jumps back. I didn't mean to scare her, but come on, she was with me when I discovered Libby's body—well, not with me, with me, since she was in her own stall when I started screaming, but come on.

Penny holds up both hands and then swipes at her cheek with the left one. Oh, geez, I spit on her. Well, I'm sorry, but you don't go accusing people of stuff like that.

"I'm not saying *I* think you did it, Amy," Penny says with a nervous chuckle. "I was just asking if the *detective* thought you did. I mean, of course you didn't do it. I was with you the whole night practically. You wouldn't have had any opportunity to do it." Penny's brow wrinkles and she lowers her voice as if she is talking to herself. "Well, I did go get the drinks, but you wouldn't have had time to do anything then. And plus, we saw Libby after that…"

"Penny!" I am really and truly flabbergasted by her accusations right now. Even if she's saying she's not accusing me of anything.

"What?" She peers at me with giant brown eyes.

"I didn't do it," I hiss.

"I know you didn't. I just told you that." She looks at me with confusion. "I told the police I didn't think you did it."

"You talked to them?"

She nods. "Yeah, well I mean, I guess they're talking to everyone. They just wanted to know what happened when we went into the bathroom." She lowers her voice and leans closer. "They really wanted to know why it took you so long to scream after going into the stall."

My mouth drops open. Detective Garfield didn't ask me any of this. "What do you mean it took me a long time to scream? It didn't take me a long time to scream."

Penny turns red. "Well I told them I was almost done in my stall when you started screaming so I assumed—"

"I didn't go into the stall right away because I was waiting for you to come out!" I snap. "I didn't want to use the handicapped stall."

Penny's gaping mouth snaps shut. "Oh, I didn't know that. Sorry."

"Yeah, thanks," I mumble as I dig my phone out to check the time. *Where the hell is Jason?* I'm so mad I could spit…again. There was no reason for Penny to tell the police that there was a delay from the time she went into the stall till the time I screamed. That just makes me look guilty, plain and simple. I have no doubt that I have not seen the last of Detective Garfield.

Of course, they'll discover there's no way I could have done it, you know, with no blood on me and all that. Still, he's going to need to interview everyone at the crime scene and people like me—with the dubious honor of being the one to discover Libby's body—are most likely going to be brought in repeatedly for questioning until they catch the culprit.

Ugh and when they do catch them, this will no doubt go to trial. I will have to conjure up this hideous night over and over.

I facepalm myself at the thought.

"What's the matter?" Penny asks, taking a tentative step toward me. I'm not sure if she's afraid I'm going to explode or spit on her again.

"Nothing, just…" I scrub at my face and come away with a palm full of black streaks. Of course, I have mascara on. The benefits of never wearing makeup in your everyday life include being able to rub your face whenever you want without looking like the raccoon I'm sure I look like right now. "I'm going to have to talk about what happened repeatedly until they catch the killer. And even afterward. It's…it's a nightmare."

For a brief second, I feel a stab of guilt. Sure it's inconvenient for me to have to repeat my tale of woe, but for Libby, this is far worse. I mean, she's dead. Doesn't get much worse than that. Someone hated her enough to kill her.

A horrific thought occurs to me then. *What if this was just a random killing? What if I could have theoretically been the victim had I gone to the bathroom a few minutes earlier?*

I must look like I'm putting a puzzle together in my head because Penny cocks her own head to the side as she asks, "What?"

I quickly tell her my theory and even as it's coming out of my mouth, I realize it sounds ridiculous. Who would be randomly stabbing women in the restroom at a high school reunion? It makes no sense whatsoever.

Penny seconds this conclusion and then she gets a faraway look in her eyes.

Now it's my turn to ask, "What?"

"This is amazing," Penny tells me, eyes sparkling.

I stare at her in utter disbelief. Did she really say what I thought she said? We're knee deep in a crime scene...no, not just any crime scene, but the actual murder of one of our classmates...a classmate who I found, and she thinks this is amazing?

"Amazing? What could possibly be amazing about this? You're not the one who came face to face with her dead body!" I hear my voice tipping up a couple of octaves, but I can't help it. Granted, this is not my first dead body; heck, it's not even my first murder, but it's not something that gets easier each time. Well, maybe if you're a medical examiner or something. Penny must be mentally unhinged to think such thoughts about the current situation.

"Shhh, keep your voice down," Penny says, gripping my arm and glancing from side to side as she pulls me to the fringes of the crowd. "People will hear you. You're overreacting."

"Penny, I couldn't care less if people heard me. I just found Libby Farrington dead in a bathroom stall. *How am I supposed to be reacting?"*

Penny's face falls. "Oh my goodness. I'm so sorry. How insensitive of me." Her lip trembles and the corners of her eyes start to crinkle up. She releases her tight grip on my arm and then pats it as if she is comforting a child. "I know this must be terribly difficult for you."

I gaze down at her hand and then back up at her face. This night has taken a turn for the weird, that's for sure.

"Yes, yes it is."

"I hadn't realized. I mean, I know you've come across dead bodies before so I just assumed this wouldn't be as shocking to you as it was. Again, I apologize."

"Well, first off, it doesn't ever get easier," I tell her. "And secondly, I've never actually come across the body of my best—" I cut myself off before I finish the sentence.

Because Libby is no longer my best friend. She hasn't been my best friend in thirty years. I shouldn't, after all this time, be thinking of her in those terms. But yet, it still hurts. It feels like yesterday that we were giggling in the tent her father had pitched in the backyard for us to camp in (only to have us rush into the house at one in the morning when we thought we heard a wolf…turned out to be the neighbor's dog, but heck, we were eleven and we weren't taking chances) and hanging out at the food court in the mall sipping Orange Julius. I felt like Libby and I were actually getting somewhere this evening and yes, I did briefly imagine us picking up our friendship where we left off, old wounds healing. We could have had lunches together and gone to the beach and maybe even in a few years, our families could have gone on vacation together. But not now. Now my second chance of friendship with my childhood best friend has completely gone up in smoke. She's dead and we're never going to have that.

I can't help the tears that prick at my eyes, but I attempt to force them back before they break through and end up streaking down my face.

Penny squeezes my arm again. She has quite the grip for such a mousy-looking woman. I welcome the distraction and try to smile at her.

"I was just thinking in terms of while it is unfortunate that Libby met her end here, it was fortunate that *you* were the one to find her. And that I was here with you."

I jerk back from her touch as if her hand has seared my arm like a hot poker. "What?"

Penny shakes her head and smooths her hair, all while laughing nervously. "Oh geez, I'm not selling this right at all, am I?"

"Selling it?" I practically shriek. "What the hell would you be selling? We almost witnessed a murder! There's now a murder investigation that we—" I wave my hand between the two of us, "are now part of."

"Amy, calm—"

I start muttering almost incoherently. "What the hell is it with me? Why do I attract murder and other crimes like some other women attract sugar daddies? Do I have some sort of cosmic sign across my forehead that says, *hit me*? What did I do in some former life to deserve this karma?"

Penny wrinkles her nose. "I don't think very many women attract sugar daddies and the ones that do have fake everything and twenty-four-inch waists." She glances down at my middle and then quickly back up again, a flush creeping up her neck. "But if it's any consolation, I don't think this is karma or anything. Unless it's the good karma."

Again, my mouth drops open and I stare at her, incredulous.

She quickly waves her hand in front of her face. "Dear God, I keep opening my mouth and inserting my foot tonight, don't I?" She lets out another chuckle.

"Ya think?" I reply, unable to keep the annoyance out of my voice. Penny is grating on my last nerve. If I weren't waiting for Jason, I would definitely be hightailing it out of here ASAP.

"What I meant to say is you have experience with this sort of thing and that will be helpful with our investigation," Penny says to me.

"Huh? Our investigation?" I stare at Penny. "What investigation are you talking about?"

"The investigation of the murder," Penny replies matter-of-factly.

"Penny," I reply, just as matter-of-factly, "the police tend to frown upon civilians getting involved in their investigations."

"That hasn't stopped you before, Amy," Penny says with a wry cock of her brow, which seems so out of character for her that it startles me.

"Well, I um…" I stammer. How do I explain that I haven't purposely engaged myself in these investigations in the past, that they have just seemed to find me, like the same way I seem to be flypaper for freaks…Penny as a case in point.

"The police are so careless and incompetent," she continues with a casual wave of her hand. "They miss all the clues and half the time they don't even solve the crime. Hell, most of the time they only solve the crime because the criminal is even more incompetent than they are, thus allowing them to have the upper hand by default."

They do?

"This crime needs a much more in depth and character driven investigation. One that we can really sink our teeth into and get to the heart of the matter with."

Character driven? What is she talking about?

"This is perfect for the podcast. True crime podcasts

are even better when the podcaster is right in the middle of the action," Penny bursts out.

My eyes widen. "True crime podcast?"

Penny nods her head vigorously. "It's all the rage right now. My sister and I have been working on a true crime docu-series, but it's not the same when you're totally removed from the scene and all that's going on. This," Penny says, rubbing her hands together, "is the perfect opportunity to be right there, on the ground floor, so to speak, and solve this murder before the police even know what hit them!" She grips both my arms. "Do you know what this could do for the podcast? It'll blow it up!"

"Podcast?" I repeat again, sounding like a blithering idiot. "What podcast are you talking about?"

"Oh, I thought I told you. My sister and I have a podcast. *Sisters in Crime*."

"Really?" I wrinkle my nose as I always do when confused, and Penny misinterprets it as disgust.

She waves her hand dismissively again. "Yeah, I know. We should have work-shopped the name a bit, but what's done is done." Her eyes light up. "We don't have a huge following right now, so maybe with this murder we can change the name and rebrand ourselves."

"Penny, I'm confused," I say waving my own hand in front of my face. "I thought you were a librarian?"

"Oh I am!" Penny says. "And my sister is a phlebotomist at the hospital. But we dabble in podcasting on the side." She giggles in a way that makes me consider that she is seriously unhinged.

"So your sister podcasts about true crime with you?" I ask, hoping I'm getting this straight. A phlebotomist and librarian sitting around talking about true crime doesn't seem very interesting to me.

I realize I said that last bit out loud when Penny's face falls. I cringe, cursing my slightly buzzed and shocked state. It has me saying things I wouldn't ever normally say out loud.

"Sorry, I didn't mean to demean your podcast."

"No, it's okay. It's totally true. We don't have the most exciting podcast. Hence why we don't really have that many followers."

"Excuse me!" A police officer is pushing us aside so a woman in a Tyvek suit can get through. *Medical examiner, maybe?* I shudder at the thought of someone examining Libby up close, and the vision of the nail file in her neck comes back, sending an extra chill up my spine.

"Even though we don't have a huge following, we love doing it," Penny says as we move aside, oblivious to my distress.

"What made you get into podcasting?" I ask, slightly grateful for the distraction of talking to Penny about this podcast so I can ignore what's going on around me.

Penny claps her hands. "The library I work at built a podcasting studio in the basement! And then my sister and I were like, well, we have to try it out. Both of us are die hard podcast listeners, so it seemed perfect."

"They built a podcasting studio in the basement of the library?"

"Well, it's really a recording studio. Local artists and audiobook narrators rent it out, but we thought it would be perfect to record a podcast in!"

"Oh, wow," is all I can say. I thought about recording an audiobook to go with the Lexie Maxwell series and tried a couple of times to record in the house. It was a nightmare of epic proportions. The dog started barking at a squirrel on the front lawn and finally stopped when I closed all the blinds in the living room and he couldn't figure out how to see through them. Then when that finally died down, the neighbor's lawn service started mowing…and leaf blowing…and doing every other damn thing a lawn service could do. I finally managed to record one entire chapter and then listened to it to edit and discovered that the entire time you could hear the forced heat whirling loudly in the background. I tried the next day to record with a blanket over my head, but I nearly died of heat stroke, so I gave up. If I had only known the library had an available recording studio, I could have saved myself a whole lot of trouble.

"So we started our podcast, like I said the title needs work and we don't have a huge following, but something like this…" she sweeps her hand toward the crime scene tape, "being at the actual crime…well that's the sort of thing that sponsors love, you know? And if we could get sponsors, maybe we could keep doing the podcast."

"But what does this have to do with me?" I ask.

Penny gasps and grabs my arm. "Oh, Amy! You're a local…no, you're a *national* celebrity. And you have experience with solving murders—"

"I haven't actually solved any murders," I point out.

"Nonsense," Penny says, swatting my arm. "That lady who killed her friend with the Fentanyl? She'd probably still be running around murdering the rest of the playgroup moms if it hadn't been for you! And that doctor who murdered the girl at the bachelorette party? Who knows how many people she would have murdered to keep anyone from finding out her secret! You're responsible for saving the lives of at least a half dozen women!"

"Well, I—" I can't help the blush of pride that's creeping up my neck as Penny points out all my accomplishments. "But just because I've been successful with *assisting* the police with murder cases in the past…" I am sure to point out that I have not single-handedly solved the murders on my own. Okay, maybe I have done it without the help of the police, but every time I solve a murder, I have *someone's* help along the way. Joey and I were held at gunpoint in the supermarket when we figured out who had killed the mom in the playgroup, and my mom was hiding in the closet with me when we cracked the case of the woman who killed the guest at Joey's bachelorette party.

"You need to come on the podcast, Amy!" Penny interrupts me before I can even finish my sentence. She grips my arms and shakes them again in that disarming way of hers (oh, wow, I made a pun and I didn't even mean to). "Our podcast! *Crime Family*!"

I wrinkle my nose. "I thought you said it was called *Sisters in Crime*?"

Penny releases her grip on me and waves her hand in front of her face. "I told you we needed to workshop that title. What of you think of *Crime Family* as the new title?"

Quite honestly, I think it's terrible, but I'm too stunned to speak my mind. "Um, it's great."

"So if you're on our podcast then we can pick your brain about the murder…you know, see where you're going with your investigation and…"

"Wait." I hold my hand up. "Penny, I don't have an investigation. The *police* have an investigation. You should be talking to them, not me."

Penny rolls her eyes. "Oh yeah, like the police are going to talk to some no-names on a podcast they've never heard of. Oooo, what do you think of *Crimes of Our Lives*?"

What I think is that it's even worse than the previous two she mentioned and she should stop trying to come up with podcast names. But of course I don't say that. I just smile tightly at her and hope she takes it as a positive sign.

She pulls at her phone and starts tapping away as she speaks. I have no idea if she's texting her sister or just making a note of these awful podcast names.

"But when you start investigating…and you know you won't be able to resist," she waggles a finger at me when she finishes typing and I feel myself getting warm, like a chastised child caught with my hand in the cookie jar, "then you can be on our show and it'll be so great for the listeners to solve the crime along with you!"

I open my mouth to speak because I must speak, right? I have to tell this woman she's bonkers, nuts, a couple sandwiches shy of a picnic. But I find my vocal cords are essentially paralyzed because I can't speak.

But fortunately, I don't have to.

CHAPTER FIFTEEN

"Amy!"

I hear my name being called behind me and I swivel my head around. And then I see him, storming his way toward me, fists clenched at his side, face bright red.

Damn it. He looks like a fire-breathing dragon right now.

"Jason, uh, hi!" I stammer as he approaches.

"What the hell is going on here?" he asks when he has caught up with me. If I'm not mistaken, he's breathing a little heavily and there are beads of sweat dotting his hairline. *Wait, is the Great Jason Collins out of shape like the rest of us mere mortals?*

"Are you okay?" I ask. "You're breathing heavy."

"Don't change the subject, Amy," Jason says through a series of ragged pants. "What happened here and how are you involved?"

"Jason!" I say with a nervous laugh. "What makes you think I'm involved?" I offer him a sunny smile I don't feel. Oh who am I kidding? Jason probably knows exactly what happened and how I'm involved. He's testing me, I bet. And if he's not, do I really think I can keep this a secret from a member of law enforcement?

He crosses his arms over his chest and peers down his nose at me. "Because there are police and crime scene tape, and from what I've been told…" he jerks his head toward the barn entrance where the cops are still swarming, "...a murder. It reeks of Amy Maxwell."

"Now wait just a minute," I say, puffing out my chest. "That's hurtful."

"Well, hurtful or not, it's true." He leans toward me and stage whispers. "The cop at the entrance is a buddy of mine. He said you found the body."

A sharp intake of air comes out like a gasp from my mouth.

"I don't know what to say," I stammer. Because I don't. There is nothing to say that will get me out of this. I will never unsee the body of Libby Farrington on the toilet with a nail file sticking out of her neck. Oh crap, I'm gonna cry.

Jason starts to open his mouth and looks at me. "Oh geez, are you crying?"

"No," I whimper, choking back tears. I feel a tap on my arm. Penny hands me a tissue. I take it gratefully.

Jason glances at Penny and then scowls at me. I can tell he's fighting off the urge to grab my arm and drag me to the car kicking and screaming, but that definitely won't bode well for his image. "Can we go now and talk in the car?" he practically hisses at me.

I glance over at Penny who makes no move to leave my side. "Um, yeah. Sure."

Where's your enthusiasm, Amy? A few minutes ago you were dying to leave.

"Good," Jason says with a nod of his head and pivots on his heel before stomping toward the parking lot.

Okay, I guess this is my cue to follow obediently like

a good little wife?

And then I recall, I'm not really Jason's wife. That's just an act for the reunion and the reunion is over. No need to pretend anymore. I don't have to listen to him.

He turns and glances at me over his shoulder. "Are you coming or are you going to stay here all night?" Oooo, he looks scary.

"Coming!" I call and start to scurry after him as fast as my heels will allow me to go. Okay, maybe I do look like a dutiful little wifey.

I am catching up to Jason, when I hear a set of footsteps on the gravel behind me. I don't even need to turn back to look to know it's Penny.

"Amy, I need your phone number!" Penny calls after me, a little breathlessly.

Jason halts in his tracks, and because I turn around briefly to look at Penny, I end up walking right into him and slamming my cheek against his back.

Is that some sort of woodsy bourbon cologne?

"Jesus, Amy." Jason faces me and runs his hand through his hair, the impact now bringing tears to my eyes.

"Sorry," I mutter, tears streaming down my face. Before I know what's happening, I'm full-on sobbing, snot and all. I futilely dab my face with the shredded tissue.

Jason sighs and wraps his arm around my shoulder. I'm too upset to even enjoy it. "Come on, we should get you home."

We start to walk again when Penny grabs my arm. I

turn with a curt "What?"

It's dark in this part of the parking lot, but I can see Penny turn crimson just the same. "Sorry, I need your number," Penny stammers.

"Um, I…" My brain scrambles to come up with an excuse for why I can't give Penny my number. And there truly isn't any excuse that doesn't make me come off as completely rude. So I smile at her and hold out my hand for her phone. She hands it to me and I add my contact information. I press call and my own phone rings. That last part was unnecessary, but strategic. If I have her number in my phone, I can choose not to answer it. Still rude, but at least I'm not doing it to her face.

"Thanks," Penny says with a wide smile when I hand the phone back to her. "I'll be in touch in the next couple of days."

"Um, yeah, okay," I reply. "Good to see you. Bye." I pivot and start toward the car again, this time, ahead of Jason, thankful to have managed to disentangle myself from a would-be disaster. I can't imagine what Jason would have done if Penny started babbling about the podcast. Jason quickly joins my side and we are almost to the car when Penny calls out.

"I can't wait to get started on the podcast! We're going to solve this thing because we've got Amy Maxwell on the case!"

I feel Jason stiffen next to me and now I know I am truly screwed.

**

I guess I should be thankful he waits until we get *in* the car to start screaming at me—apparently he has enough sense to not want to look like a stark-raving lunatic in front of all these people.

After sliding into the car, I close my eyes and count backward from ten, waiting for Jason to situate himself in the driver's seat before he loses his mind. I get to one and there is no screaming. Also, the car has not started moving yet either, so I crack my eyelid to see what's going on.

Jason is sitting quietly in the driver's seat just staring through the windshield at God knows what. I open my eyes all the way to try to figure out what's caught his attention, but all I see is the darkness of the night swallowed up in the woods surrounding the parking lot. Squinting, I wonder if there's some sort of animal coming out of the trees and am momentarily thankful that I'm sitting in the car with him instead of outside in the parking lot.

"What?" I ask finally, looking at him. I glance into the night and then back at him. "What are you looking at?"

He doesn't answer me but instead drops his head in his hands, resting his elbows on the steering wheel.

Now I'm concerned and reach for his arm. "Do you have a headache or something?"

Jason pulls his hands away from his face and turns to

gape at me. Like his mouth is actually hanging open as if he has no control over his facial muscles.

Oh no. He's having a stroke.

Quickly my brain scrambles to remember what to do when you think someone is having a stroke. It's ABCs, right? No wait, that's CPR.

"Do I have a headache or *something*?" Jason finally asks me incredulously. "Do I have a *headache*?" he repeats, his voice getting close to soprano range. He leans toward me, madness in his eyes and I instinctively grip my phone in my hand to call 911. Not because I'm scared of him, I'm scared *for* him. Jason has never acted this way and I'm taking this as a clear sign he's having some kind of episode. Maybe a seizure.

"Calm down, Jason. I'm going to call—"

"Let me tell you, Amy, every time I'm with you I get a headache," Jason says, interrupting me. He closes his eyes and pushes the bottoms of his palms into his eye sockets.

"Well that's…*hurtful*."

He drops his hands and stares at me. "It's true. It's like you're personally trying to kill me by adding to my mounting stress so I'll keel over and have a heart attack."

Oh, heart attack. I didn't think of that. But wouldn't he be clutching his chest if he were having a heart attack?

Still, I should call 911…

"What are you doing?" Jason peers at the screen where I have already dialed 9 and 1. He snatches the phone out of my hand. "Are you calling 911? What is wrong with you? I'm not actually having a heart attack."

"Oh." That's comforting. I just give him chest pains then.

He sighs and runs his fingers through his hair before leaning his left elbow on the steering wheel and shifting his body toward me. "Amy, do you realize this is the *seventh* time you that you've managed to get yourself involved with a murder?"

Before I make some snarky remark about lucky sevens, I squint my eyes and count in my head.

The drug ring, my sister's lover, the playgroup killer, the murder at Joey's bachelor party, the conference debacle, and now tonight. That only adds up to six.

"It's only six." And then I realize he's counting the time I was kidnapped in the Caribbean. "When we were in the Caribbean, I didn't get involved in a murder," I tell him triumphantly.

He rolls his eyes. "The point is, being around you it's statistically impossible to not have to save you from a murderer…" I open my mouth to protest again and he holds up a finger, "...or a kidnapper. And wait…you're wrong. Someone did die that time."

Oh yeah, forgot about that.

"It's also becoming more statistically possible that at some point in time, *you're not going to be able to get yourself out of a murderer's clutches*."

"I've handled it very well up until this point, thank you very much," I reply indignantly.

He cocks an eyebrow at me. "No you haven't. I've saved you every single time. What happens to you if I'm not there to save you next time? You'll be toast."

Tears start to prick at my eyes. I can't believe Jason has such little faith in me. And he acts like I *want* to get involved in these cases. I haven't inserted myself anywhere I don't belong. Well, not really. Okay, maybe the first couple of times, but seriously, lately they just fall into my lap. I mean tonight all I was doing was going to the bathroom!

"I just happened to be in the wrong place at the wrong time, Jason. It's not like I have anything to do with this murder."

"Do you promise you won't go on some crusade to solve this murder and then end up in a dumpster in a back alley?"

I roll my eyes. "I'm not going to—"

Jason holds up his hand before I can deny getting involved. "What was that back there about a podcast?"

I cringe. And here we go.

"That was just Penny talking about the podcast she and her sister have." I wave my hand to dismiss his concern. Even if Penny does have a true crime podcast, and even if she did ask me to be on it, I'm not going to do it. This murder has just been way too close for comfort for me. Not only did I find Libby's body, but we were also actual friends once upon a time. I don't want to go on a podcast and talk about it, exploiting her death for ratings. Well, ratings for Penny and her sister. It's ridiculous that she would even ask me to participate.

Even though she did say it could help solve Libby's murder. Wait, how can I say no to helping solve the murder of my former friend? That's un-American, right?

No. I will absolutely not go on that podcast. The police can do their job. I have confidence in their abilities to solve this crime and put the person responsible for it away for life.

Besides, it probably won't make for a very interesting podcast anyway. I'm sure it was Preston who killed her. It's always the husband and after witnessing the way Preston and Libby were interacting at the reunion, there's no doubt in my mind that it was a contentious relationship.

But wait, the police never asked about any of that. *I will have to make a point to call them in the morning to let them know...oh geez, this is exactly what Jason is talking about, isn't it? Okay, I will not get involved.*

I'm sure that wasn't the first time Libby and Preston got into it in public and there will be plenty of other witnesses to their marital strife.

Although Libby did confide in me that she wished she hadn't married Preston. *Hmmm, I think I should probably make sure Detective Garfield knows about that...*

"Amy!" Jason barks, jolting me back to our conversation.

"What?"

"Why do you look like you're being hypnotized?"

"Um, no reason. You were saying?" I try to sound cool and casual, but I know it comes off as strained and out of place for this very intimate conversation in the front seat of my SUV.

"I was saying," Jason replies with an eyeroll, just to let me know how uncool I actually sound, "what was that woman…Penny, is it? What was Penny saying about you solving the murder?"

I laugh, again trying to sound cool and breezy. "Oh she's just being…crazy."

Although, now that I think about it, maybe she's not. I mean, yes, I should leave this to the police, but now that I'm going back over my conversation with Detective Garfield in my mind, there were a lot of questions that he didn't ask. Will he eventually get around to asking those questions? Plus, this area probably doesn't see a ton of murders, so how experienced would a guy like that be with a case like this?

Jason sighs with relief and runs his hands through his hair *again.* I glance up at him…is his hairline receding? Probably from running his hands through his hair so much.

"I'm glad to hear it," he says.

I wrinkle my forehead. "Glad to hear what?"

"Glad to hear that you're not getting involved in the podcast. It makes things easier for me."

"Makes things easier for you how?" I'm wracking my brain to figure out what any of this has to do with Jason at all. Aside from the fact that he is here.

He chuckles as he says, "Well, I was thinking I was going to have to forbid you to be on the podcast."

My wrinkled-up forehead springs back into place as my eyes bulge. "Forbid me?" I gawk at him and repeat, "*Forbid me*?"

He laughs again. "Yeah, but it seems like you're definitely getting smarter and I don't have to tell you what to do in these situations anymore. You can figure it out on your own."

I purse my lips and then twist them to the side while Jason puts the car in gear, the gravel crunching under the tires.

Yes, Jason, I can certainly figure out what to do on my own. I don't need your help and I certainly don't need you forbidding *me to do something. You must not know me very well.*

CHAPTER SIXTEEN

Simone felt hands on her arms and even without turning around, she knew they belonged to Raul. The electricity between them pulsed through his fingers, causing currents to run up and down her body. She was trembling with pleasure from his simple touch. He had that much power over her. He pushed his pelvis into the small of her back and she gasped at first, feeling his manhood against her. But then she sighed as she felt her body melting with his, the rhythmic rocking of his—

"So….how was the reunion?" Lexie asks as she flops onto my duvet. I look up from my laptop and cringe at the sight of my almost eighteen-year-old daughter sprawled on it. Not that I don't want her sprawled out on my bed…considering the fact she's been all but ignoring me for the last few months, her presence is more than welcome. It's the fact that I'm writing soft porn on my laptop while she does. Okay, spicy romance, but still…don't want my child reading it over my shoulder.

I slam my laptop closed and try to smile at her. How was the reunion? Well that's certainly a loaded question. I don't even know how to respond.

It was great honey, until my former bestie got murdered with a nail file to the neck. How was your night? Did you go to the movies like you planned?

"It was…interesting," I finally settle on.

Lexie raises her eyebrow and stares at me. "Interesting? You've got to give me a little more than that, Amy."

I scowl at her. Suddenly in the last few weeks she's taken to calling me Amy instead of Mom. I really have no idea why. Although, it ironically started around the same time her college acceptance letters started rolling in.

Hmmm, I wonder if she's trying to push me away in an attempt to try out her newfound independence or whatever she feels getting into college is. Well, she better cut it out. I've been down this road before, and she still has to finish out her senior year and make it through the summer without me wringing her neck to actually get to college.

"It was lively."

"*Lively*?" Lexie mimics a snoring noise. "Sounds like a real snoozefest."

"Snoozefest? Um, yeah it definitely wasn't snoozefest," I reply with a laugh.

Lexie sits up and rubs her hands together. "Was there drama? There had to be drama if a bunch of people who haven't seen each other in years get together under one roof with alcohol."

I cringe. "Yeah, you could say there was a little drama."

Lexie bounces on my bed. "Tell me all about it," she

says, clapping her hands together.

"Okay…" I say slowly. "One of my classmates was murdered at the reunion." Okay, so I decided to shock her. Sue me.

Lexie's eyes practically bulge out of her head.

"You're lying!" she says with a laugh when she recovers, shoving my arm playfully.

"I swear to God," I say solemnly with a hand on my chest.

Lexie face goes through various stages of disbelief until she settles on awe. "That is so cool!"

"Lexie!" It's my turn to slap her arm. "It is not cool! A woman died last night! A woman I went to school with!"

Lexie ignores my chastising and asks, "How did it happen? Poisoning? A single gunshot to the heart? Bludgeoning?"

"Oh my god, you watch too much *Forensic Files*," I say, rolling my eyes.

"Was it a catfight?" Lexie asks hopefully.

"No!" I shake my head. "She was stabbed. With a nail file." I cringe, not sure if I was supposed to divulge that tidbit.

Lexie's eyes grow to the size of saucers. "So it was a catfight!"

I shake my head. "No…well…not that anyone saw. I found her in the bathroom stall after it happened."

Lexie leaps off the bed and stares at me. "You what?"

I realize my mistake and cringe. I had not meant to

tell her that I was the one who found the body. Now she'll never let up. She will badger me until I give her every single detail about this murder.

Lexie leaps back on the bed, bouncing on her knees and rubbing her hands together like a villain in a movie. "So how did you find her? What did she look like?"

"Christ, Lex, this isn't a movie or a book. This was a real person. I person I knew and grew up with." Tears are brimming over my lower lids. *Damn it, I'm going to cry. Why can't I stop crying?*

Lexie's face falls. "Shit, I'm sorry. I didn't mean to be callous." She reaches for a tissue on my nightstand and hands it to me.

"It's okay," I reply as I dab my eyes with the tissue. "I know you're just curious."

She shrugs. "Yeah, but I should have thought about it before I asked. That had to be hard, seeing someone you know like that. I mean, not like it hasn't happened before."

"Yeah, but Libby was my friend. It was a special kind of difficult walking in on that. In the bathroom stall, no less." I shudder, the memory resurfacing. I downed a copious amount of shots last night when I got home so that I didn't think about the murder scene I had stumbled onto. Okay, by shots I mean Zquil shots. If I had done tequila shots I would still be puking right now. But I knew if I didn't take something to sleep, the moment I opened the stall door and saw Libby would play on repeat in my brain.

"Wow, that's crazy," Lexie says, scooting closer to

me, our knees touching. I know I should stop there…this is a murder investigation after all, but this is the first time in almost two months that Lexie has shown any interest in my existence other than to ask me what's for dinner.

So, needless to say, despite my better judgment, I find myself telling Lexie the whole sordid story, including Penny's request to come on her podcast.

"That's crazy," she says when I finish. "What's the podcast called?" She pulls her phone out of the front pocket of her hoodie.

"What are you doing?" I ask, craning my neck to see her phone screen. "You can't tell anyone what I just told you!" I grab for her phone.

She pulls it out of my reach. "I'm not going to tell anyone. Just chill. I'm going to check out the podcast. See how many subs she has."

"Subs? Like sandwiches?"

"*Subscribers*, Mom," Lexie tells me with an eyeroll.

But I don't mind. She called me Mom instead of Amy. That's a giant win as far as I'm concerned.

**

"It's a little formulaic, but it's got potential," Lexie tells me the next day as I'm scrambling eggs that Colt may or may not eat. He's been on a scrambled egg kick for the last two weeks, asking for them every morning. I'm trying to get ahead of it this morning, hoping that I can get everyone out of the house on time for school, but it's a gamble. Generally, Colt goes on food kicks for roughly two weeks (Cheerios, apples, pasta, bagels) before he declares he never wants to see that food again. Usually it's right around the time I completely lose my mind and stock up on whatever he's been eating.

"What's formulaic?" I ask as Lexie pours coffee into a travel cup.

She takes a sip of the coffee and makes a face. "That lady's podcast," she tells me, opening the fridge door and taking out the creamer.

I stare at her. "How do you know?"

She rolls her eyes and adds the creamer to her coffee. "I listened to it last night, Mom. Duh."

"Oh."

"She's got potential, like I said," says my daughter, evidently the podcast expert, "but she needs to get a good, recent murder to get more interest in the series. The twenty-five-year-old cold cases she's talking about on there aren't fascinating enough to generate interest." She grabs the sugar bowl and starts heaping spoonfuls of sugar into her coffee.

"Oh, of course, a new murder. What every podcast needs," I say with sarcasm, but Lexie doesn't seem to pick up on it.

"I mean, don't get me wrong, people love unsolved mysteries, but they're not doing enough on-the-ground research to figure out who actually committed these murders they're talking about. I mean, the one was in California and took place before they were even born for heaven's sakes. Looking up newspaper articles about old mysteries in the AV room of the library isn't the same as doing real research on them," she points out matter-of-factly. "You need to interview people, get access to police reports…hell, watch footage of interviews with suspects if you can. This armchair detective solving is for when you're reading Miss Marple, not for when you're trying to solve decades-old murders."

"Um, okay." I stare at her in shock. How does she know all this?

"I listen to a lot of true crime podcasts," she says with a shrug.

Colt stumbles groggily into the kitchen and staggers over to the stove. He stares into the pan and then at me. "Eggs. Ewww. I'm not eating that." He turns and stumbles away, rubbing his eyes.

I scowl at his back as he grabs a bowl from the drying rack and reaches for the boxes in the cereal cabinet. "We're all out of Rice Krispies," he tells me, dumping the remains of the Rice Krispies box in the bowl. He grabs the milk from the fridge (leaving it open in the process…can't he hear the gosh darn beeping noise that thing makes?) and pours it into his bowl, sloshing it over the sides like a dam in a hurricane. No wonder we go through a gallon of milk a day.

I shake my head, slide the eggs onto my own plate, and return to my conversation with Lexie who is still spooning sugar into her coffee. Jesus, can you say Dia-beet-us?

"Okay, well I don't think Penny is looking to make this a career or anything. She has a job. She's a librarian."

"She should definitely pursue it. It's a cool side gig." Lexie takes another sip of her coffee, nodding with satisfaction. "Besides, her voice is perfect for a true crime podcast. And that other woman that's on it…"

"Her sister?"

"I think so. Actually, they don't use names so I'm not sure who is who. The one calls the other Dear Sister, and Dear Sister calls *her* Sister Dearest. It's weird. Anyway, the one called Sister Dearest sounds super creepy. You would think she actually committed the murders they're talking about." Lexie lets out a laugh, but a shiver crawls up my spine. When Lexie sees the look on my face, she rolls her eyes. "Relax, Mom. It's impossible. They're talking about murders that happened ages ago. In different states, too. None of these crimes take place around here."

"I know that," I say with a huff. She shrugs and grabs her backpack from the chair where she dumped it when she first walked into the kitchen.

"Well, I got go or I'm gonna be late, Amy."

Great. She's back to calling me Amy again.

I stab my fork at the eggs in front of me and as I bring it to my mouth, I decide to meet Penny at the library today to record the first episode of the podcast.

CHAPTER SEVENTEEN

Detective Garfield stands at the podium and addresses the audience of over a thousand spread before him in the vast ballroom.

"Welcome, friends," he says opening his arms out to the crowd. The crowd responds by clapping with fervor. Detective Garfield waits until they have settled down to continue. "It is with great pleasure that I stand before you tonight to honor a special woman."

Now the crowd starts clapping again, but this time, even more enthusiastically. Is that whistling I hear? I turn my head to see my sister Joey at the other end of my table, putting her fingers in her mouth and whistling with a cocked eyebrow. I turn away, slightly embarrassed by her behavior. This is an upscale venue after all. I'm surprised Beth doesn't tackle her to the ground.

Detective Garfield pats his hands toward the floor, indicating that the crowd needs to quiet down. He's smiling though, so I can tell he isn't annoyed.

"Without the help of this individual, we would have never solved the murder of Libby Farrington...may she rest in peace."

There are murmurs from the crowd that sound like "God bless" and "rest in peace." Detective Garfield continues. "She used her sharp wit and cunning intellect to piece together the puzzle of Libby's murder that evaded our police force, and because of her dogged persistence, the murderer was swiftly brought to justice."

Now the room erupts into cheers, whistles, and foot-stomping. My entire family is on their feet. I feel my cheeks burn, but I listen carefully for Garfield's cue.

"Without further ado, I would like to present to you, Mrs. Amy Maxwell!"

The applause is deafening as I shakily rise to my feet. Feeling a hand grip my elbow, I glance down to see Jason with an apologetic expression on his face. He leans closer to me as I become steadier. "I'm so sorry I doubted you, Amy. I should have let you trust your instincts. But in the end, your judgment was solid and it's only thanks to you that Libby's murderer was put behind bars." He cocks his head to the side and gives me a sheepish grin. "Can you ever forgive me?"

I stare at him for a moment, trying to get my bearings, tears threatening to well over. He had to do this now? When I'm getting ready to stand up in front of a thousand people and give a speech with mascara on? No matter. I can forgive him. I am the one getting the key to the city tonight after all. And it was sure worth it to hear Jason eat crow.

I pat his arm. "Sure Jason."

He clasps his hands together and beams. "Thank goodness! I wouldn't be able to bear it if you were mad at me." He squeezes my arm. "Good luck up there. Picture the audience naked."

I groan. Of all the lousy advice...

**

I step into the elevator at the library and shudder. Ever since I got stuck in the elevator with Mrs. Kringle, my least favorite teacher in high school, I've hated elevators and I try to avoid them if I can, especially if it's only a flight or two. Sure, it was only about fifteen minutes before the fire department came and used their key to rescue us, but let me tell you, it's a long fifteen minutes when you're trapped in an elevator with a woman who had a tuna and pickle sandwich for lunch, and wants to tell you everything you got wrong on your *Tess of the D'Urbervilles* final paper. Wretched woman and wretched book. It's a wonder she didn't turn me off reading for good. As it is, every time I hear the name Thomas Hardy, the faint aroma of tuna nauseates me.

But the staircase is currently being fixed (something about a step caving in) and it's only to be used in emergencies for the foreseeable future, so I have no choice but to put on a brave face and step into the elevator. Thankfully the ride to the basement is swift and the doors slide open quickly, revealing a long, brightly lit corridor. I breathe a sigh of relief. I have never been to the basement in a library, so I wasn't sure what to expect—a dark and dank space that smelled of mold and everyone needs to duck to avoid smacking their heads on the ceiling, even a shortie like me? In addition to despising elevators, I'm not a big fan of basements either.

It's a wonder I get myself in as much trouble as I do while simultaneously trying to avoid both elevators and basements.

I follow Penny's directions and head down the corridor toward the last door on the left. As I get closer, I notice a long panel of windows and of course, I peek inside. Penny is bustling around the room, gathering up papers and shuffling them. She frowns and glances around on the ground as if she has lost something. Her eyes light up as she must have spied what she's looking for, and she places the stack carefully on the table before bending down to retrieve the lone piece of paper on the floor. She's holding it in front of her with a huge grin on her face when she catches a glimpse of me through the window. Continuing to smile, she waves at me and then points enthusiastically toward the door. I nod and reach for the handle, opening it just as she reaches the other side.

"Hi!" I didn't think the smile on her face could get any broader, but it does. She is lit up from the inside out. The meek and quiet woman I met at the reunion is completely gone. This must be how she is when she's in her element. I can understand. I feel the same way when I get into a groove with writing. Not that that has happened much lately.

"Hey, Penny," I say as she backs away from the door to allow me to pass. I step inside the room and Penny whirls around and immediately heads into another room deeper in the space.

"You can follow me in here."

I step inside and nod my head in awe. This must be the actual recording studio. In the center of the studio several microphones are suspended from the ceiling and there are high desks set up underneath them, tablet screens glowing. A long table with some sort of control panel sits to the side, buttons blinking and knobs glowing. The walls are lined with dark egg crate material—to block any sound, I guess. It's very overwhelming.

"This is where we record," Penny tells me as she closes the door and silence swallows up the room.

I nod my head and stand in front of one of the desks. There is a set of headphones draped across it.

"Wow, this is really impressive," I tell Penny as I shed my lightweight cardigan and search for a place to deposit it.

"Thanks," Penny says, that million-watt smile surfacing again. "It's not nearly as high-tech as many recording studios are because we didn't have a huge budget, but I helped design it and I think we did a pretty good job with what we had to work with."

My eyes widen. "Wow, now I'm really impressed. You're like a Jack of all trades."

"A Jill of all trades," Penny corrects me as she leans down and starts fiddling with the buttons on the control panel. "You can put your sweater on a chair."

"Right," I reply as I toss the cardigan on the nearest chair.

"So," Penny pops up, obviously done with fiddling. She rubs her hands together and beams at me. "Are you ready to get started with your new podcasting career?"

I smile back weakly. As fun as podcasting sounds, I don't have time for a new career. I barely have time for the one I have. I've been trying to write something for weeks and end up hitting a wall at every turn. The last thing I need is to add something else to my schedule. Still, Penny is super excited and I don't want to disappoint her.

"Sure," I reply, trying to summon up as much enthusiasm as I can for this endeavor. This is Penny's baby, and she was kind enough to invite me to take part in it so the least I can do is be gracious and enthused. On the outside, that is.

"Great." Penny presses her hands together in prayer before pointing to the desk closest to me. "That's going to be your mic. You can stand or sit."

"Oh, okay." I step closer to the desk and notice that the microphone is pretty high up in the air.

Penny notices and frowns. "Ah, I asked Francis to make sure the microphone was at an appropriate height, but…" She makes a motion like jazz hands. "I guess that's what you get when you hire the board director's kid as your sound tech."

"Well, I'm sure with some experience he'll get better. Kids are—"

"Francis is fifty-two," Penny says matter-of-factly, cutting me off.

Oh. I guess Francis is at the end of his career rather than at the beginning.

"Yes," Penny says grimly. "When we got the

funding for this recording studio, his mother insisted that the library hire her son for the tech work. We had to go along with it. She was the deciding vote. If she had voted no, the whole project would have been nixed before it even started. We figured it would be fine—I mean, how hard can it be to adjust a few mics? But alas, Francis is completely useless. Probably would have helped if we had checked the guy's references a little more closely before agreeing. He's been fired from his last seventy-two jobs."

"Twenty-two?" I can't help but squawk. I haven't had twenty-two jobs in my entire life and this guy has been fired from twenty-two jobs?

"Yes." Penny reaches up to my microphone and plays around with the lever on the side. Like magic it drops lower, in line with my mouth. Penny steps back and examines it before nodding with satisfaction. And then she clasps her hands together. "Okay, so a few basic rules. Number one, don't get too close to the microphone."

"How close is too close?" I ask.

"As long as your lips aren't touching it, you should be good," Penny reassures me. "But don't get too far away either."

"Too far?" My voice cracks. I had no idea there would be rules I'd have to follow. Maybe I should just—

Penny shakes her head and waves her hands dismissively. "Don't worry about it. Just act naturally."

Oh great. Does she want me to break an appendage or get trapped in a murderer's lair while I'm here?

Because that's pretty much acting natural for me. I am one hot mess.

She must sense my discomfort and leans over, placing a hand on my arm. "It's fine, Amy. We're just going to record the podcast like we're having a conversation, just you and me. If you need to take a break then we can always—"

I wrinkle my brow and interrupt her as a thought occurs to me. "Wait, I thought your sister was going to be here too?"

Penny frowns. "Yeah, she was supposed to be, but she got called into work and has to miss this episode. An unavoidable emergency. She'll be here for the next one," Penny assures me. Then she reaches over me and points at the tablet. "So these are some notes on today's episode. You can just swipe the screen to turn the pages. Better than paper because it doesn't make noise."

I nod as I quickly flip though the pages and see what resembles a script written out.

I'm supposed to follow a script? I got kicked out of acting club in the fifth grade because I couldn't memorize three lines after three months of rehearsals!

The sweat under my armpits trickles down my sides and my face flushes, my heart galloping a little faster.

My distress must be obvious because here comes Penny's hand on my arm again with a reassuring pat. "I know it looks like a lot, but we're not going to be following it verbatim. They're more like talking points." She points to several highlighted sections. "I just want to make sure I hit these key points and whatever your response to them is fine." Then she wrinkles her nose. "Well, actually, the pink highlighted sections are what I'd like for you to make sure you hit on."

I flip through the pages, my mouth agape. There are *a lot* of pink highlighted sections. I glance up at her.

"Penny, I would have liked to have a day or two to review this…I can't…I'm not good at memorizing lines."

Penny waves her hands again. "Amy, don't worry. You don't have to memorize anything. All you really have to do is follow my lead." She places her hand on my arm, presumably to help ease my mind. "And plus, this all is going to take place over several episodes. This is just a template so to speak. We go with the flow on this podcast. It's going to be very easy. No pressure."

I want to tell her that by saying no pressure, it does nothing to alleviate the mountain of pressure I feel on my chest. Not only do I have a horrible time with line memorization, I hate public speaking…even public speaking that takes place in a studio where no one else can see me. It makes me so nervous that I not only sweat bullets, I start rambling like my vocal cords are on those runaway ramps you see on mountain roads…you know, for the trucks to brake.

I want to explain this to Penny, but I can't actually speak right now to tell her that. Instead, I just open and close my mouth like a goldfish gasping for air after it's been removed from the tank with the owner's intention of cleaning the tank, except the goldfish is just going die because I'm going to put it in a cup and then someone is going to call me to wipe their butt and then the phone is going to ring and then Roger will ask where is dinner and only then will I realize I forgot to put the goldfish back in the bowl. Or even clean the bowl for that matter. And then I will have to flush the goldfish and immediately run to the store for a new one. Not that I know from personal experience or anything.

Penny tilts her head and examines me curiously. After a moment she sighs and says, "Listen, I need to do a little intro first. It'll probably take me ten or fifteen minutes to do that. Do you want to go back out in the waiting area and go through the notes so you feel more prepared when we chat?"

I nod my head, relief spreading all over my body. Okay I have brought myself a reprieve. At least for a few minutes. After all, that's all I need…a few minutes to study the notes Penny has made so I'm not stammering and sounding like I have no idea how to speak.

Penny opens the door and sweeps her hand toward the waiting room. She offers me a tight smile as I grab the tablet and step through. For a second, I'm worried that I have made more work for her. The people pleaser in me does not like that and I start to berate myself. Until I remember that Penny is the one who begged me to do this podcast and not the other way around.

After she closes the door, I settle down at the table and try to get as comfortable as I can. As I glance over the pink highlighted sections on the pages, my mind drifts to the last time I spoke in public, at the Women Entrepreneur workshop that my sister Beth dragged me too. The one where a woman was murdered, and I crashed and burned on stage in epic fashion. I shudder as a vignette of that weekend plays in my head.

"Hello my darling listeners!" A polished and commanding voice jolts me out of my daydream (or should I say nightmare?). I glance around, startled, thinking someone has entered the recording studio waiting area.

I realize with a start that Penny is the one who is speaking. I peek through the glass between the waiting room and studio to see that she is seated cross-legged in a high-back chair, microphone at mouth level, speaking into it effortlessly, as if she does this all the time.

Well, I guess she does. She is a podcaster after all. Great. I am going to sound even more idiotic when trying to talk next to such a professional. It'll be like Penny is trying to interview the woman who discovered fire or something. Ugh. Great.

My hands are sweaty and I'm trying to tune out Penny's voice as I sift through her notes.

Interview Isabella Napolitano
-is she a viable suspect?
-when was the last time she saw Libby before the reunion?
-does she have a motive?

Interview Libby's high school boyfriend
-what is his name?
-when was the last time he saw her?
-was he at the reunion?

-Why did they break up?
-harboring a grudge?

Don't forget RT
-fight with Libby at the reunion
-use photos?
-pull up articles

Interview the detective on the case (Garfield?)
-will he allow us an interview?
-if not, talk to Joe Ramsey in the PD to get a copy of the autopsy and other pertinent information
-need to know if they have a suspect

Theories about Preston, Libby's husband
-will he allow us an interview or will he feel too guilty?
-why would he kill his wife? Having an affair? Him or her?
-he's running for reelection next year...a dead spouse might harm him...unless she's killed by his opponent OR it's staged to look like she's been killed by his opponent.

I glance up from the pages and wrack my brain to figure out why that last theory not only sounds utterly ridiculous, but familiar. Then it comes to me. Oh yeah, that's the plot of *The Princess Bride.* Or at least the plot the Prince is trying to sell to create a war.

I stare back down at the pink highlights and I feel a headache coming on. Despite my desire to solve this crime, I know this is going to open a whole can of worms.

Not only will the police be absolutely furious with our intrusion, Jason's words are echoing in my head. I don't doubt that he will kill me if I meddle in this crime. Well, maybe not actually kill, considering he's a government agent and I assume he likes his job and doesn't want to do anything illegal, but I have a feeling he could make life pretty intolerable. Considering he's my brother-in-law and he knows where I live.

"You ready?"

Once again Penny's voice seems to come out of nowhere and jolts me out of dreamland.

"Ready?" I squint at her as if I can't exactly understand who she is or what I'm doing here. Well, this isn't far from the truth. I have no idea what I'm doing here. I feel like I was lured here under false pretenses and now I'm like a butterfly caught in a net. I lick my lips, trying to figure out how to prevent my butterfly self from being pinned to the board for inspection. It never works out well for the butterfly, does it?

"Yeah, I did my intro?"

"You did?" I glance at my watch as if that is going to answer my question. I have no idea what time it was when she started recording her intro in the booth.

"Yeah."

"Oh, that was quick." Yes, I am stalling for time. Or an earthquake so that I don't have to do this.

She beams at me. "Yeah, I've got it down to a science now. It's really quick."

"Uh, huh," I nod.

"So, come on, let's get back in there." She jerks her thumb toward the recording studio. "I don't have to pay to use the recording studio, but my bosses don't like me to monopolize it, you know?"

"Right, right, of course," I say, getting to my feet and smoothing my hands down the front of my jeans. My palms are oozing more sweat than a fat man in a sauna. "Let's do this!" I try to muster up as much enthusiasm as I can.

We enter the studio and I stand in front of the mic, listening to the rest of Penny's directions.

"The headphones aren't necessary, but it makes it easier to hear what's going on," Penny instructs me, while sweeping her hand toward the pair draped over the desk in front of me.

Wordlessly, I slip them over my head and the room around me becomes even more muffled, like the sound of the world after a snowstorm. I have to admit, it does help calm me a tad bit.

I can see Penny opening her mouth and speaking, but with the headphones on, I can't hear her. I slip them off and say, "What? Sorry. I couldn't hear you."

"I was just saying that you can put the tablet down."

I gaze down at my right hand. I'm clutching the tablet for dear life, my fingerprints all over its screen.

"Oops, sorry."

"No worries," Penny says with a smile. "Any other questions?"

This is your chance, Amy. Ask her what the hell she's thinking and then get out of this before she drags you down with her. Instead, I nod my head, no.

"Great," she says with a nod, pulling her own headphones on. "Now I'll count down like this," Penny holds up three fingers. "Three," she drops the third, "two," and then second, and then without any words, she points the one finger at me.

"Um, okay?" I say after she stares at me expectantly for a moment. "I got it?"

"Perfect," Penny says with a nod. And then without any further fanfare, she proceeds to repeat the counting down process. I quickly pull my headphones back onto my head and inhale sharply. Now I don't hear the quiet after-snowfall-peaceful noise I just heard.

Instead I hear my own heartbeat thrumming in my ears. Great. I hope the microphone isn't picking that up.

"Welcome back to *Sisters in Crime*!" Penny says, the smooth, podcaster voice back. I guess they're going with the original podcast name. Probably easier. Change is so difficult. Especially with branding and marketing and—

"Amy Maxwell!"

Shit. I have not been paying attention and Penny has just introduced me. I don't even know what she said about me.

Did she ask me a question? Jesus Amy! When are you going to learn to pay attention! No wonder you have such anxiety.

"Um, hello," I stammer, hoping that this is an appropriate response to whatever lead up Penny has spat out.

"So anyway, the reason we have Amy on the show

this season is because Amy is something of an expert in the field of murders."

"Oh no, I wouldn't say that," I blurt out with a nervous chuckle. *Christ. Are people going to think I'm a professional murderer or something?*

"But you are, Amy," Penny says, giving me a dazzling smile. "Amy has single-handedly solved several cases that have stumped the authorities, making her our very own Miss Marple in town."

I didn't single-handedly solve those murders. "Well, I had help. My own sister—"

"Not only that, but Amy has recently been an eyewitness to a crime that took place in our very own town!"

She beams at me, and I fight off the urge to correct her. I didn't actually witness it. I discovered the body. It's slightly different.

"Well it wasn't technically in our town," Penny says. "But…it was at our high school reunion, one of our very own dear classmates cut down in the prime of her life." Penny's voice grows solemn, and I feel a tear prickling at the corner of my eye. The memory of Libby in that stall…everything that we lost that night…the second chance at friendship. Damn she's good. She's almost like Barbara Walters. I hope I don't cry here in the recording studio.

Penny goes on, her voice more forceful now.

"Amy had the misfortune of making the gruesome discovery of our former classmate Libby's body and not only was it incredibly traumatic for her, but Amy has vowed to get to the bottom of this murder if it's the last thing she does."

I have?

I open my mouth to contradict Penny, but she's still talking. "So Amy, let's talk about Libby. What was she like when she was younger? Was she the studious type or was she a wild one, getting drunk at parties in the woods on weekends?"

Recalling Libby when we were younger pushes me over the emotional cliff. Tears prick my eyes and the next thing I know, I'm sitting there with tears streaming down my face. Penny's eyes grow wide and she reaches for a tissue box on the table behind her, offering me one. I thank her silently and pull out a tissue, certain the microphone is going to pick out that rough noise. As I dab at my eyes, I assume that Penny is going to halt recording, allow me some time to get myself back together, but no, she's smiling at me encouragingly, as if she wants the audience to know I'm crying and upset.

And then I get it. I'm here for the emotional angle. She's hoping if I talk about the murdered woman, I can paint the picture of her being a sympathetic character and have the audience demanding justice for her murder. Sly and cunning that Penny is. One wouldn't expect it with her librarian bun and sweater set, but she knows what she's doing. Maybe she will be a world-famous podcaster after all.

"Libby and I were the best of friends," I hear myself say. "Well, we were best friends until the night of her thirteenth birthday party."

CHAPTER EIGHTEEN

Libby, as you might have gathered, was wildly popular. I was never "popular" by anyone's standards, but because Libby had dubbed me as cool back when we both ate paste (don't judge…you know you did it too), everyone else just seemed to accept me. That is, until our friendship imploded in a most epically bad way.

As I said, it was the night of her sleepover, a Saturday night. We were in seventh grade and I know most people hate seventh grade, but up until that point in time, I had been enjoying middle school and all its glory. It was March and Libby was the first one of our friends to turn thirteen. Our friend group consisted of me, Libby, Gennifer (with a G) Meyersen, Kelly Martino, and Rita Singh. Kelly and Rita were best friends since kindergarten much like Libby and I had been, but Gennifer was new to our school that year and had integrated herself into our friend group seamlessly. Libby had taken an instant shine to her, even though the rest of us had been a little leery of the girl who was allegedly twelve years old but built like a bronze goddess. The boys, puberty stricken at the time, nearly fell over themselves the first day Gennifer walked into our school.

No, that's not quite right. Most of them actually did fall over themselves. If I recall correctly, Justin Rogers tripped up the stairs while ogling her and broke his nose.

Anyhoo…Libby and I had once been inseparable, but with Gen's arrival, Libby slowly started to change. She was of course, in awe of Gen, just like everyone else was, but there was something more. It was like Libby wanted to *be* Gen. She started doing her hair in Dutch braids like Gen did and wearing makeup like Gen did. Libby had always worn a little bit of makeup…even in third grade her mother had let her wear it (my mother wouldn't let me wear makeup until I was in high school…which was ridiculous if you ask me), but this makeup was totally different. Very…glam. Libby, who had always looked nice and dressed well, *really* started to care about how she looked and whether her clothes were designer or not.

This obsession with appearances was exactly what led us to the situation that imploded our friendship. You see, before the sleepover party, Libby and I had plans to go to the mall. Just me and her, just like it had been every weekend before Gen waltzed into our lives. I had really been looking forward to it, so imagine my surprise when Mrs. Farrington pulled up to my house with Libby in the front seat next to her…and Gen in the backseat. I reluctantly slid in next to Gen who gave me a tight smile.

To say I was fuming all the way to the mall would be an understatement. My ire radiated off me, causing Gen to shift away from me in the backseat—I'm sure you could have felt it in the front seat, but Libby didn't seem to notice. She was too busy chattering all the way there to her mother about Gen this and Gen that. As if the holy Gen wasn't sitting right there. And Libby's mother, who had normally been very astute as far as I was concerned, just sat there and smiled, completely oblivious to my pain as Gen gloated next to me.

When we got to the mall, Gen immediately went into this clothing store that neither Libby nor I had ever shopped in before, probably because it was ridiculously expensive and all we could afford on our five dollar a week allowances was stuff from Sevens & Eights…cheap stuff that fell apart the second time you washed it. I looked at Libby, mouth agape when Gen started pulling things off the rack and piling them in Libby's arms. She looked so at ease doing it, like this was not her first rodeo.

Libby looked shocked, but she didn't question her hero…she never would. I, tired of this hero worship however, opened my mouth. "What are we doing here, Gen?"

"Shopping," she replied, snapping her gum and not even giving me the courtesy of looking at me. "What size are you, Libby?"

"Um, seven," Libby had replied and Gen went back to the rack, pulling off size sevens.

My eyes widened as I stared at Libby. She widened her eyes back at me, silently telling me to shut my mouth. But of course, I couldn't.

"You know we can't afford anything in this store, right?" I pointed out to both of them.

This time Gen looked at me, still feverishly chewing her gum.

"Good thing we don't have to," she told me, gum

snapping.

I admit that at first, I had no idea what she was talking about, but then when she marched Libby into the dressing room and shoved me inside, I was beginning to get the idea. She pulled a pair of pliers out of her purse and it became abundantly clear what she intended to do. Skillfully, she pried off the security tag on a sweater while I watched in horror.

"Here, put this on," she said to Libby, shoving the sweater at her.

"Now?" Libby asked, her voice squeaking a little.

"Uh, yeah," Gen said with a roll of her eyes.

Libby immediately began to comply while I backed out of the dressing room. "I'm going to wait for your mom at the pickup spot, Libby." And so I stormed out of the mall and over to the wall outside JCPenney's where Libby's mom had told us to meet her. Granted, she told us to meet her about three hours from the time I got there, but I definitely didn't want to miss my ride home. What's more, I didn't want to have anything to do with what Gen and Libby were doing.

When they emerged from the mall a mere minute before Mrs. Farrington pulled up, Libby was wearing the sweater and a new pair of jeans while carrying a bag stuffed with her clothes in one hand, and a cup with an Orange Julius in the other. She didn't look happy, but as soon as she saw me, she plastered a fake smile on her face, hip checked Gen, and started laughing as if Gen had said something hilarious and Libby wanted me to know I had missed out on it.

Once we got back to her house, she did nothing but give me the cold shoulder. She and Gen ignored me while they set up the rec room downstairs for the party (a job that had once been Libby's and mine only for past birthday parties). I had nothing left to do but set up my own sleeping bag and wait for the rest of the girls to show up.

When they did, they brought a couple of boys from our class with them. This was planned…they were going to hang out until it was time for us girls to go to sleep and then leave. This wasn't supposed to be some creepy boy/girl sleepover party.

Well, that *had* been the plan. As soon as they got there, Gen started angling to sneak them back in once they had "left" out the front door. I was mortified—I had no desire to sleep with one of the smelly boys from our class five feet away. For a few minutes, I considered going home, but I wasn't sure if Libby would ever speak to me again if I did. I was just going to have to put up with the boys being there and sleep with one eye open.

But it didn't stop there. Gen opened bottles of Mr. Farrington's liquor and got behind the bar, pouring drinks for everyone. I didn't drink anything, but Libby sure did. Within a half an hour, Libby was so drunk she couldn't even stand up without falling over and laughing. It was funny for about thirty seconds, but then I remembered that the reason Libby was drunk was because of Gen.

I don't know what came over me then, but I had had enough. In the middle of a rousing game of Seven Minutes in Heaven, I pulled Libby aside and told her if she didn't tell Gen not to sneak the boys back in and stop drinking, I would tell her mother.

And that was all it took for me to lose my best friend of eight years. Gen overheard me and started laughing and calling me a baby. She told the other kids at the party that I was such a baby I was afraid the boys would try to feel me up if they stayed. One of the boys, Brian Parker, I believe, laughed and said, "Don't worry, we don't want to feel up Miss Itty Bitty Titty!"

With tears in my eyes, I gathered up my sleeping bag and ran out of there, all the kids laughing.

On Monday, I had expected Libby to apologize or at least act normal. Instead, she and Gen launched a smear campaign against me. I was called "IBT" for years (until tenth grade when my size C cup kind of made that insult null and void) and for many months after that sleepover I was spit at, had gum put in my hair, and had my books knocked out of my hands as I walked to class. It didn't matter that Gen moved back to where she came from after eighth grade. The irreparable damage had already been done. Libby and I never spoke a civil word to each other again.

Until the night of the murder.

**

I stop talking and look at Penny who is peering at me curiously. My face flushes and I pat it.

"What?" I finally ask, lowering my hands to the desk. "Do I have a booger hanging out of my nose or something?" I glance up at the microphone and remember that we are recording. I hope Penny will edit this out.

"No, no!" Penny shakes her head, horrified. "I didn't mean to make you self-conscious. That's a sad story. The one about you and Libby. It sounds like you guys were really good friends."

"Yeah, well Gen wrecked that," I say bitterly.

Penny continues to look at me with pity. "But Libby should have valued a true friendship with you over a fake one any day."

I shrug. "Well, we were barely teenagers."

"But it must have made you so mad," Penny continues, that smooth podcaster voice returning. "After all, those other kids picked on you and made your life at school uncomfortable because of it."

I consider this for a minute before answering. "It did at the time, but, I don't know, in some ways it was best that it happened then, you know?"

Penny squints at me. "Best how? Sounds like it was a terrible way to go through school."

I shrug again and throw my hands up in a defeated gesture. "Sometimes even though things seem like they're bad at the time, it works out for the best in the long run. Sometimes what you thought you wanted and what you really needed are two different things. Fate intervenes so you can get what you need instead of what you want, you know?"

Penny looks at me thoughtfully before she says, "I think I do."

CHAPTER NINETEEN

"I've been waiting for you my whole life, Simone," Raul said.

Simone felt her insides turn to molten lava. "You have?" Her voice peaked at the end of the word. Her excitement was palpable. She chewed her lip nervously and recalling how cliché it was, she hoped that Raul wouldn't think less of her.

He didn't because he was a huge cliché himself. Instead, he took a step closer to her, running his tongue over his lips and making seductive eyes at her. Her back arched as he grabbed her in his arms, pushing her against the wall and her....

**

The doorbell chimes and I breathe a sigh of relief. I hate this erotica writing in the worst way. The idea that someone I know could read it, even if I use a pen name, sends shivers down my spine. It's definitely holding me back. Every time I get to what *should* be a sex scene, my characters end up baking a cake or adopting a puppy. And no, that is not a euphemism for anything.

The bell rings again and Jeter, who slept through the first round of doorbell ringing because he was sound asleep on my bed upstairs, comes bounding down the steps with the zeal of the Energizer Bunny and the grace of a hippo.

"Coming!" I call out at the door after slamming my laptop shut. Penny is coming by and there is no way I want buttoned-up Penny seeing this garbage. Not that all spicy romance is garbage, but mine certainly is. And it's mostly because I have absolutely no idea what I'm doing.

I open the front door and Penny is standing there alone, attaché case slung over her shoulder.

"Hi!" Penny says before she oh's and ah's over my no-way-is-this-impressive house, and gives Jeter an obligatory pat on the head after he relentlessly whines and dances around her. She then proceeds to sneeze approximately forty-two times, waving off my repeated offers of tissues and antihistamines.

Penny pats the bag at her side and says, "I have notes."

I nod as I show her into the kitchen, Penny sniffling as she follows me, Jeter trotting after us, tongue lolling out of his mouth.

She places the bag on the table and unzips it as I shove my laptop to the side like she has X-ray vision and can see the smutty document on the computer. Yeah, there is no way I can pursue this. I can't even cope with the idea that someone might find out that I wrote that stuff, let alone if someone wanted to read it.

"You want some tea?" I ask. I don't even wait for Penny's answer before putting the kettle on. I grab two mugs from the cabinet before rummaging through the pantry and discovering I only have green tea or sleepy time tea.

"Green tea okay?" I ask Penny who has pulled a stack of papers from her bag.

"Sure," Penny says as she shuffles through the papers.

Good. *I really need to get to the grocery store*, I think to myself as I notice the rest of the cabinet is nearly bare. I feel just like Old Mother Hubbard as I stick one tea bag in each mug.

"So I have a printout of the transcript from the episode we recorded the other day. Along with notes." Penny points to all the red and blue ink dotting the sides of the pages.

"Wow, that's…that's a lot of notes," I say with a frown, not sure why she has made notes for an episode that has already been recorded. I get cold and clammy at the same time, considering that maybe she wants us to rerecord some of the sections.

Penny sees the horror on my face and quickly says, "Don't worry! They're just notes to help us with the future episodes!"

"Oh," I reply as I slide into the chair next to her. With my left hand, I shove the laptop even farther away. "Why are they different colors?"

Penny beams. "I'm glad you asked." Then she lets out a girlish giggle. "I'm a little bit of a nerd when it comes to organizing notes and things of that nature. It just makes me feel so much more in control."

I nod my head because this is logic I can get behind. Considering ninety percent of the time I feel completely out of control, any semblance of order I can get a grip on is a godsend for me.

The kettle whistle blows and I stand up to retrieve it and pour the hot water into our mugs. Penny goes on as I bring them to the table and set a mug in front of her.

"The notes in red are some things that we have to watch for," Penny explains, pointing her finger at the many lines of red ink on the first page.

"What do you mean?" I ask, as I sit. I glance at the notes, squinting at them and then looking back up at Penny. They are written in some kind of shorthand I don't understand.

Penny laughs and shifts in her seat, avoiding my gaze. "Just stuff like saying *um* or stammering or leaving dead air between us during dialogue." She points to another section. "Here you rambled a bit and I'm not sure it made much sense so I cut it. It wasn't necessary anyway."

"Oh." My face falls. I thought I had done pretty well with the first podcast. These critiques are a bit more hurtful than I imagined.

Penny waves her hand at me. "Don't worry about that kind of thing. Those are just suggestions."

I nod, still a bit dejected, and Penny takes it as a sign to go on.

"And the notes in blue are avenues I'd like to explore in future episodes, like different paths we can go down. Suspects we can speculate about. For example…" She flips through several pages and points to the notes on one of the pages. "We ended the podcast episode by saying the police interviewed everyone at the reunion after Libby's body was found." She looks at me for confirmation that I am following. I nod encouragingly.

"Yes, we just kind of ended there, right?"

She nods. "This is the perfect place to segue into the next episode. Did you know that Isabella, was conspicuously absent then?"

"She was?" I do not recall Isabella being missing, but I do recall her trying to help me after I discovered the body, telling me to breathe and offering to get me water. But maybe I imagined that. I was quite shaken up at the time, so my memory of the events are quite foggy.

Penny raises her eyebrows. "She was. A bit suspicious, don't you think?"

I open my mouth to point out that even if Isabella had left early, if the police needed to talk to her, they could have certainly gone to her house to do so. It's not like she fled the country or anything like that. At least I don't think she did.

But I don't get a chance because Penny starts flipping pages. "And here I made a note that while I was waiting for the police to be done interviewing you, I noticed Preston had rolled up the cuffs of his shirt sleeves and he smelled like soap." There go the eyebrows again. "Like he had scrubbed them as a surgeon would. Why would he do that?"

"Well maybe he's a germaphobe and didn't want to eat any of the passed hors d'oeuvres without washing his hands really well?" I don't add that if Penny knew what grew on those hors d'oeuvres trays, she probably wouldn't want to eat them either. I saw an expose once and I had to push it far back in my mind whenever I was at a wedding or an event where trays were being passed around.

"It's always the husband," Penny says, pointing to those exact words written in the margins.

"Um, right…"

"And this note," she squints to read it, "says Penny's ex-boyfriend Neil was also waiting to be interviewed by the police."

"Oooakkkyyyy." I don't mention that *my* ex-boyfriend was also at the reunion and probably was asked a few questions as well. In fact, most people's exes from high school were at the reunion. It would have been difficult to throw a spitball in that room and not hit someone's ex.

"Libby and Neil broke up under suspicious circumstances at the beginning of their senior year," Penny tells me, matter-of-factly with a slight waggle to her eyebrows.

"They did?"

This is news to me. Not that they broke up. I knew that. But we live in a relatively small town and let's face it, small towns get boring. Anything anyone did when we were in high school was gossip fodder, and it didn't take long for the entire high school to be privy to the intimate details of any and every breakup, especially that of Libby and Neil, who were supposed to be prom queen and king. If there were "suspicious circumstances" surrounding their breakup, you better believe the entire senior class would have heard about them. And what, other than one cheating on the other, what would constitute *suspicious* circumstances with two seventeen-year-old high school seniors?

Penny nods. "Yeah apparently Libby dumped him for an older. Seems like Neil had been broken up about it."

"Oh." I recall the man Libby seemed to be arguing with at the reunion. Was that Neil? No, that guy was too old to be Neil.

Penny looks at me with a sly expression. "Broken up enough to seek revenge?"

"Over twenty-five years later?" I can't help but sound like I got my finger caught in a vice. Penny really is pushing the confines of logic here.

She shrugs. "We're gonna keep him on our suspect list for now."

I look at the list on the page—there are about twenty names on there.

"These are a lot of suspects, Penny. I think we might be reaching here." I point down at the list.

"I know. But we can have one episode per suspect," she reasons. "It'll stretch out the podcast longer."

"Twenty episodes? It'll take forever to solve the murder! Why are we stretching this out if we want to figure out who killed Penny?"

Penny chews her lip as she looks at me. "It wasn't my idea. I didn't make this list."

I stare at her. "Well it didn't make itself," I reply with a chuckle.

She offers me a weak smile in return. My own smile slides off my face. "If you didn't make it, who did?"

"Paula," Penny replies, without elaborating.

"Speaking of, when will I meet the elusive Paula?"

"She uh, wanted to be here today, but she couldn't make it. She has a migraine."

"Oh."

"She'll be with us tomorrow when we record the podcast," Penny assures me.

"We're recording a podcast tomorrow?" This is news to me. We haven't even aired the first podcast episode that we recorded the other day; Penny said we were going to wait to record them all before airing them...something to do with police procedure?

"But seriously, I do have some good news," Penny says, pushing the notes out of the way and reaching for her mug of tea. She stares into it as if she's trying to determine whether it's clean or not. Or maybe poisoned.

"What's that?" I take a sip of my own tea to show Penny that everything is above board.

"Isabella has agreed to be on the podcast tomorrow," she tells me, taking a long sip as I digest this information.

Isabella? Why are we wasting time interviewing her? Does Penny really think her absence after the murder is telling? Unless she's just looking for some insight into Libby's current life. Isabella would know Libby now better than I would.

"Okay, so that's good news. Shouldn't we be going over what we're going to say to her?" I recall the notes about how she had disappeared and am wondering how

Penny will spin that without sounding accusatory.

Penny, who looked like she was going to put the mug down, lifts it back up to her lips and takes another long sip. If I didn't know better, I would think she was trying to avoid talking to me.

"Penny?"

"We can just wing it," she tells me after she lowers her mug to the table. She lets out a giggle that sounds completely unnatural.

I haven't known Penny long and I can't remember how she was in high school, but based on the color-coded organizational system she has presented to me, I'm going to go out on a limb and say that Penny is not the type of person to just "wing it." In fact, I'm thinking that "just winging it" would cause someone like Penny all sorts of anxiety and quite possibly a panic attack.

I attempt to cock my eyebrow unsuccessfully. Geez, you would think I had Botox or something the way I can't get any of my facial muscles to cooperate.

"That's how Paula wants it," Penny says, shoving the mug in her face again. "Mmmmm, this is really good tea."

Now I'm really suspicious. The tea is just a generic brand and there is absolutely nothing special about it. Her deference to Paula is also concerning. Is Paula bullying her sister?

I lean closer after she finishes what appears to be a gargantuan swallow of tea. "Do you need help?"

"Need help how?" She glances down at the pile of notes. "With my notes? Oh, no I'm good."

"Not with your notes," I say as I lay my hand on top of hers. I notice it's trembling slightly.

"With your sister. I know what it's like to have a domineering sister."

Penny's face turns bright red and she recoils, pulling her hand away from mine. "Oh no, no, I don't need any help with her," she stammers. Leaping to her feet, she starts shoving her notes back into her attaché case. "I've gotta go. I forgot I told Paula I'd meet her for lunch."

"Oh well, okay," I manage to stammer myself and I rise to my feet. "I'll show you to—"

Penny waves me off. "No need! I got it!" She bundles everything together and pulls the strap over her shoulder before giving me a cursory glance and scurrying from the room.

I stare after her for a long while, even after I hear the front door slam and Jeter barks with disappointment.

Didn't Penny say that Paula couldn't come because she had a migraine? Yet, she's rushing off to meet her for lunch?

There is something very odd about Penny's relationship with her sister. My radar is tingling…but of course, I'm going to ignore it. After all, we have a murder to solve.

Chapter Twenty

The next day, I arrive at the library bright and early, even before it's open to the public. Penny sent me a text last night apologizing for rushing out like she did. She asked me to meet her at the library at eight am and to text her when I arrive. I have to admit the fact that I'm going to get to see the library in a behind-the-scenes sort of way is making me geek out a little bit. Like going backstage at a rock concert. It's excited me enough that I've all but put my misgivings about Penny and Paula out of my head. I'm going to meet Paula today and see that her relationship with her sister is normal and there's no cause for my concern. Shut those alarm bells up once and for all.

As I climb the steps of the library, I send Penny a quick text. She must already be waiting for me, because the front door pops open.

"Hi!" she calls out, enveloping me in a hug when I reach the door. It's a tad uncomfortable since I'm not a hugger, but whatever.

"Hey."

Penny releases me and holds the door open as I step inside. A shudder of delight crawls through me as I glance around the nearly vacant library, certain that I'm going to be privy to some secret goings on. To my disappointment, all I see are a handful of librarians pushing carrels of books that need to be reshelved and two reference librarians at a counter talking and drinking coffee.

What the heck did you expect, Amy? A Freemason's meeting?

I trail after Penny as she heads to the elevator and steps inside. Cringing, I reluctantly follow suit. When the doors close, she says, "Oh, I forgot to tell you. The podcast episode, um, the first one we recorded? Well it dropped yesterday."

"Oh. I didn't know you were going to drop it so soon," I reply, a little hurt that she didn't share this information with me yesterday at my house. Or even in the text she sent last night. "I thought we were going to record them all before dropping the first episode."

"Yeah, it was a decision that…well, Paula wanted to drop it last night. Drum up some interest in the podcast."

I frown. Paula again.

Penny catches my expression in the mirrored door of the elevator before it opens up so I quickly try to reorganize my face. "I can't wait to finally meet her today!"

Penny doesn't reply as she steps out of the elevator and scurries down the hall toward the recording studio. "That's the Archive room!" she says with a wave of her arm toward the closed door across from the recording studio.

"Oh, good to know," I say, as I hurry after her, my heckles rising. There she goes again, evading any mention or questions about Paula. What is going on?

Penny attempts to unlock the door of the recording studio, her fingers trembling. Dropping the keys, she lets out a nervous chuckle. "Oops!" she says, bending down to retrieve them. Rising, she fumbles with the keys again, but this time manages to get them in the lock and unlock the door. Instead of stepping back so I can enter, she pushes the door open and shoves it against the wall to hold it open. I step in, eyeing her suspiciously. She pulls open the door between the waiting room and the studio and ushers me inside before closing it firmly behind us.

"So, let me show you how to use the equipment," Penny says, placing the keys on the table as I drop my own bag on one of the chairs.

"Use the equipment? Why would I need to use the equipment?" Using the equipment is seriously above my pay grade. Especially since my pay is zero dollars.

"Well sometimes it takes two people to run the control board. You know, when we have a lot of guests or an outside caller," Penny explains.

"Well, isn't that what Paula is for?"

Penny turns away and busies herself with one of the microphones.

I glance around the room. Again, there is no sign of Paula at all. Suspicion runs through me as I watch Penny dart all over the recording studio, flipping switches and turning knobs.

Did she make Paula up? Is she even crazier than she appears at first glance? Am I in the basement of the library with a seriously unhinged woman?

"Penny?"

She doesn't look at me and I almost miss her words because she's mumbling like she has marbles in her mouth. "Paula isn't going to make it today."

"What? Why the heck not?" My voice is screechy, but for heaven's sake, there's only so much of this getting jerked around that I can take. I'm really starting to wonder if Penny is off her rocker, making up an imaginary friend…er, imaginary sister…and she has some form of schizophrenia.

"She really wanted to be here…" Penny starts.

I hold up my hand, even though Penny hasn't looked up and can't see it. "That's exactly what you said the last two times she was supposed to meet us to do something with this podcast and she never seems to be able to make it." I cross my arms over my chest. "Does Paula really exist?" Sure it's mean, but I want my cards on the table. I've got to know what I'm dealing with here.

Penny's head whips up so fast that I'm certain there's a chiropractic visit in her near future. "What? Why would you say that?" She stands up straight and smooths down her shirt. "Of course she exists. She's just…" she trails off and then sighs. "Paula is…well, she suffers from extreme anxiety…sometimes she's even a bit agoraphobic if you know what I mean. She hasn't left the house in a few days now."

I squint at Penny. "So she's just going to stay home for good?" I have no idea how agoraphobia works or even how one would become agoraphobic. I mean, quite honestly, I get the appeal of it…not having to deal with people? It's like a dream come true. Maybe I can convince everyone in my life I'm agoraphobic so I don't have to go anywhere. No, that won't work. My extended family will just set up camp at my house and come and go as they please. I'll end up running away from home screaming.

"No, she…well, it comes and it goes. She's good for a while and then something will trigger her and she'll spend a few weeks inside. And then the same thing seems to happen in reverse. She wakes up one morning and decides to go to the grocery store and work or the library and it's like the previous few weeks never happened." Penny shrugs. "She's been like that as long as I can remember. That's why we decided to start this podcast."

My face clearly indicates my confusion as to the natural progression of those items, so Penny goes on.

"That way she can record episodes even if she can't leave the house."

"I don't understand. How can she record episodes if she can't leave the house and come down here to the recording studio?"

"Just like this."

A voice fills the recording studio and I stagger backward, hitting the backs of my thighs against a chair on wheels, which goes careening in the other direction. I grab onto the desk before I end up falling flat on my ass.

"What was that?" I stammer, my head swiveling around the room, trying to make sense of the sudden noise. I look at Penny but she's poking around on the control panel again and has slid the headphones over her ears.

"That…" says the disembodied voice, "is me."

I stare up at the speaker on the ceiling where I think her voice is coming from.

Is this some sort of joke? Some Wizard of Oz moment?

I look at Penny again, but she seems to be oblivious to both the voice and my distress.

Wait, can she hear the voice? Maybe it's just me? Oh great, now I'm the one who is going nuts, not Penny.

"So anyway," Penny says, ignoring the literal voice in the room. "This button here is what starts the recording." She points to a bright red button. "Now that's if you want to record and edit it later. If you want to go Live…"

"Why would I want to do that?" I glance over my shoulder expecting the "voice" again, but it's quiet.

"Well this studio is also used for radio shows," Penny tells me.

"It is?" I can't imagine what radio shows would be recording in the basement of a small-town library.

"Well, it can be." Penny shrugs. "There was a cooking show that recorded here once."

"Only once?"

"Turns out it's not so easy to do a cooking show on the radio in the basement of your local library."

I laugh, momentarily forgetting the disembodied Wizard of Oz voice I heard just a few moments ago.

"Put your headphones on so we can start recording," Penny says without looking up from the control panel, bringing me back to reality. "I, uh, think Isabella is going to be calling in soon."

I slide the set of headphones off the desk in front of me and slip them over my head. Penny presses a few buttons and says, "Okay, you're patched in, Paula."

"I've been talking for twenty minutes. I hope I'm patched in." I can't see the woman's face, but I'm pretty sure she's rolling her eyes.

"Amy," says Penny, ignoring the snark in the woman's voice, "this is Paula. She's called in to participate in the podcast today."

I think about that for a second, understanding dawning. Okay, so this is how she does the podcast with Paula if she can't be in the studio because she doesn't want to leave her house.

"Great, um, nice to meet you," I reply.

"You have to talk into the microphone," Penny says, pointing at it. "She can't hear you otherwise."

"Oh, yeah, of course." But as I lean into the microphone, I remember that Paula heard me loud and clear a few moments before and I was definitely not leaning into the microphone.

"So Amy, I listened to the last podcast episode," Paula tells me, not even waiting for a segue. "I've got to say, it was pretty eye-opening."

"Oh really?" I chuckle nervously. I don't know why it's so unnerving to be talking to Paula when she's not in the studio…it's just like talking to someone on the phone. Actually, it's exactly like talking to someone on the phone. "Eye-opening how?"

Paula laughs and it immediately sets my teeth on

edge. "Well for starters, it was interesting to learn that you and Libby were so…*close*."

"Well, I wouldn't call us…close. Not now anyway. We were much closer in our early years. Middle school year. Not anymore. No big deal, really," I ramble. I don't know why I'm getting defensive. No wait, I do know why. I'm nervous and I'm allowing this woman, who is not even in the room, to unravel me.

God, I can only imagine what she'd do to me if she were here. I guess it's a good thing she's got soul crushing anxiety then, right?

"Oh that's not the impression I got from your confession the other day," Paula says, her voice causing the hairs on the back of my neck to stand on end.

"Confession?" My voice squeaks. "That wasn't a confession. That was just…me talking about Libby when she was younger." I glance at Penny, my eyes widening, hoping she'll sense my unease and shut Paula down, but once she sees me looking at her, she becomes entranced with the wires underneath the control panel, successfully selling me out to the demon that is her sister.

"Sounded a lot like a confession to me," Paula says. I can't see her face, of course, but I swear I can see her smirk in my mind. Which is doubly crazy since I have no idea what Paula even looks like.

"Well, I don't know what to tell you. It wasn't," I shoot back. "Why are we talking about me? I thought we were going to talk to all the suspects." I glance at Penny who has lifted her head, watching me with the same intensity one might watch a car accident in progress. "I thought we were going to talk to Isabella."

"You know, you're right, Amy" Paula says. "We should be talking to all the suspects."

"I thought that was—"

"Especially the most suspicious of all the suspects," Paula continues. "Where were *you* when Libby was killed, Amy?" Paula asks, her ominous words echoing in my headphones. My chest tightens, the accusation suffocating me.

"What?" I must have heard incorrectly. "What are you asking me?"

Paula sighs the sigh of a mother whose children have gotten into the cookie jar at nine-thirty at night and are on a sugar high with no intention of going to bed in the next century. "It's a simple question. Where were you when Libby was killed?"

"I was at the reunion." I glance around the room with a disbelieving look. As if there is an audience who can commiserate with me. Like, is this lady for real or what?

"Exactly," Paula says with emphasis. "So you had the means to kill our friend Libby."

Our friend Libby?

"I certainly did not."

"Why not? You were at the exact place where she was killed," Paula replies.

"So were about a hundred other people!"

"Yes, but very few of those people knew about the bathroom where Libby was found," Paula reports triumphantly.

Wait a minute. How does she *know about the*

bathroom where Libby was found? That was not in the many news reports about Libby's death. In fact, the only people who knew about that bathroom were me, Libby, Isabella, and...Penny.

"Penny," I hiss as I rip the headphones off. "Did you tell your sister about the secret bathroom?"

Penny gawks at me wide-eyed. "Well, yeah I did…she's…we're investigating the crime."

"I don't think you were supposed to tell anyone that."

"Sorry, I didn't know." She shrugs before pointing to the microphone in front of me. "She can still hear you, by the way."

I frown at her and pull the headphones back over my ears. I have half a mind to storm out of here.

"So," Paula is saying, oblivious to the fact that I've had my headphones off for the last minute or so and have no idea what she has said. "I also think it's rather convenient that you were the one who found Libby's body."

I stare at Penny, my eyes bugging out of my head. *Tell her!* I try to send Penny telepathic messages. *Tell Paula that you were with me when I found Libby's body. Stop this ridiculous line of inquiry right now!*

"And from what I heard, you entered the stall and didn't call for help for almost five minutes. Plenty of time to kill Libby."

I glower at Penny who shrinks back in her chair.

"I didn't go into the stall until I was certain Penny wasn't coming out right away. I didn't want to use the handicapped stall." No good deed goes unpunished apparently.

"And I bet you had a nail file in your purse as well," Paula says, ignoring me.

"What? That's…"

How did she know about the nail file? That's another fact that has been kept from the press and I didn't tell anyone about it aside from Detective Garfield and Lexie. I didn't even tell Penny. At least, I don't think I did.

Still, this is ridiculous. "I'm pretty sure ninety percent of the female population has a nail file in their purse."

"Which makes it a really great weapon to use, right?" Paula prods. "Virtually untraceable, I mean, a million women must use that brand, right? And with all those fingerprints filed off it?"

I open my mouth but snap it closed. I have no idea how fingerprints would be retrieved on a nail file, and I have no interest in making myself look even more ridiculous than I already do by saying something stupid. I pull my T-shirt away from my body, the sweat curling down my cleavage in rivers. I lift one thigh and then the other—I'm so sweaty I could probably slide off this chair and right out of this room. Which is what I should do. There's nothing keeping me here, right? Except for the fact that if I leave, it's going to make me look guilty. But then again, what do I care what Paula thinks? She's not even here. She's a woman who's afraid to leave her house and I'm worried about what she thinks? That's so stupid.

I'm about to stand up to leave when Paula says, "So there you go. What's that little saying about murder? You need the means, the method, and what's the last part?" I hear a popping noise from her end of the conversation, like she's tapping her finger against her lips. "Dear Sister? What's the last part?"

"The motive," Penny says timidly. I shoot daggers at her with my eyes—she quickly glances down at the control board and starts playing with the dials. As I fan myself with my hand, I wish she would press the button that would disconnect Paula. *God, why is it so damn hot in here?*

"Well it's a good thing we're looking into the motives of all the suspects," I say, hoping to bring this whole circus back around.

That's it, Amy. Segue into the motives of the other suspects...wait, not the other *suspects...the actual suspects. You're not an actual suspect, Amy! No matter what this crazy lady is leading you to believe. You're not guilty!*

"That is true," Paula says, agreeing with me for the first time during this entire sordid affair. I glance at the clock. *It's only been fifteen minutes?* It feels like I've been grilling on a spit for an eternity. "Motive *is* one of the biggest factors in murder."

"Um, right," I say, hoping she continues in this direction. Away from me.

"What are the main motives for murder, Dear Sister?" Paula asks, cuing Penny to pop her head up.

"Money, sex, and revenge," Penny says dutifully.

"Money, sex, and revenge," Paula muses. "Yes. And in fact, Amy now not only has the method, the means, she's got the motive as well." Paula adds with a shit-eating grin.

Again, I have no idea what Paula looks like, but I'm picturing a shark who has just feasted on a fish that it has tricked into being its friend…like in *Finding Nemo*.

"What are you talking about?" I can barely stammer out the words.

"Revenge. One of the oldest reasons for murder in history," Paula says. "You have revenge as your motive for killing Libby."

"Revenge?" I sputter. She can't be serious.

"You had every reason to seek revenge against your former best friend. Maybe you had to wait years to enact it, but you finally made it happen."

"Because she decided not to be my friend in seventh grade?" I could probably break glass at this octave range. "Do you hear how ridiculous that sounds?" It's even more ridiculous than Neil seeking revenge for Libby dumping him our senior year.

"But is it? I mean, you did admit that it shaped the rest of your middle school career."

I am stunned. I said nothing of the sort. Well, perhaps I implied that middle school was not my favorite point in my life, mostly because of what had happened between Libby and me, but in no way did I imply that it was bad solely because of that. I mean, who knows? I might have been as equally miserable even if Libby and I had remained friends. Middle school is notoriously rough for almost everyone. Just because I'm looking back at it now as a blight on my life doesn't mean anything really. Hindsight is twenty-twenty.

"Middle school can hardly be called a career," I manage to snort with disbelief. "It's a two or three year time span in a person's life. Most of whom will probably tell you that it was the worst years of their life."

"But how many of those people had a falling out with their best friend?" Paula asks.

Again I snort. "Probably a good number of them. My own daughter had a falling out with her best friend when she was in eighth grade." I'm glad I can pull this useless fact from the recesses of my brain to prove my point.

"Still, how many of those people ended up regretting their life in the future?"

"I don't regret my life!" I interject, jumping to my feet. Now this is getting way too personal. Okay, yes, I have been having some woe-is-me moments lately, but I certainly don't regret my life. And even if I did, I'm sure I wouldn't regret a falling out with a friend thirty years ago to the point that I would blame it for my failings and kill her.

"Even if that's true, you have to admit, your life hasn't been so hot. Killing Libby would be like a rebirth for you...a second chance of sorts. Metaphorically speaking of course, because if you killed Libby, you actually go to prison and your life will really suck then."

I don't wait another moment. I rip the headphones off my head and toss them on the desk. I push the chair back, strap my bag over my chest, and storm out of the recording studio.

"Amy!" Penny calls after me before I can get out the door. "I'm sorry!"

I whirl around to face her. "*Sorry?* You tricked me into coming here today thinking we were making a legitimate podcast episode. That we were interviewing someone else who was at the reunion. But no. Your sister called in and…" I clench my fists at my sides to prevent myself from trembling, "...accused me of killing Libby simply because we were friends once upon a time. And you sat there and didn't defend me at all. You just let her do it." I turn on my heel. "I'm done with this whole podcast. Don't you dare air that episode." I wave my hand in the air before storming out of the recording studio.

"Amy!" I hear Penny calling out after me.

I don't turn around, but I halt in my tracks, hands clenched at my sides. "What?"

"I'm sorry, but I was just doing what she told me to do."

I don't speak, but I continue walking toward the stairwell until she says one more thing that causes my blood to run cold.

"And Amy? Paula wanted the episode live. It's already dropped."

CHAPTER TWENTY-ONE

The doorbell rings for the umpteenth time today and I groan. Another reporter? Another nosy neighbor looking to see if the rumors about me are true? I don't care. I'm not answering the door anymore. If it's any of my friends...okay, Laura*...or my sisters, they would have called before coming over.*

I ignore the ringing and go back to my dusting.

Two minutes later, my cell phone rings. I pull it out of my pocket and stare at the caller ID. Number Blocked. *As much as I would like to ignore this call, I can't. Maybe one of the kids are hurt and this is the emergency room calling me. I press* Answer Call.

"Is this Amy Maxwell?"

"Depends on who's calling," I reply with a lot more confidence than I am feeling.

"This is Detective Garfield with the Brookside Police Department."

My heart thrums loudly in my chest as I lower myself down into the nearest chair. "Detective Garfield! How nice to hear from you again," I lie, lacing my words with sugar. "What can I do for you today?"

"Well, Mrs. Maxwell," Detective Garfield says, "we're outside your house right now, so you can open the door and let us in."

I gasp involuntarily and dash over to the living room

window, cautiously peeling back the curtain. Detective Garfield is indeed standing on my front porch. With five other officers. I rush over to the front door and throw it open.

"Detective Garfield!" I say in a cheery voice that completely belies the butterflies batting around in my belly. "To what do I owe this pleasure?"

Detective Garfield reaches into his back pocket and pulls out a pair of handcuffs, which he slaps on my wrists before I can even blink.

"Amy Maxwell, you are under arrest for the murder of your former best friend, Libby Farrington. You have the right to remain silent, but knowing you, it's physically impossible. Anything you say or do can be used against you in court, and since it's you, Amy, you'll make this an open and shut case for us. Considering you admitted to killing Libby on the podcast yesterday."

My mouth falls open in protest. "But I didn't—"

"Save it for the judge," the detective snaps at me.

*Garfield tugs on my handcuffs and pulls me through the front door toward a waiting...*litter box*?*

I glance up at him and realize he's turned into a furry orange cat.

Sleep eludes me the night after the podcast, so I'm up before dawn when the idea strikes me to go to the grocery store early and get it out of the way. Apparently, though, it isn't early enough. There are enough people in the grocery store to make me regret my decision. This is where it starts...the hushed whispers when I pass by in the cold cut aisle. The stares behind the display of grapefruit. The not-so-hushed whispers when I'm comparing toothpastes in the hygiene aisle.

It seems as if the entire town has heard the podcast. And suddenly, the entire town knows who I am. I have never craved anonymity more than I do as I'm checking out, shoving my unbagged groceries back into the cart because of course I forgot my recyclable bags in the car.

By the time I get in the car, I'm actually sweating. It's not as if grocery stores aren't stressful enough as it is—throw in a few town gossips to stare at you while you shop and it's a recipe for an anxiety attack. Or worse…a heart attack.

And that isn't made any better by the sight that greets me when I pull onto my street. Lined up in front of my house are three different news vans…all from the three major networks. There are several reporters milling about on the sidewalk, drinking coffee and chatting with the cameramen.

"What in the actual hell," I mutter to myself as I pull into the driveway and crane my neck to see down the block.

Was there an accident or a fire or a robbery on this street? Why would all three major news networks be on our street? Oh gosh, I hope everyone is okay.

I get my answer as soon as I step out of my vehicle and pop the trunk. The reporters come swarming toward me, and it's not to help me with my bags.

"Mrs. Maxwell!" A curvy blonde in a hot pink wrap dress is the first to reach me, waving a microphone in the air. "Erin Randall from TBC news. Can you comment on the allegations of your involvement in the murder of Libby Farrington?"

"Mrs. Maxwell!" Another voice interrupts before I can even wrap my brain around what this woman is asking. "Tamara Frank from PCS news. How does it feel to be accused of murdering your former best friend?"

My mouth hangs open and I swear a squeak escapes my lips, but currently, I'm completely unable to form any words.

"Mrs. Maxwell!" The final reporter is a man and apparently the most ruthless because he doesn't even introduce himself before shoving the microphone in my face and asking, "Why did you do it, Amy? Why did you kill your best friend?"

Again, I try to speak, but my words are drowned out by the sound of a motorcycle pulling into my driveway and stopping.

"Back off!"

I turn and gawk at the motorcyclist, who is the last person I expected to see pull in my driveway this morning. After these reporters, that is. He parks, swings his leg over the side, and pulls his helmet off. Jason comes striding toward the back of the SUV and the reporters suddenly become interested in him.

"Who are you?" Erin Randall asks in a tone of voice that makes it unclear whether she's asking for the story angle or because she wants to get his number and have his babies.

"I'm the person who's going to arrest you if you don't get your asses off this private property pronto," Jason says as he pulls his badge from his jacket pocket. The reporters collectively lean forward to read it, but he doesn't give them the opportunity before he tucks it back into his jacket pocket.

Without another word, Jason grabs two bags of groceries and shoves me toward the house as the reporters begin their barrage of questions again, this time keeping a safe distance behind us. Jason whirls around and fixes them with a steely stare, causing a hush to fall over the crowd.

"Open the door," he says to me with a clenched jaw. I scowl without turning around and punch in the code on the door.

I reach for the handle to open the door, but Jason beats me to it, reaching around me to push it open, shove me inside, and drop the bags on the floor, in one fluid motion. Before I can blink, I am standing in the living room, front door closed, Jeter pawing through the grocery bags, and Jason Collins frowning at me.

"What?" I ask, throwing up my hands.

He jerks his thumb toward the street. "The reporters?" he says with a cocked eyebrow.

I frown at him as I snatch the handles of my grocery bags, push Jeter out of the way with my hip, and stomp off toward the kitchen. "I didn't invite them here," I tell him without looking over my shoulder, the weight of the bags making it impossible to turn around.

Did he pick the two heaviest bags to carry in? What the hell is in here?

"You practically did by going on that stupid podcast. Here, give me that. You're going to hurt yourself," he says, following me and reaching for the bag in my left hand, but I don't give him the satisfaction of helping me. "Didn't I tell you to leave this whole thing alone?" he asks as he trails after me, helplessly stuffing his hands into his pockets. Jeter nudges his elbow with his snout, looking for pets, but Jason doesn't budge. He must really be mad at me—he usually loves Jeter.

My arms squeal with pleasure when I unload the bags onto the kitchen island, spilling them everywhere. I ignore the can of soup that rolls off the island and smashes onto the floor, right by Jason's foot. I wish for a second that it smashed his foot.

"How did you know they were here anyway?" I ask, suddenly realizing that Jason doesn't normally show up for weekday morning visits unannounced.

"Tom called me and told me there was something weird going on," Jason says, gesturing toward Tom, our neighbor's house.

I grunt and shake my head.

Why does he always have to do this? Act like I'm a damsel in distress that needs saving? It's a bad romance novel cliche and I'm tired of it playing out in my real life all the time. Although, he did shut the reporters up…for now. What is he going to do? Be my bodyguard?

"I think I should stay with you until this dies down,"

Jason says after bending down to retrieve the can by his foot and setting it on the counter.

I squint at him. *Can he read my mind or something?* I turn a lovely shade of eggplant. If Jason Collins could read my thoughts, I would need to flee the country and go live in that convent where Maria Van Trapp came from. I wouldn't talk at all…I swear. I'll take a vow of silence. It would probably be best for me considering the mess I've gotten myself into with my mouth.

"Why would you do that?" I ask Jason when I recover from my shock.

"Oh, I don't know," Jason says, folding his arms across his chest and leaning a firm butt cheek against the counter. *Stop it, Amy...stop it!* "Maybe the shit show on your front lawn led me to believe it isn't exactly safe for you to be on your own right now."

"That's ridiculous. I'm fine. Everything's fine. I don't know what you're talking about," I add, my damn voice pitching up to the rafters at the end. *Ugh, just stop talking Amy!*

To his credit, he doesn't laugh at me. He just raises his left eyebrow ever so slightly. "Really?" This is not a question. This is Jason trapping me somehow. I've known him for a long time. I'm on to him. "Well then riddle me this…*detective*…why is there a Kill Amy Maxwell group on social media right now if you're so safe?"

My own eyebrows meet my hairline. "What?" I pat my pockets, frantically searching for my phone. "That's not allowed! They would never—"

"It's called *Get Maxwell* actually," Jason says, retrieving his own phone from his pocket and clicking a few buttons before holding it up to my face. "But you get the gist."

With shaking hands, I take the phone from him and start to read, my blood vacillating between running ice cold and boiling.

Did you hear that podcast…the Sisters in Crime one? That woman has the absolute gall to go on a podcast after what she did to her friend!
She's obviously the killer…why don't the cops see it?
That Amy Maxwell should be shot on sight!
To kill your best friend and then go bragging about it on a podcast? What the hell is wrong with this world?
Amy should be killed the same way her friend was killed!
I have a nail file!
I have two!
Ooo, I have a better idea. How about poison? It's a slow and painful death so she has time to think about what she did?
Or the heel of a stiletto through her neck?
That's incredibly gruesome. I love it!
And I have her address!
We ride at dawn!

It's the second to last message that sends me into a frenzy.

"What is this?" I ask Jason, shaking the phone in his face. "They know where I live? Some random people who follow a podcast know where I live? Are they serious about all of this?" My lip quivers as I speak, so I'm surprised Jason can even understand my babbling.

Jason gently reaches out and steadies my shaking hand, taking the phone from it with his other hand. "They might. The reporters don't help the situation, that's for sure," he says releasing my hand and sweeping his own toward the front window where we can still see the reporters lurking. "Or they may be full of it. The internet it chock full of people with fake bravado behind a keyboard."

"I know that but…" Quivering lip again. "This is personal."

Jason starts to smirk in an *I told you so* gloat, but seems to think better of it, a gentle expression crossing his face as he takes the crook of my arm and leads me to the nearest chair.

"This is exactly why I suggested—" His face contorts and I know he's having trouble not saying *you stay out of this mess to begin with*. If anyone has earned an "I told you so," it's Jason in this situation. But he opts to go with a more mature response. "Why I told you I should stay here for a little bit and keep watch for you. Until this blows over."

My face crumples just then, my emotions overtaking me. It's such a generous offer…I don't think anyone has ever cared for my well-being the way Jason is caring for my well-being right now.

That's why I start bawling. Oh, that and the fact my period was due two days ago and this perimenopause thing has me playing emotion roulette on a daily basis.

Of course, Jason doesn't do crying and leaps away from me as if I am toxic. Which, I guess I am in a way. I have like the opposite of the King Midas Touch. It's the Amy Maxwell Touch…everything I touch turns to crap.

God, how have I made such a mess of things again?

"Amy, Amy…listen…don't…cry…Amy…" Jason says from his safe distance of approximately seven feet.

"I can't stop!" I wail. "I've screwed this up so bad!"

There's a pause and once again I know Jason is checking his maturity card. "Maybe so, but that podcast was not totally your fault. Those women tricked you into coming on it and then they ambushed you."

I don't have a response to this. He's, as usual, one hundred percent right. It's so irritating, especially in this situation. Paula knew what she was doing, and Penny must have known what she was going to do. That's why she never argued with her and said, "No! Amy is innocent! I was with her all night!" Penny could have totally put a stop to this whole thing and instead she completely fed me to the wolves.

"That's why I'm staying here until this dies down," Jason says.

"Jason, you can't stay here," I protest.

"Why not?" He takes a few steps into the living room and points at the couch. "Does that thing open up? I can sleep there. Or if it doesn't open up, I can just sleep on the sofa. I'm used to sleeping on sofas."

I shake my head. "No! I would never have a guest sleep on the couch like that. Allie's room is empty and her sheets are clean. But that's not what I mean. I meant, you can't actually sleep here. Roger…" My voice trails off, not sure how to gently put this.

My husband is incredibly jealous of you because you're supremely hot? Even though you're my brother-in-law and nothing would ever happen between us, you sleeping in my house might give me embarrassing sex dreams?

There is just no way to say what is ruminating in my head and how this situation would not work out. Unless…

"I think Roger might get offended that you think he can't protect me." When in doubt, throw Roger under the bus and blame his insecurity.

Jason shakes his head. "Don't worry about that. I'll handle Roger. You just go handle this." He points to the melting carton of ice cream on the counter.

CHAPTER TWENTY-TWO

By the time Roger got home from work, the rumor that I had killed Libby had pervaded our small town so intricately that Roger, he of zero social media accounts and oblivion that rivaled a deaf and blind cloister, had heard about it. He came tearing up the driveway immediately after school, which is nearly unheard of since he usually stays for a few hours after the students and staff have gone home to answer emails and generally avoid the chaos that is our household.

But not today. Today he storms into the house at precisely four o'clock in the afternoon, bursting through the front door like a raging river crashing through an ineffective dam.

"Amy?" His voice holds a measure of fear that I don't think I've heard since the time we were kidnapped by criminals in the Caribbean and held captive by a nearly naked native wielding a spear.

Geez, is he worried about my safety with the jackals out in our neighborhood, or is he afraid of me? Does he really think I killed Libby? I muse as I take a deep breath and wipe my wet hands on a dish towel, anticipating Roger's entry into the kitchen.

Jason is sitting at the kitchen table with a cup of coffee when Roger enters the kitchen, Colt next to him toiling away on his math homework, something he never does. When he came home from school and discovered Uncle Jason was visiting, he immediately set up camp next to him at the table and hasn't left his side since, making Jason's one visit to the bathroom quite awkward for both of them. Evan is off playing somewhere, not nearly as impressed by his DEA agent uncle as his brother is. He's more impressed that his aunt is currently building a fashion empire and has asked repeatedly if he can model clothes for Jason so he can take his ideas back to Joey. Unfortunately, he is not in her ideal demographic. He's about five inches too short and about twenty pounds too light…missing boobs, hips, and a butt as well.

"Oh hi, Roger," I say as he stands in the doorway between the kitchen and the living room, red-faced and panting. *Did he run here*

"What is this about a murder, Amy?" His tone is accusatory but now that I can see his eyes, I can tell he's actually scared. Like I said before, not sure if he's scared for me or *of* me. Which pisses me off…you think you know a person. Roger should know by I would never kill another human being or animal for that matter…well, not intentionally. There was that squirrel I ran over a few months ago that traumatized me. The fear that I have gotten in over my head, however…that's a valid one. I have definitely, once again, gotten in over my head.

"Roger, I—"

I don't even get a chance to speak before Roger is unwinding his tie and reaching into the fridge for a beer, continuing his tirade. "Mrs. Goldstein told me there was a murder at the reunion, Amy! You didn't tell me there was a murder at the reunion!"

Ugh, Mrs. Goldstein, I should have known. Mrs. Goldstein is one of the teachers in Roger's school. She's been there so long that she taught me when I was in high school. In fact, she's been there so long that she's taught almost everyone who grew up in this town. Heck, I think she even taught my father…okay, maybe not. But she has been a fixture at the school forever, garnering such respect that none of her colleagues, including Roger, the principal of the school, can call her by her first name and everyone calls her Mrs. Goldstein. Actually, I don't even think she has a first name. She was born before people had names. Okay, that's just silly, but seriously—a pillar of the community for sure—and the most busiest busybody there ever was. If something goes down in this town, Mrs. Goldstein is the first to report it at the school. If Roger had even a modicum of interest in gossip, Mrs. Goldstein would be where he would go for the dirt. Forget the water cooler, the woman *was* the water cooler.

"I thought I did. You must have forgotten about it," I reply nonchalantly as Roger closes the refrigerator door and turns to look at me, frowning.

"You know you didn't. I wouldn't forget something like that."

He might. He's getting old and forgetful.

"Well remember you called asking when I would be home and why there was a motorcycle in the driveway and I told you it was Jason's and that we were going to be late because the police wanted to talk to me?" I wave my hand at Jason, who to his credit, is trying his best not to get involved in this conversation at all.

Roger doesn't respond to me but notices Jason for the first time. He does a bit of a double take but doesn't ask why Jason is there. Instead, he jerks his head toward the bottle in his hand and asks, "You want a beer?"

Jason shakes his head and holds up his mug. "No, thanks, I've got coffee."

Roger shrugs as if to say *your loss* and then continues to glower at me. "Yes I do remember that, but you conveniently left out the part where there was a murder."

"Well honestly, Roger, what do you think happened to bring the cops there?"

Roger thinks for a moment and then shrugs. "I don't know. A rowdy crowd?" He twists the top off his beer and tosses it into the trash.

I roll my eyes. "Well, sorry I forgot to mention it, but there was a murder. A girl I went to school with."

Roger points an accusatory finger at me as he takes a swig of his beer. "And that's the other thing," he says when he pulls the bottle away from his mouth. "You didn't tell me it was your best friend! I had to hear that from Mrs. Goldstein too! She said she heard you on a podcast talking about her!"

God is there any end to Mrs. Goldstein's reach of gossip? I had no idea a ninety-year-old would even know what a podcast was, let alone how to find one and listen to it. But then again, this is Mrs. Goldstein we're talking about. She probably drinks the blood of virgins in order to stay alive, hence why she works in a high school.

Again I roll my eyes. "She was my best friend in *middle school*, Roger. Like over thirty years ago. Back when you had to call people on the telephone and speak to their parents before you could actually talk to them? A million years ago."

That wasn't entirely true…Libby had had her own private line. I can still remember the number, I dialed it so many times. I was so jealous because my parents wouldn't even let me have a phone in my room, let alone a private line. I had to do all my gossiping and squealing about boys in the living room for my sisters and parents to overhear. But I better not let that information get out, or there will be a rumor that I killed Libby over her teen line that she had in 1991. Insert eye roll here.

"Still, it wouldn't hurt to actually mention that sort of thing to your husband." He takes another swig of beer and his eyes float over to Jason. "I bet he knew," he says, jerking his head toward Jason.

"Well, yes, because he was there, Roger."

"Another thing you forgot to mention. That Jason was going to the reunion with you," Roger says as if Jason and Colt aren't sitting right in front of us. "I thought you were going with Joey."

"Proof that you don't listen," I interject, happy to be able to bring up this point. "I told you Joey was on bedrest and couldn't go."

"Yeah, but you—" Roger starts to say, but Jason speaks up for the first time since being offered a beer.

"If it's any consolation, Roger, she wasn't very

forthcoming with me either. I came back to the reunion after being called away for a work crisis, and I found out about the murder from one of the detectives that were on the scene."

Roger stares at Jason, considering this information. I can practically see the wheels turning in his head. Will he now consider Jason a friend instead of a foe? Or rather, a friendlier foe?

Unfortunately (or fortunately, depending on how you'd like to look at it), we don't get to find out the answer to that question because my cell phone rings. The four of us stare at it like it's a bomb, watching it skitter across the kitchen table with each buzz.

"Aren't you gonna get that?" Roger asks after it stops ringing and buzzing and then starts up almost immediately.

I shake my head. "I don't know who it is." I don't add that I've had several unpleasant encounters with strangers today and I have no desire to replicate that experience in my own home, thank you very much.

The phone is in front of Jason so he leans closer to the screen and announces, "It's Beth."

"Oh I'll take it." It's after four in the afternoon and that's the time Beth plays tennis at the club. She never makes phone calls during tennis time. If she is calling me now, it's serious. Someone might be hurt…or dying even.

"Hello?" I put my phone to my ear—all the men in the room stare at me, including my child. I'm tempted to turn my back on them but that would be really rude. Wouldn't it?

Instead I busy myself at the sink, rewashing a mug that I previously washed. Hey, you can never be too careful about cleanliness, right?

"Amy is that you?" Beth asks, as if I routinely have random people picking up my phone to answer it.

I bite my lip to hold the sarcasm back and try for my most casual, neutral voice. "Hi, Beth. What's up?"

"What's up? What's up? *What the hell, Amy*?" Beth screeches into the phone, her voice echoing like she's in a tunnel.

"Where are you? It's very…echo-y."

"I'm at the club," Beth replies, lowering her voice. "I'm in the locker room. What. The. Hell?"

"Um, is everything okay?" I ask, knowing full well that it can't be if she's calling me from the locker room, of all places, and has already asked me what the hell twice.

"No, everything is not okay," she hisses. "Brandy Lowenstein and Francesca Picarelli not only stared at me…gawked at me, in fact, when I walked in before…I heard them talking in the locker room when they didn't know I was there. Do you know what I heard them talking about?"

I chew my lip having a pretty good idea about what those two old fish wives were gossiping about. "Um, who they're going to vote for for governor?" I take a stab in the dark.

"Oh no, Amy," Beth replies in what I would refer to as her "just bit a sour lemon with maggots crawling out of it" voice. "They were discussing something a bit more salacious. They were talking about a certain local podcast. One that featured *my sister*."

I seize the opportunity to take one final stab at humor. "Oh, Joey was on a podcast? Cool, which one?"

Beth, predictably, does not laugh. In fact, judging by the lack of noise on the other end of the phone, I'm not even sure she's breathing.

"Beth? Are you there?"

I hear a deep suck of breath and then, "Yes, I'm here. Unfortunately. You know it wasn't Joey. It was you. They were saying…you killed Libby Farrington."

"Well you know that's not true." You would think making such statement would be unnecessary, that my family would assume, no that my family would *know*, that I of course did not kill Libby. But no. Obviously not.

"I didn't think so, but—"

"You didn't think so?" Jason and Roger cringe at my high-pitched voice. *Sorry*, I mouth at them.

"Well of course not, but Amy…there's more."

I wrinkle up my brow. "What do you mean there's more? What more could there be?"

Again, Beth is silent for a moment before clearing her throat. "There's a rumor that you're writing erotica."

I swear my heart stops beating at that moment.

How the hell would anyone know I was writing erotica? That was private! That was for my eyes only!

It was…on Writepod…the document writing program. There's a setting for writers to share their work so you can get other people's opinions before publishing. People can comment on your work by sending you messages. But I never shared it. It was set to private.

Wait...the last time I was on there, I noticed a bunch of messages in my Inbox folder but I thought they were just nonsense from the Writepod company. You know, hey for an extra five hundred dollars a month, you can have your own website. That kind of nonsense. They must be messages from people who have read the spicy romance. Oh god, I thought I had set it to private! You really need to get a handle on technology, Amy!

I feel nauseated as the realization that people are going to read…*are* reading…the steamy, yet poorly written sex scenes that I crafted in my brain. Oh god, the mortification. This might be even more embarrassing than being accused of murder.

But wait, how did anyone connect it to me? I don't use my full name on Writepod. I only go by Amy M. Come on, there has to be a million and one Amy Ms writing on there. Why would anyone think it was me? Can people somehow figure out the IP address from my profile? That is one terrifying thought. There has to be a way to block that, right? That doesn't sound safe.

I'm about to ask Beth when she interrupts my thoughts.

"Amy, do you have any idea how embarrassing it is to have your sister accused of murdering her best friend? *And* writing that…*stuff*? What will my clients think if they find out? You think the women in this club won't tell my clients that my sister writes smut? That's exactly the thing they would love to tell them!"

I scowl. "Gee Beth, you have any idea how

embarrassing it is to be accused of a murder that you didn't commit," I add. I don't defend the smut comment. Maybe if I don't talk about it, it'll go away.

"Mom is going to have a heart attack when she hears this, Amy. If she hasn't already. And the smut…geez, you better hope she never gets wind of that. That'll give her stroke on top of a heart attack."

"Well then maybe you should get off the phone to free up the line in case the hospital is calling to say she's had a heart attack and a stroke," I snap back.

"Oh that's hysterical. Maybe you should become a comedian. I heard they need entertainment in prison. Oh maybe you can read them your writing. That'll be good for some laughs."

My face burns. What a horrible thing to say. I don't know what hurts more, the prison comment or the reminder that my writing is that bad. "Wow that's harsh. I'm not going to prison. I haven't done anything wrong."

"Plenty of innocent people go to prison, Amy," Beth says with a haughty laugh.

Of all the hurtful things Beth has slung at me this afternoon, that's the one that hits the hardest.

She's right. Innocent people do go to prison all the time. But, I'm like, super innocent. I can't go to prison for something I had nothing to do with. I can't go to prison just because some podcaster has accused me of something…right? God, I hope not. I am not prison material. I absolutely would not last a day. I mean, not only would the orange baggy jumpsuit look horrible on me, I have absolutely no street skills or knowledge whatsoever.

"Maybe you should start listening to Roger and Jason and mind your own business from now on," Beth says, snapping me back to reality. "That is if you're not doing twenty to life."

"I have to go, Beth," I announce, and I don't wait for her reply before ending the call. I am not doing twenty to life. I am not even going to trial for something I didn't do. I am going to fix this once and for all. I am going to find out who killed Libby Farrington if it's the last thing I do.

I scan the faces of the three males sitting in front of me, all of them with their mouths hanging open.

"Who wants pizza for dinner?"

CHAPTER TWENTY-THREE

Thunder rumbles in the distance and occasionally, a flash of lightning brightens up the living room, creating an eerie atmosphere. I shiver, pulling my cardigan tight against my body before wrapping my hands around the steaming mug of tea in front of me.

Despite the lightening, it seems like it's getting darker by the minute, the grandfather clock in the living room chiming out the hour…two in the morning already, but I refuse to stop. I place the cup of tea on the coffee table and resume combing through the stack of paper I have printed out from the computer—the transcripts from the podcast interviews, with all the suspects that Penny and Paula have spoken to. I've been poring over them for hours, my eyes shifting from the papers to the laptop in front of me. My eyes have grown heavy, and I haven't even stopped to pee, but yet, I continue on. I must find out who killed Libby and I know the answer is here somewhere. One of these people is guilty (not me) and I will not rest until I figure out which one it is.

I pick up the yellow marker to highlight a passage in the transcript of Libby's husband, when it hits me like a ton of bricks. Gasping, I re-read his interview, each word that he says painting a clearer picture than before. How did no one spot this? How did the police not see it? How did I not see this the first hundred times I read this interview? It's a clear as the nose on my face...heck, it couldn't have been any clearer if he had said out loud, "I killed my wife."

"He killed her," I say to the empty room. "Of course he did."

I pick up my phone to call Detective Garfield and tell him what I have found, but suddenly there is a knock at the front door and I rush over to open it. On my doorstep in the pouring rain stands Detective Garfield.

He doesn't have an umbrella, but somehow he isn't getting wet at all. "Mrs. Maxwell. I came as soon as I got your call," he says, stepping into the house.

I stare at the phone in my hand. I didn't call him...did I? This is all quite strange.

"What is it you needed to tell me, so urgently at this hour of the night?"

I forget the strangeness of it all and grab Detective Garfield's hand, dragging him toward the couch and my discovery. I snatch up the pages of Preston's transcripts and shake them in his face. "It's here, it's been here all along. The most obvious answer has been staring us in the face this whole time!"

He frowns as he accepts the papers from my outstretched hand. I watch with bated breath as his eyes scan the words in front of him, my chest fluttering with delight when I see recognition dawning on him. With wide eyes, he lowers the paper and grins at me. "Do you know what this means?"

I nod my head rapidly. "I do! It means that everyone will know I didn't kill Libby and her murderer will be behind bars..." I point at him, "...as soon as you go and arrest him!"

He bobs his head up and down. "I'm going to do that right now." He beams at me as he dashes toward the door.

"You're brilliant, Amy! This murder is solved, and we owe it all to you. How can we ever repay you?"

I open the door and lean on the door jamb as he steps out into the now sun-filled morning. "It was nothing. After all, it's always the husband."

**

The sound of thunder rumbling in the distance wakes me from my bizarre dream. Well, that and the fact Jeter is standing on me. Correction, he is standing on my already fragile bladder, his body trembling with fear.

"Oh geez, buddy." I attempt to untangle myself from the bedsheets while he shakes and refuses to move. "I'm sorry, I didn't realize it was supposed to thunder tonight. I forgot to put your thunder shirt on."

I click on the light and Jeter is giving me a look that says, *You better be sorry, lady*.

Jeter is terrified of thunderstorms. He's also terrified of fireworks, the grandfather clock in the living room, the chiweenie next door, and yellow flowers. I can understand the first couple of items—the chiweenie is terrifying, but we have no idea where the fear of yellow flowers came from. And yes, this includes the dandelions which completely pervade our backyard in the spring months—Jeter literally hops around the backyard trying to avoid them, so I have to take him for walks to do his business from April to June. If it were not completely annoying, it would actually be comical.

I open the closet to pull Jeter's thunder shirt out of the drawer where it is stored along with the kids' baby blankets that they don't use anymore. Roger thinks the thunder shirt is ridiculous, but it really helps, and it's not *his* bladder that Jeter stands on when he's scared.

I pull the shirt on the dog and tuck him back into bed beside Roger, who is snoring, despite the booming thunder and the lightning. I swear that man could sleep through the apocalypse. And he will wake up in the morning and tell me how he hardly slept at all.

I pad into the bathroom to do my business and catch sight of myself in the mirror. I have to bite my lip from screaming. No, seriously—I barely recognize myself. My skin is sickly pale and I have dark purple rings underneath my eyes, probably from my lack of sleep and shitty nutrition the last few days. Not only have I been considering apple cider donuts as part of the fruit food group, it's been five days of Jason following me around like he's one of the President's secret service agents and I'm the President's very fragile and impulsive teenage daughter who he has to save from danger at every turn. I swear he practically threw himself on my body when the smoke alarm went off this morning when I was making breakfast.

Yes, I know. In the past I probably would have appreciated such attention from Jason Collins, but I have to tell you, it gets old pretty quickly. And on top of it, he's commandeered my phone, under the pretense that he wants to screen my calls in case someone is threatening me. I protested, but he took it regardless and shoved it deep into the pocket of his cargo shorts.

I sigh as I go back into the bedroom, realizing that I am now wide awake and not likely to fall back asleep any time soon. I stare longingly at my spot on the bed, occupied by a now-calm Jeter. Despite the fact that I desperately need sleep, it seems pointless to try to squeeze in next to Roger and the dog just to toss and turn for the rest of the night.

Remembering my dream, I wonder if there is some way that I could actually do some research from my living room couch to help the police uncover the real murderer.

My eyes skid over Allie's door when I step into the hallway, wondering if Jason is a deep enough sleeper that I can sneak in and grab my phone without him noticing. Oh yeah. Did I forget to mention that he is still sleeping at our house? Pregnant wife on bedrest and two toddlers running around and he thinks it's more important to sit vigil for me. Although if I had two toddlers like Sebastian and Amelia running around, I would probably want to find someplace else to hide out too. And considering my mother has now camped out at their house permanently—or until the baby is born, whichever happens first—I definitely don't blame Jason. I would want to be anywhere but there.

Even though Penny and Paula have dropped two more episodes with potential murder suspects, the media and the public have not given up on the idea that I have killed Libby. The circus isn't camped out in front of my house twenty-four seven anymore, thank God, but they show up at six in the morning like clockwork and I've been getting threatening calls, social media messages, and even letters shoved through the mail slot. One particularly frightening one used cutout newspaper and magazine letters to spell out "Amy Maxwell is a murderer."

Shaking my head, annoyed with myself for even considering going in that room and taking my phone off a sleeping Jason, I shuffle past the door and down the stairs toward the kitchen, Jeter is now hot on my heels, having abandoned Roger and the comfy bed, his thunder shirt worn proudly.

After fixing myself a cup of coffee (Sleep? Who needs sleep? I'm burning the midnight oil here, trying to solve a crime.), I remove my laptop from the charger and pad off to the couch. I watch the home screen come up and eagerly attack the keys until I realize, I have no idea what I'm doing. *How can I find a murderer from the comfort of my own living room, hiding behind a keyboard?*

Then I remember my dream. I pull up the podcast website and navigate it, searching for the transcripts of the interviews. I find them and try not groan as I see the cheesy titles for the episodes. I never looked at the podcast website before and I guess when I listened to the podcast episodes I hadn't really paid attention to the names of them. It's super cringy. Someone died and they're making puns? In a way it seems almost disrespectful to the dead.

My eyes land on my episode. Well, the episode that has people thinking I'm a murderer anyway. The title is *Max Suspicion.* I frown with annoyance and bypass it. That's not the episode I'm looking for anyway. I know exactly what was said in that exchange, and besides, I'm not guilty. Studying what *I* said isn't going to do me any good.

I find the episode featuring Libby's husband (*The Moore the Merrier*) and yell "Yahtzee!", glancing around the living room after I've said it because it came out much louder than I had intended. Fortunately the only reaction I have gotten is Jeter thumping his tail in his sleep, thrilled to hear the sound of my voice.

Clicking on this episode, I rub my hands together in anticipation. This is it! The answer to Libby's murder is somewhere in this twenty-page transcript. As daunting as that seems, I'm determined to put the work in and figure out what the police and everyone else on the planet have missed. It's got to be him. It's always the husband, right? In a few short minutes, I will have this mystery solved and I can call Detective Garfield, just like I did in my dream.

Nearly an hour later I finish poring over Preston's words and Penny and Paula's ping-pong-like questions, and I am no closer to figuring out the truth. In fact, I am more confused than ever. Reading through the interview, I've learned next to nothing. Even though Penny asks pretty direct questions of the man, ones that ought to set the record straight and help the police (and me) figure this out, Libby's husband has managed to artfully dodge every one, and in a roundabout way, brings the whole thing back to his campaign for reelection. I guess that's a politician for you.

I'm getting nowhere fast. It seemed so much easier in my dream. Despite drinking a 16 oz mug of coffee, I feel my eyelids growing heavy, my body begging to go back to sleep. Sighing, I close my eyes and rub my temples, warding off the inevitable migraine I will have tomorrow from lack of sleep.

I suddenly hear the chime of a message landing in my inbox and my eyes snap open. I stare at my laptop, the envelope icon dancing with one new message on the edge of the screen. I'm confused until I realize I never removed the social media messenger from my computer.

I glance up at the clock. It's close to two in the morning. Who could possibly be messaging me at this time of the night?

My brain screams at me to ignore the message, close the computer, go back to bed, and try to get some sleep, but of course my soul is curious. And curiosity always trumps logic. At least in my world.

I open the app and see the message is from someone called Poisoned Penn. Recognition tugs at the recesses of my brain. Do I know a Poisoned Penn? I don't want to open a message from someone I don't know, like one of those crazy stalkers that Jason's supposedly protecting me from. But I feel like I've seen this name before, but where?

It takes me a second, but then it dawns on me. *Oh geez, Amy, you really need some sleep.* Of course, Poisoned Penn must be Penny.

Now I'm really conflicted. Do I open this message, even though I'm furious with Penny for putting me in this situation to begin with? Or do I let it languish here, sending her the message that I'm still mad and I'm not going to forgive her anytime soon? And what if I open the message and I get even angrier? Will she know I saw the message if I open it?

I debate about it for all of ten seconds before my curiosity wins out and I click on the message, consequences be damned.

Hi Amy. I hope you're still online and you can see this message as soon as I send it as time is of the essence in this situation.

This first line gives me pause and my eyes shift uncomfortably toward the living room windows. The blinds are drawn tightly but I can't help but wonder if someone is watching me. Is Penny watching me? Maybe her sister Paula is spying on me?

A shiver runs down my spine as I wrap the throw blanket around my shoulders and continue to read Penny's message.

I've tried to contact you several times over the last few days but your phone just goes to voicemail and you aren't responding to my texts so I figured I would try here after seeing you were online.

Again with this. *How did she know?*

My eyes drift to the tab that's still open on my laptop. *Oh geez, Amy, you're dim tonight. Of course! She saw that little green light that indicates you're online.*

A wave of relief crashes through me. For the first time ever, I'm glad that I'm just dopey instead of being stalked.

I know you're mad at me and I don't blame you.

Gee, that's magnanimous of you, Penny, I think bitterly. It takes me a second or two of staring at the words on the screen to realize there is a blinking cursor after each line I read and words suddenly appear. It takes me a few more seconds to realize it's because this is live and in real time and Penny is currently typing as I read.

But I want you to know, it was all a mistake and we're sooooooo sorry!

Oh. Is sorry going to get the hordes of reporters off my front lawn and Jason Collins out of my house? I don't think so. And who is this *we*? Is she referring to Paula?

Quite honestly, this was all Paula's doing. I didn't even

know she was going to accuse you of killing Libby. I know you didn't kill Libby...heck I was with you the entire night! You didn't kill Libby any more than I killed Libby. But Paula said she did it to create a buzz for the podcast in the hopes that it would draw out the real killer.

It created a buzz all right. A buzz right around my hive. And now everyone in town thinks I'm a murdering lunatic. Thanks a lot for that, Paula.

We're going to fix that, I swear. We've been doing some digging and we think we've found something! We know who the murderer is!

My blood runs cold. They know who the murderer is? How? Is it Libby's husband, like I suspected?

We're actually at the library right now with the evidence. We're going to record a podcast revealing the killer and then call the police so they can surprise the killer at their home. We feel terrible for what we did...we had no idea it would blow up like that...and we want you to be a part of this very special podcast episode as an apology. After people hear this episode, there's no way they'll think you're the killer because the real killer will be locked up and in jail! So what do you say? Come to the library and help us reveal the killer on the podcast?

I glance at the grandfather clock that has recently

chimed two. Is this woman crazy? She wants me to come to the library and record a podcast in the middle of the night? Who does that?

But then my eyes drift to the front door and the lawn beyond it. The reporters have left for the night, and this may be my only chance to get out of the house with them not around.

Amy, I know you're reading this. Please come. I'll leave the front door unlocked and you can join us down in the archive room. We want to show you the evidence before we record.

I stare at the blinking cursor for what feels like forever before I lift my trembling fingers and type.

I'll be there in twenty minutes.

CHAPTER TWENTY-FOUR

"Penny?"

I step into the darkened library and glance around, shuddering as a draft from an open window skates across my skin.

Why is that window open? Shouldn't it be closed if the library is closed? That's really strange.

I shake my head, dismissing the weird feeling and rubbing my hands over my arms where goosebumps have erupted. I hope it's from the cool breeze on my skin and not some odd premonition.

"Penny?" I call out again as I inch forward into the atrium. I've never been here when it's empty and dark—I have to admit, the library is a creepy place when it's devoid of all its human occupants. Although, it should have at least one other human occupant in the building right now. Probably two. Didn't Penny say that Paula was here too? My mind begins working overtime.

What if Penny went to let Paula in and someone accosted her at the door? Or what if Penny left the door open for me and someone came in and hurt her? Or what if they climbed in the open window and then dragged her out and left the door unlocked? Would that be better or worse than if they were lying in wait for me? What if it's the murderer?

What if the murderer is on to them? I mean, they

have been asking quite a few questions and even though the podcast hasn't gone viral or anything like that, it only takes the murderer to listen to it in order to know what Penny and Paula have been up to.

Even though there are panel lights lit up along the base of the checkout counter and the ceiling is glass in the atrium, the main floor is quite dark and again…creepy. I find myself stumbling, catching my foot on some uneven pieces of the carpet, and I knock into the welcome table with a display encouraging the library patrons to sign up for the summer book club, scattering the pamphlets everywhere. I bend down to pick them up and hit my head on the rack.

Standing up, I rub my head and stare down at the pile at my feet. It's difficult to see and I think this would be a project better suited for a time when there is light in the atrium. As much as I hate to leave a mess for the day librarian, I need to meet up with Penny.

Where did she say they were again? The Archive room?

I bypass the elevator, because…of course I bypass the elevator. Can you imagine if I get trapped in an elevator in the library when it's closed? Pushing open the door to the stairwell, the hairs on my arm stand on end. I tell myself it's because of the draft I created when I opened the vacuum sealed door. Yup, it must have something to do with physics, and damn if I understand physics. I failed physics senior year of high school. I only took the class because the physics teacher my *junior* year was this smoking hot guy just out of college, Mr. Tanner.

Imagine my disappointment when I showed up the first day to the class to find out he had been replaced by Ms. Mudrack, an eighty-year-old curmudgeon with a face like a wrinkled up Shar-pei puppy. And no, not in a cute way. Mr. Tanner was transferred to an elementary school because he was, and I quote, "A distraction to the female population of the school." Like he wasn't a distraction to the female teachers and PTA moms at the elementary school? So unfair.

Anyway…the stairwell. It's dark and I recall the reason it's off-limits is because of the broken step. Damn, I wish I had my phone so I could use the flashlight. I run my hands along the wall to see if there is a switch anywhere and am dismayed to discover it's one of those switches that needs to be turned on with a key. The janitor must turn it on every morning before the library opens.

Again, I wonder why Penny didn't wait for me up in the main part of the library. They must be working on whatever they found in the Archive room, figuring out some way to work it into the podcast.

After carefully feeling my way along the staircase (and nearly busting my ankle on the broken stair), I push open the door to the basement and discover it's just as dark down here as it was in the stairwell, despite the panel lights running the length of the hallway. I rub my arms with my hands and shiver. It's freezing down here, even though it was almost eighty degrees outside today and crazy humid.

"Penny?" I call out as I creep down the hall.

"We're in here!" I glance around, trying to gauge where the voice is coming from.

"Where's here?" I ask, squinting in the dark.

"Follow the sound of my voice!" Penny calls out. I am relieved to discover that her voice is coming from the room on my left. I go through the propped-open door and discover the Archive room is huge, but there is only one light on in the room, and it comes from the microfiche machine in the corner.

Why don't they turn the lights on? And how the heck can they see in the dark anyway?

"Hello?" I call out as I approach. Penny is standing behind a woman in a chair, scrolling through the machine. The woman must be Paula, so I use this opportunity to check her out. All I can see from here is that she seems rather tall (she's sitting so it's hard to tell for sure) and her hair is pulled into a high ponytail on top of her head. Kind of like *I Dream of Jeannie.* With one hand on the back of the chair, Penny turns to greet me. The other woman remains seated and doesn't turn around.

"Hi, Amy," she says in a perfectly friendly tone, but there is something about her voice that seems…off. As I get closer, I see her face looks puffy. Was she crying or is it just the light from the microfiche machine?

"Hi, Penny. Are you okay?"

She gives me a forced smile. "Yup! Everything's fine!" she says in a chipper voice that indicates to me that everything is not fine.

"Here it is," the woman sitting at the machine says

and Penny waves me closer.

I peer at the machine where the woman has her finger pressed up against the screen, pointing out an article.

"Whatda ya think of that?" she says triumphantly, without turning around so I still can't get a good look at her face.

I lean closer and read the headline, "Teacher Accused of Inappropriate Relationship with Student."

Hmmmm, what is this and what could it possibly have to do with Libby's murder?

I scan the article, hoping it'll make sense when I'm finished, but even after hitting the highlights, I'm still not sure what any of it has to do with Libby's murder.

"Okay, so a teacher was accused of an inappropriate relationship with a student? What does that have to do with Libby?"

"It was at your high school," Penny tells me.

"So, that's…" I trail off as I realize she said "your" not "our" high school. Stunned, I stare at her. Was that just a slip of the tongue or does it mean something?

Frantically, I try to recall memories of Penny in school. She says she was quiet, but how quiet could she have been that no one at the reunion recognized her? Well, no, that wasn't true…Libby did seem to recognize her. Or at least, she said something like *don't I know you*? Which was a silly question to ask someone at a high school reunion.

I stare at Penny. *There was a Penny Whitaker in the yearbook, but there was no picture, like she was absent the day they were taken. Did this Penny Whitaker in front of me really go to high school with us or did she make that up? But why would anyone make something like that up?*

"Look at the date," the woman says, jerking me away from my suspicions about Penny.

I squint at the screen. *Jesus, has the print always been this small or is my vision getting worse?* I make a mental note to make an eye doctor appointment on Monday.

"June 27, 1996," I read the date out loud.

"When did y'all graduate?" the woman asks.

I don't even wait for Penny to answer. Not sure if she can actually answer that question or not. Heck, it'd be a good test, but I only realize after I blurt out, "June of '97."

The woman taps the screen again. "So this happened the year before you graduated."

I nod even though she hasn't turned around and can't see me nodding.

"Obviously the girl in question isn't named, but we did a little more digging and we think it was Libby," the woman says.

I take a step back. "Wait, that doesn't makes sense. Wouldn't we all know if it was Libby? I mean, the rumor mill around that place was vicious."

"Maybe, maybe not. But this…." she scrolls down a few pages to the section of the paper that recognizes charitable donations, "...says a Mr. and Mrs. Richard Farrington made a sizable donation to the school the same week that the teacher was suspended and moved to the elementary school. Hush money perhaps?"

For the first time since I walked in, she turns around, leaning her arm over the back of the seat and raising an eyebrow at me. I gasp involuntarily. She's so familiar, but I can't place where I know her from. I feel like I saw her recently and not some twenty years ago in high school. Maybe her hair was a different color?

"I'm sorry, I forgot to introduce you two," Penny says, her voice sounding a little twangy, almost copying the other woman's. "This is my sister Paula."

The other woman is frowning and I'm waiting for her to shake my hand or say it's nice to meet me, but then she instantly jumps back to the article.

"It was Libby," Paula says definitively. "And did you look at the name of the teacher that was suspended?"

I squint (really who's idea was it to make print this small on microfiche????) and read the name out loud. "Robert Tanner." My skin erupts into goosebumps at the coincidence.

I was just thinking about Mr. Tanner! Did I somehow know about this in the recesses of my brain and conjure up thoughts of Mr. Tanner before coming down here?

"Look at the picture of him on the next page," Paula says, reaching for the control pad and scrolling down.

I nod as a picture of Mr. Tanner in all his glory fills the screen. My breath hitches as I take in that luxurious mop of dark curls on his beautiful head, his sculpted cheekbones, his full, and I'm certain, kissable lips, a lazy smile curling at the edges. Even his trademark seersucker suit with the dorky arm patches was hot on this guy. I feel a giddiness in my chest that reminds me of the feeling I used to get whenever I'd pass Mr. Tanner's room between classes and he'd be standing out in the hall. God, he always had a gaggle of girls surrounding him, all of them pretending they had urgent questions they had to ask him about physics or the chess club he hosted at the school. There was a moment in time that I even considered joining the chess club, but then I came to my senses because I have no idea how to play chess and wasn't about to embarrass myself in front of Mr. Tanner.

I wonder for a brief second where they got this picture from and if there's a copy somewhere online, when Paula thrusts another picture in my hand.

"What's this?" I ask, startled.

"Just look at it," Paula says gruffly.

I frown at her before I glance down at the picture and see a middle-aged man standing at a bar. The place looks familiar and so does the man, but I can't seem to place either of them.

"Who's this?" I ask Penny, avoiding Paula all together. I still can't help but feel salty about what she did to me on air, regardless of whatever the purpose was.

Penny opens her mouth, but Pushy Paula jumps in. "Look closer. You know who it is."

I purse my lips, refusing to look at Paula. She and Penny cannot possibly be related. I've never met anyone so pushy in all my—

Then it dawns on me. Where I know Paula from. My

head snaps up and I glance at her face. Of course! The pushy lady in the grocery store that asked me for my autograph a few months ago! But wait, why would she—

I don't even get time to ask Paula why she wanted my autograph before she snatches the picture from my fingers.

"It's Robert Tanner," she tells me.

"Um, okay, but…"

"The picture was taken at the reunion," she further continues.

My blood runs cold, and I suddenly get the connection. "Wait, the reunion where Libby was killed? Our reunion?"

Paula looks at Penny with an amused expression on her face. "Wow this one catches on fast, doesn't she?"

"Yes, at our reunion," Penny says quietly. "Mr. Tanner was at the reunion," she continues, eyes cast downward.

"And he's our killer," Paula finishes. "He killed Libby."

My eyes nearly bug out of my head. "Wait, what?"

"Robert Tanner is Libby Farrington's killer," Paula repeats, enunciating each word much more than necessary. Obviously she thinks I'm an idiot for not understanding.

"But that makes no sense. Why would he kill her?"

"Because she's the reason he lost his job," Paula says in a tone that *clearly* indicates that I am dense for not understanding.

I shake my head and point to the article on the screen

in front of us. "He didn't lose his job. He was transferred to the elementary school." I poke the screen. "It says it right here in this article."

Paula shakes her head and rolls her eyes. "Well it's a good thing we read *all* the articles." She scrolls down a few pages until she comes to another article. "Go on, read it."

I glance uneasily at her before turning my attention to the new article on the screen. The first line instantly grabs me.

Teacher accused of inappropriate conduct with high school student is fired years later after affair with an elementary school student's parent is revealed.

I skim the article and deduce that after leaving the high school and going to the elementary school, Mr. Tanner had an affair with a mother of one of his students. He thought it was a consensual relationship while she accused him of coercing her into having the affair, threatening to fail her son if she didn't.

"That doesn't sound like Mr. Tanner at all," I say to Paula and Penny after reading the article. "He wouldn't ever—"

"Oh you know him so well, do you?" Paula asks in a mocking tone.

"No, but—"

"The woman said he forced her. Do you not believe *women*?" Paula asks with a sneer.

"I do but—"

"The paper reported he coerced her and he was fired. I'm sure the school board did their research before firing him," Paula says firmly before looking at me with pity. "Oh what's the matter? Don't want to admit that your precious Mr. Tanner was not only a killer but a rapist as well?"

I gasp at the crude accusation. "Mr. Tanner—"

She cuts me off again. "Robert Tanner was at the reunion. He had a heated conversation with Libby Farrington in front of the building about an hour before she was killed. There's a witness to this confrontation."

I whirl my head around to look at her. Recalling the man Libby was talking to. Was that Mr. Tanner? "How do you know this?"

"Because I'm the one who witnessed it," Paula says triumphantly.

It takes me a second, but when the implication of Paula's statement hits me, it crushes me like a ton of bricks.

"How did you witness it? You would have had to be at the reunion to witness it." I eye Paula suspiciously.

For the first time since I've met her, Paula looks uneasy. She licks her lips and glances at Penny, whose own face looks like that of someone who has just lost her best friend. She's wringing her hands and cringing repeatedly. It's very…weird.

Finally, Paula waves her hand impatiently. "That's not important. What is important is that Robert Tanner killed Libby Farrington. I have the proof right here and we're going to record a podcast right now and let the world know." She waves a stack of papers in the air and jumps to her feet. She's almost out the door when she turns around to stare at us. "Well, what are you two slowpokes waiting for? I want this recorded and ready to go before rush hour." Her eyes sparkle. "Imagine…all the people getting up and getting ready for work and we reveal the killer as they're on their morning commute! We'll be a national sensation!"

I glance at Penny who still wears that pained expression on her face. She glances back at me and offers me a weak smile.

"Let's get the show on the road," she says before turning around and leaving the Archive room.

I follow her out the door and into the studio, a nagging voice begging me to leave this alone. Funny, the nagging voice sounds a lot like Jason.

Penny pulls her keys from the pocket of her sweater and unlocks the recording studio door with trembling hands. We all step into the waiting room together, but then Paula pulls Penny to her side before we enter the studio. She smiles brightly at me, waving her hand toward the open studio doorway.

"Go ahead. I just want to go over a few notes with Penny before we start recording.

Now I'm going to have to chalk this lack of judgement up to the fact that it is now after three in the morning, and I haven't slept in close to a week because of the swarm of reporters hounding me. To say my judgment is clouded would be an understatement. As I step inside the studio, I feel a sting on my neck, and the next thing I know, the world goes dark.

CHAPTER TWENTY-FIVE

When I come to, I have to blink several times to orient myself. The room that I'm in is dimly lit, except for tiny little lights that are dancing around the periphery of my vision. I squint several times to clear my eyes, and it's only after my third blink that I can see I am in the recording studio.

It takes about three more blinks for me to realize that I'm sitting in a chair, my head lying atop a desk. Drool has pooled underneath my cheek, so I try to lift my hand to wipe it off my face, but I can't.

Is this...am I tied *to this chair?*

"Amy? Are you okay?" A loud voice fills the studio, but there is no one there. At least, I don't think there is anyone there.

I lift my head and turn it toward the sound—it's coming from the waiting room. Penny is peering at me through the window, her big brown eyes welling up with tears.

"I'm tied up, Penny! Why am I tied up?" I yell as Penny's eyes meet mine and they soften with pity.

"You're not tied up," Penny says softly. "You're handcuffed."

"I'm what? Where did you get—"

"What are you doing? Don't stare at her like she's an animal at the zoo." Another voice, this one mean, cuts in.

It's hard to see clearly into the window from the angle at which my body is tilted, but I can make out a taller figure standing behind Penny, pulling her away from the window. "Come on, we have to get that concoction ready." It's Paula, that witch.

"Are you really going to do this?" Penny asks as they both disappear from sight. I crane my neck to see where they have gone to no avail. Yet, I can still hear them talking. Penny must have turned on the microphone or I wouldn't have been able to hear her through the glass otherwise, since this is a sound-proof room.

"We have to. She knows too much. Besides, this was our original plan, Elaina."

Elaina? Who's Elaina?

A loud sigh is followed by, "This wasn't the original plan, Paula. The original plan didn't have Amy confessing to murder before killing herself."

Wait, what? Killing myself?

"No, but this is even better. She's already the most suspicious person. When they find her dead in the studio after recording a confession, it'll be an open and shut case. The podcast will be a smashing success, and no one will be the wiser. They will have no idea who really killed Libby." There's a pause before she adds, "Isn't that what you wanted, Elaina? To get rid of Libby and get away with it?"

"No! That's what you wanted! You're the one with the grand plan of revenge against Libby! You're the one who wanted her dead!"

There's another moment of silence and then Paula

says, "For you. I wanted her dead for you. I wanted her dead because she ruined your life." A loud sniffle. "And this is the thanks I get?"

"No, that's not…come on, I'll…"

I hear shuffling, like someone bumping against a chair, the sound of its feet scraping against a linoleum floor. Cringing, I strain my ears to hear more, but their voices are getting farther and farther away until I can't hear them at all.

Oh my God. They're going to somehow get me to confess to killing Libby and then kill me! I'm going to die and people are going to think I'm a murderer and that I've killed myself! There cannot possibly be a worse outcome to this situation!

My chest starts to constrict and before I know it, I'm hyperventilating. Which does not help the situation at all.

Okay Amy, you need to focus. Close your eyes.

Now, imagine a meadow. A green, lush meadow with long blades of grass. Imagine you're lying in the meadow on your back. No, don't worry about the grass stains, just relax. You see the white fluffy clouds overhead? Look at those clouds and inhale and exhale slowly. Watch the clouds pass overhead. As they drift by, you will feel yourself getting calmer and calmer with each passing cloud.

Repeat until calm. Repeat until calm. Repeat until calm! Why aren't you calm? This is supposed to make your heart rate slow. Supposed to ease your stress. Stop your spiraling panic. Why the hell isn't it working?

Stop.

You can do this. You've done this more times than any normal person should ever have to. You've gotten out of more jams than a traffic helicopter. Which is exactly why you're in this situation to begin with. It's your uncanny knack for getting in and out of snafus that's led you down this path—trapped in the basement of the library. I mean, the library, Amy! There's no place more benign on earth, and somehow, you've managed to make this the place you'll meet your maker! How do you do it?

No.

I refuse to believe this is the end. There is some way out of this, and I will find it. *But um, God, I could use a little help here. Could you maybe show me the way? And I don't mean* to *you. I definitely don't want to see you in person right now, no offense. I need a way out of this mess.*

I will, in fact, vow to become a nun and join a convent if I get out of this one. Seriously, God...I will not let myself get sucked into murder and mayhem ever again. I will be the best damn nun you've ever seen, God.

Oh wait. I don't think nuns can curse. Not that damn is really a curse per se, but I doubt it's something they're supposed to be saying. Wait...do they have to take a vow of silence? I don't think I can take a vow of silence. In fact, I know I can't take a vow of silence.

No, wait. I'm wrong.

It's monks who take a vow of silence. I'd be okay talking as a nun. But they probably don't want me. I mean, why would they? I'll probably bring a plague of locusts upon their parish or something with the luck I have. Is it a parish? Is that what you call a church that nuns work at? I probably should have this information figured out before I apply to the nunnery.

Although, I couldn't apply until all the kids are grown. There's no way Roger can get those demon seeds out of the house in the morning without having a stroke. Ugh. I don't think I can become a nun. *Sorry, God. I'll have to make another deal with you.*

Ooo! How about I give up technology? Specifically, listening to podcasts? That would have been a good thing to give up say, a month ago. If I hadn't become a podcast-listening junky, I would not be in this predicament. Although, one hardly knows where one's decisions will ultimately lead them. Life is just a series of decisions. We can't foresee where we will end up because of those choices. Some regrets are inevitable. It's just a fact of life. We often don't realize we've made the wrong decision until it's too late.

Like the choice to go to my high school reunion. If I could just go back to that day in February when I decided to go, I wouldn't be here right now. I know that *for sure.*

I hear muffled voices and my heart rate kicks up again. They're coming back and they're going to put their diabolical plan in place. My eyes flick around the windowless recording studio. No windows, only one door. No way out.

Or is there a different way out? I need to think outside the box here.

My eyes drift to the recording equipment in front of me and my mind flashes back to the day that Penny (or should I call her Elaina?) taught me to use it. The button to record is right in front of me, and I can press it with my nose, recording whatever Paula and "Penny" say to me when they come back in to kill me.

Maybe the police will find it when they investigate, but Paula might find the recording and get rid of it. And even if the police do find the recording, I'm still dead. That doesn't help me get out of the situation.

What does help me get out of the situation is the big green button on the far-left side of the control panel, the one that I can just about reach with my elbow if I stretch my arm to the point that I feel like it may pop out of my socket. The one that will record live if I press it.

"Help!" I call out after I nudge the button, watching it light up green. "I'm trapped in the basement recording studio in the…"

My pleas are interrupted by the studio door opening with such a loud bang that I try to duck under the desk because I think it's gunfire. Which of course I can't do with the handcuffs around my wrists, and I cry out in pain as I twist my arm.

"What are you doing?" Paula asks as she stalks toward me, red-faced, nostrils flaring like a bull's, blonde hair escaping her ponytail and flying all around her like a halo.

"You can't keep me here, chained to the desk of the recording studio in the basement of the Fairfield Ave. Library," I tell her while resisting the urge to glance at the button to assure it is still lit up and broadcasting our words out over the air to the world. I don't know what station it plays on, if it even plays on a station at all, but I've got to hope that someone is listening. Even if it is three-thirty in the morning. Hey, we're close enough to New York, the city that never sleeps, that I can dream, can't I? After all, it's my only hope.

"Oh we won't be keeping you here for long," Paula says, adding a maniacal laugh. I shudder. She reminds me of every Disney villain ever created. "You'll only be here long enough to confess to killing Libby Farrington, which we will record…" she sweeps her hand toward the equipment and I hold my breath, praying she doesn't see the On-air button lit up, "…and then you will be on your way to meet your maker. You see, you'll be so distraught about killing your former best friend that you won't feel like you can go on." She holds up a coffee mug. "So you'll sit right here and end it all."

Even though I had heard part of the plan and assumed it would go something like this, I can't help but gasp. This is hardcore diabolical. I glance at Penny-not-Penny. I haven't known her long, but this doesn't seem like something she would do or go along with at all. She looks miserable, but that could be an act. She might be really amazing at acting. After all, I thought her name was Penny. She had me fooled about that at least.

"I'm not going to confess to something I didn't do," I say with a confident scoff that sounds much more confident than I actually feel. I jerk my head toward the mug. "And I'm sure not going to drink any concoction that you brewed up for me."

Paula laughs that spine-tingling laugh again. "I

didn't think you would. That's why this is so helpful." She reaches her other hand into the pocket of her hoodie and pulls out a shiny gun.

I can't help but gasp and recoil. A gun was not factored into my original equation. Then again, no part of this was ever in my original equation. Damn Jeter for waking me up tonight. I'd still be asleep in my bed if it were not for him, and I certainly wouldn't be handcuffed to a desk in the basement of the library contemplating how to outwit my would-be murderers. You don't ever think a golden retriever is going to inadvertently kill you, but here we are.

"Paula! You didn't say anything about a gun!" Penny-not-Penny gasps.

Paula rolls her eyes and turns to her sister. "Really? How did you think we would subdue her and get her to do what we wanted? With our wily charms?"

"What we wanted?" Penny-not-Penny's voice rises an octave. "What *we* wanted? No, more like what *you* wanted. I didn't want to have anything to do with this whole plan."

Paula's mouth sets into a hard line. "And here we go with the ingratitude again."

"I don't understand why you think I should be grateful that you killed Libby! I didn't ever ask you to kill Libby!" Penny-not-Penny wails.

"You went along with the plan, Elaina!"

"I didn't know you were going to kill her! I thought it would just scare her a bit," Penny-not…maybe I should just call her Elaina?...whimpered.

Paula rolls her eyes again and tilts her head back before laughing. "Really? You expect me to believe that? What did you think was going to happen when you poisoned Libby's wine then? Did you think it would just scare her?"

"No, I did…you said it would just make her sick. You didn't say it would kill her!"

Paula laughs again. "Nice one, dear sister. You're naive, but you're not that naive. You knew it would kill her. You wanted her dead and you were content to pretend you didn't know you were going to be the one to kill her." Paula pauses and looks pensive. "Or maybe I'm wrong. Maybe you did know and that's why you spilled the wine. So that I would have to swoop in with Plan B."

I gasp again as I remember the night of the reunion, when Penny, well, Elaina brought us the wine and then ended up spilling it. Was the glass intended for Libby poisoned?

"I spilled it because the poisoned glass ended up in front of Amy," Elaina says, lifting a trembling hand toward me.

I recoil, recalling how I had the glass in my hand, bringing it to my lips. *How close I came to death! How scary!*

Until I remember that I'm pretty much hanging by a thread at the moment as well.

"How convenient," Paula scoffs. "You forced me to come up with plan B on the spot. You're lucky I can think quickly in stressful situations."

"You're the one who stabbed Libby in the neck with

a nail file?" I ask. Even though I had already put this together, I really wanted her to admit it out loud and on the air. You know, in case anyone was listening.

Paula stares at me for a second but then says, "Well yeah. Thank God there's always that basket of toiletries in bathrooms at those hoity-toity places like the winery. Free murder weapon that can't be traced back to me." She laughs, her shoulders shrugging at the same time.

Yeah, I doubt God is the person to thank for that. Probably was more like Suzy Sunshine.

"I was going to just use the heel of my pump, but that would have been messy…physically messy and logistically messy as well. The metal nail file was much easier and slid right into Libby's neck." She pauses for a moment as if contemplating her act. "I would definitely recommend it as a murder weapon. I mean, she didn't even get a chance to scream. Well, she opened her mouth to scream but no sound came out, so I guess I was lucky on that front. And minimal blood splatter on me as well. I was even able to get the stain out of my shirt." She shrugs again. "It really was my lucky day."

I shudder, thinking of how it was anything but Libby's lucky day and how callus Paula is being about the whole thing.

"Anyway," she continues, probably realizing that both Elaina and I look horrified. "It doesn't really matter how the deed got done. It's done and we have the perfect little scapegoat here to take the fall." She turns to Elaina. "See? I told you I would take care of it and tie up all the loose ends."

Elaina's face crumbles. "I didn't want you to kill anyone!"

Paula's expression turns stony. "I think you're lying to yourself there, dear sister. If you didn't want me to do anything about it, why did you tell me what Libby did to you?"

"It was over twenty years ago! I didn't—" Elaina starts to say, but her bottom lip is quivering so much that she can't even speak.

"What did Libby do to you exactly? Did she bully you in school or something?" I ask, turning to Elaina and wondering what sort of high school bullying could possibly merit murder twenty-five years later. Not that bullying is okay in any way, shape, or form, but there needs to be a statute of limitations on revenge killings for that sort of thing.

"School?" Paula doesn't even let Elaina speak, although, judging by the way her mouth is gaping open and closed like a fish, I'm not sure she could speak even if she wanted to. "Elaina didn't go to school with Libby!" She stares at me with disdain as if I'm some single-celled organism underneath a microscope. "You didn't figure that out yet?"

Crinkling my eyes, I try to think about this, but I'm starting to get really exhausted by this whole scenario, not to mention I have to pee and the handcuffs are starting to make my hands go numb. "But she was at the reunion. Our high school reunion."

Paula scoffs. "She was there pretending to be a classmate who basically fell off the face of the earth and has no social media presence. Way to pay attention to your classmates, Amy. I guess Penny Whitaker was so insignificant that no one even noticed that this Penny," she mimics air quotes with her fingers, "wasn't even someone you went to school with."

Ugh, I knew it!

I make a mental note to get in touch with the real Penny and apologize. That is, if I get out of this mess. God can consider it a penance of sorts.

"I'm sorry," I say, facing Elaina as I say it.

"Don't be," Paula says with a wave of her hand, obviously misinterpreting my apology as aimed toward her. "You made it a heck of a lot easier to get the rest of your classmates to buy the story."

"What are you talking about?" I ask with a wrinkled brow.

"Simple," Paula says, her lips curling into a smile that makes me want to peel my skin off. "You were so easily convinced that Elaina was Penny by her gushing over your stupid blog, so when she attached herself to you at the reunion, it made it a cakewalk to get others to believe it too. No one even questioned it. Although they should have. I guess they didn't realize how gullible you really are."

This last statement hits me right in the solar plexus and I'm not sure why. It's true, I'm gullible and I'm too trusting. The fact that "Penny" stroked my ego by complimenting me and my writing only added to my gullibility. I'm going to have to work on that in the future. If I get out of here, that is.

"You played right into our hands and made it super easy for Elaina to get close to Libby. Although, I have to say, that confession about what Libby did to you when you were in middle school was the unexpected icing on the cake. I mean, you were our intended fall guy from the beginning. It was so easy to stalk you on the blog. You put way too many personal details on there, by the way. Plus, you made it super easy when you came to the hospital for the sprained wrist…"

"How did you know about that?" I ask, remembering Penny, erm, Elaina mentioning my wrist at the reunion.

"Duh," Paula says with a roll of her eyes. "I work there." She shakes her head and continues. "Anyway, we set you up from day one. Remember meeting me in the grocery store?"

I nod numbly.

Paula grins and pulls a piece of paper from her hoodie, waving it in my face. "You made it really easy for me to copy your handwriting and write a confession slash suicide note."

I gasp but can't speak.

"But then Elaina got all soft on you, so I started looking for other people to blame, against my better judgement. Hell, we were going to frame Tanner since I witnessed Libby fighting with him outside of the winery—"

"Wait, Mr. Tanner was really there?" I stare at her. I missed Mr. Tanner for real?

Paula rolls her eyes. "I showed you the picture."

I shrug. "I thought maybe you were really good with

photoshop or something."

She releases a deep sigh not unlike the one I use when one of my kids have said something utterly ridiculous.

"Anyway…I initially sent an invite to Tanner just to complicate things and add an extra layer of drama, but then after witnessing the fight—I really didn't think Libby had carried a such a torch for Tanner after all these years—I was going to make Tanner the main suspect. We were even going to have him on the podcast and bring up the whole sordid affair with Libby, but then you came along and presented us with such a clear-cut motive and means…not to mention, method. There was no way I could ignore it. It was back on you."

She sets the mug down on the counter and pulls a shiny metal object out of her hoodie pocket—it's like a clown car in there. I gasp as I realize it's a nail file, just like the one that killed Libby.

Is she going to stab me in the neck right here? I would be a total sitting duck, handcuffed to the desk and all. I wouldn't even be able to fight her off.

Wait, no, that doesn't work. She can't make that look like a suicide. Plus, she has that mug full of something she wants me to drink that'll kill me. Okay, breathe, Amy. She's not going to stab you in the neck with a nail file.

But I still can't breathe because I understand what she intends to do with that nail file. She bends down and slips it into my purse that's pooled by my feet.

"There we go," Paula says in a self-congratulatory manner when she stands up, swaying a little from the rapid transition. "Now the police will also find a nail file similar to the one that killed Libby in your purse, solidifying your confession as the murderer."

"But I didn't kill Libby," I say with a slight whine to my voice. Yes, I know Paula is aware of this, considering she was Libby's actual killer, but I want to make sure my listening audience is one hundred percent certain of that fact as well. If I have any listening audience at all, that is.

I chew my lip and glance over at the clock on the wall. We've been on air for at least fifteen minutes now and there has not been any breaking down of the doors to the studio or swooping in of any police to save me. I'm starting to think that no one is listening, and I'm doomed.

Paula rolls her eyes. "For all intensive purposes, you did."

"Intents and purposes," I reply before I even think.

Oh crap.

It's probably not best practice to correct your would-be killer's grammatical errors. But I can't help it. That's one of my biggest bugaboos in life. People who say "I could care less" make my skin crawl.

Paula cocks her head. "What? What are you talking about?"

I'm in a quandary now. She didn't understand what I said.

Do I tell her that she used a completely made-up phrase and correct her again, or do I let it go and not get myself killed any sooner by pissing off the woman with a gun?

"It's all intents and purposes," Elaina mumbles,

speaking for the first time in forever. "Not all intensive purposes." She shakes her head. "You always say it wrong."

Paula turns away from me and narrows her eyes at her sister. "Well excuse me, Miss Goody-Two-Shoes librarian. You always know how to make me feel like shit about myself. Not all of us have been properly schooled in the art of who-gives-a-fuck-about-grammar." She purses her lips into a fine line, and I didn't know any better, I would think it was to prevent her from crying.

"I just—" Elaina starts, but Paula holds up a hand.

"I don't give a rat's ass," she says before scowling. "If I didn't mess up that phrase, dear sister?" She cocks her eyebrow and Elaina shrinks away. "I thought so. Anyway, it's time to get rid of one pest at least. Here's your drink. A lovely hot chocolate. You won't even taste the antifreeze. It'll go down like a charm." She glowers at Elaina. "Just like it was supposed to for Libby but someone messed up that plan." Elaina shrinks further into the wall as Paula picks up the mug and shoves it toward me, her eyes gleaming…or wait, maybe that's just the gun. Boy, it's a shiny thing. I don't think I've ever seen such a shiny gun.

Snap out of it, Amy! You can't be distracted by shiny objects right now! Paula is going to try to get you to confess to a murder you didn't commit before killing you and making it look like a suicide. Think, woman, think!

Paula steps closer and I feel like I'm in some movie. *Okay, Amy. Calm. Remember what the therapist told you? Things you can feel, see, smell, hear, and taste.*

Ground yourself now because you have to get out of this mess.

I can feel Paula's energy radiating off her, smell her breath on the side of my face—I think she had garlic at some point in the day—I see the beginnings of a mustache on her upper lip. *No, stop!* I do not think this is what the therapist meant. This is not grounding me. This is making me panic even more.

"But wait!" I call out, causing her to retreat sharply and spill a bit of the drink on her hand. *Don't murderers always want to talk about their misdeeds to the person they intend on killing next? Cleanse their soul or whatever?* "You still didn't tell me why you wanted to kill Libby in the first place."

Paula frowns and gazes at me for a moment before glancing at the cup in her hand. "I didn't *wan*t to kill her, Amy. I *had* to kill her," she says with an air of superiority. "If my sister wasn't such a coward, she would have taken care of it herself. But then again, I've been cleaning up her messes since she was a toddler."

She turns her head and glowers accusingly at her sister. Elaina, who up until this point, has cowered from her, suddenly stands up tall and stares right back at her eyes flashing with...what is that? Fury? She's clenching her fists at her sides and her nostrils flare.

I watch their silent exchange with curiosity until I remember what curiosity did to the cat. This cat needs to get to the bottom of this mystery and buy herself some time in the process.

"Why did you *need* to kill Libby?" I ask, distracting

Paula from her staring contest with her sister. Paula's attention returns to me, the gun shaking slightly in her hand. Was she unnerved by Elaina's resistance?

"Libby was a blight on humanity and she had no consequences for her actions," Paula says.

I cock my head to the side. "If you guys didn't go to high school with her, how did you know her? And how do you know she needed consequences for her actions?"

Paula laughs the laugh of someone who thinks something is definitely not funny and turns back to Elaina. My heart soars when I see the gun lower to her side. God, if I weren't chained to this desk, I might have a chance at grabbing that gun and subduing her.

"You want to clue her in, dear sister?" Paula asks with a wave of the gun.

Elaina purses her lips, shaking her head vehemently. "No. This was all your idea. You should tell her why you did it."

Paula's nostrils are the ones that flare now. "You are such an ingrate. You never appreciate what I do for you."

Elaina remains silent, crossing her arms over her chest.

Paula shakes her head with disgust and returns her full attention to me, gun and all. *Rats.*

"Libby was in a car accident several years ago, when she was home for Thanksgiving break during college," Paula tells me. "A very bad one. She was drunk one night and driving home from a party, and she hit another car head on. The driver of the other car had to be cut out of the car and medevac'd to the nearest hospital. The other driver was burnt all over and had broken their pelvis and both legs."

"Oh, I had no idea," I tell her after I realize she is staring at me expectantly.

Paula nods. "No, you didn't. Libby's father was a bigwig in the political sphere at the time and paid a lot of money to the right people to keep it hush hush. In fact, it was kept so hush hush that Libby never even received punishment for her drunk driving. Hell, she never even paid a fine for it. Not even a slap on the wrist. It was like it didn't even happen." She shakes her head again.

"Okay, I mean that's terrible but what does that have to do with you?" I squint at her. "And if it was kept quiet, how do you know about it?"

"Because the driver of the other car was me."

Elaina steps toward us, hands visibly shaking as she pushes up the sleeves of her sweater. The puckered skin all up and down both arms tells a terrible story of pain.

"It took me over six months and countless skin grafts before I was even able to leave the hospital," Elaina told me. "I had two years of PT before I could even walk without a walker."

"Don't forget the loss of your career," Paula interjected. "Elaina was a backup dancer for a pop star, but couldn't dance after the accident and lost her job. Libby robbed her of her career and livelihood. Hell, she robbed her of her dignity as well. She couldn't walk or use her arms or even feed herself for a while, so when she finally got out of the hospital, she had to move back in with our mother."

Elaina turns bright red and starts to shrink away again as Paula continues to catalogue the indignities that Elaina endured, finishing up with her mother's death and Paula's subsequent conclusion that the stress of caring for her daughter had sent her to an early grave. Elaina looks like she wants the earth to open up and swallow her whole.

"I'm so sorry," I start to say, but Paula cuts me off.

"Why? Why are you sorry? You didn't do it. And maybe Elaina is tired of people feeling sorry for her."

"I don't—" Elaina is interrupted by Paula holding up her hand.

"Just stop, Elaina. Libby paid for her mistake and unfortunately, Amy got involved so she's going to have to pay for her mistake as well." Her arm reaches out and snakes around my body, her hand groping for one of the buttons on the panel.

And that's when she sees it. Her eyes widen as she takes in the On-Air button and then her head springs toward mine, our eyes meeting, hers enormous, and dare I say, frightened, mine briefly triumphant. I say briefly, because my triumph over outsmarting her at her own game only lasts for a minute.

"You!" she growls, slamming the mug down, hot chocolate sloshing everywhere. "You shouldn't have done that!" She points to the button.

"What happened?" Elaina asks, stepping forward. But I don't hear anything else. Or smell or taste anything else for that matter. But I do feel Paula's balled up fist hitting the side of my face and I see the world going blurry. Again.

CHAPTER TWENTY-SIX

"Well, I told her to stay out of this business."

Is that Jason? It sounds like Jason. Why is Jason here?

"I know you did, Jason. We all did. It's like Amy can't listen to reason."

Wait, is that Roger? Why is Roger here too? Where am I? Why can't I move? Why is it so dark in here? What's that beeping noise?

I hear a loud sigh, followed by, "I guess this is exactly why she's in this state right now. God, I hope she pulls through. I'd hate to have to raise four kids by myself. She wasn't good for cooking or cleaning really, but at least she did the grocery shopping."

I open my mouth to scream at Roger, but no sound comes out.

That's when I realize...I'm dreaming.

Wake up, Amy! Your life depends on it!

**

"What are you going to do now?" I hear someone ask in a quivery voice.

Is that Elaina? Where am I?

I try to open my eyes but they're so heavy.

God, I could really use a nap right now. I wonder if they would mind if I took a nap right now before they...what am I doing here? Oh yeah, that's right. They're going to kill me. I definitely shouldn't take a nap or I'll be taking a very long nap. Open your eyes, Amy! Wake up!

My eyes snap open and I see Paula looming over me, ire leaching from her eye sockets.

"I'm going to get her to confess. Just like we planned. Of course, she's made things a bit complicated here by thinking she's sly and pressing the On-air button, but the joke's on her because no one heard that. It's four in the morning and it was only broadcast to a small college radio station."

Her eyes crinkle around the edges and she looks a lot like the Grinch. My heart thuds unnecessarily loudly in my chest. So my brilliant plan was obviously foiled.

"To record a podcast and drop it live, you have to press *this* button." She sweeps her hand toward a button well out of my reach with the handcuffs. "That On air button has nothing to do with the podcast audience."

The bile rises in my throat as she presses another few buttons, stands up, and pulls out the gun. She shoves a piece of paper in my face. "Now, I've taken the liberty of writing out a confession for you, so if you just read out what I've written here on this—"

And that's when I hear it. The sound of footsteps. And not quiet, haunted house, one footstep at a time kind of footsteps either. Loud thunderous steps, coming closer.

I cock my head to the side to gauge where the sound

is coming from. Paula hears it too and her head whips around toward the door.

"Lock the door!" she shouts to Elaina, but Elaina is frozen where she stands, eyes wide and frightened. "Elaina! Do it now!" Paula orders, holding the gun toward me, her hand visibly shaking. When Elaina still refuses to move, Paula rushes toward the door—she's three steps in front of it when it comes crashing open, knocking her to the side.

Paula screams. Elaina screams. I open my mouth to scream, but when I see who is standing in the open doorway brandishing their own gun, I start to cry instead. Tears of happiness, that is. I've never been so happy to see anyone in all my life.

"Jason!" I call out as he sweeps the room with his eyes and his weapon.

"Jesus, Amy, thank God," he says before stepping toward me. The police swarm the already small room and haul Paula to her feet and attempt to subdue an already subdued Elaina. "What the hell were you thinking?" He shakes his head as he examines me. "Where are the keys to these handcuffs?"

I jerk my head at Paula who is resisting arrest while shouting, "I'm innocent! I've been framed!" like some deranged villain in a cartoon movie. Without another word, Jason steps over to the deranged villain and demands the keys. She starts to protest and then looks at him with his charming smile and dimples and…well, she says, "In my hoodie pocket."

Jason fishes them out and returns to free me. I gasp

with relief when I can move my hands again, rubbing my left wrist with my right hand. "How did you find me?" I ask him in amazement when I switch hands. "How did you know I was here?"

He stares at me for a second, mouth twisted in a smirk before asking, "Didn't you broadcast this live on purpose? So that someone would hear you and come find you?"

I'm momentarily stunned. "I did, but Paula said that no one would hear it because it was the middle of the night and it only broadcasts to a small college station."

Jason rolls his eyes. "Do you think college students care if it's the middle of the night?"

I consider this for a moment. "I guess not. I can't really remember my college days that well."

"Exactly, because you didn't get enough sleep," Jason says, pointing a finger.

"I want a lawyer!" Paula shouts as they lead her away. "And my one phone call!"

Jason and I pause for a moment to stare after her and Elaina being led away and out the door, up the hall and into the elevator. And then there is silence, and Jason looks back at me.

"But still, you're not up all night listening to the radio, Jason. You were asleep when I left. How did you know where I was?"

"I may not be up all night listening to a college radio station, but college students are. And one of them happened to hear what was going on and also happens to know who you are because she went to high school with another college student you might know." His eyes twinkle. "Does the name Allie Maxwell ring a bell?"

I gasp. Allie! Of course! Allie is at college and so are most of her friends! And they would be up all night like good college students are. Maybe not listening to some small time radio station—don't they prefer Spotify and Apple Music?—but up nonetheless. Someone was listening to that station! Someone heard my cry for help.

"So this girl heard the broadcast and knew who you were because of course she did. You're infamous around here."

I ignore his dig and he continues. "She called Allie to tell her what was happening and Allie called me. Well, she called you first but you didn't answer—"

"You have my phone," I point out. "Exactly why I couldn't call for help when this situation went bad."

"A situation you shouldn't have been in to begin with," Jason says with a scowl. "But anyway," he goes on, running his hand through his hair (seriously, it's definitely getting thinner...maybe he should try one of those men's hair clubs), "she then tried Roger, but he didn't answer either—"

"Shocker. He sleeps like the dead."

"So, long story short, I notified the police as I high tailed it down here to save you." He frowns. "Again."

I cringe before wrapping my arms around him and hugging him as tightly as I can. He groans with annoyance? Pleasure? I can't tell.

"Jason Collins, you're my hero."

EPILOGUE

"Are you guys ready?" Julia's disembodied voice fills the studio.

My eyes skim over my notes as I grab my headphones, slipping them over my head in a fluid motion. If I'm not ready by now, I'll never be. I nod at Julia through the glass partition. "I'm ready. Lex?"

Lexie looks up from her notes and gives Julia a thumbs up.

"Alright then. I'll count it down from ten and when we reach three, I will just use my fingers. When I point to you, then you'll be recording. Okay?"

Again, I nod and take a deep breath, making sure to fill my lungs with as much air as I possibly can. *Don't let your nerves take over, Amy.*

When I walked into the studio this morning with Lexie to record the very first episode of our true crime podcast, surprisingly, I wasn't nervous. Lexie and I had gone over our script ad nauseum over the past week, and we were certain we were comfortable enough to try our hand at recording it today, the only day Julia, our sound editor, was free this week.

Lexie and Roger and pretty much everyone I know were nervous that I'd be uncomfortable recording in the studio at the library where I was held captive by Paula and Elaina, those two fruitcakes, and urged me to find a different location to record. They were afraid it would cause some sort of PTSD or a nervous breakdown, but honestly, it didn't trigger any bad memories. In fact, I was proud of myself for figuring out how to escape without the help of anyone else (okay…how to call for help to escape).

But now that it's come time to record, I'm feeling a totally different kind of nervous. Not necessarily about recording. I've decided that podcast recording is the most pain-free way to reach an audience…well, besides blogging that is. And I know that we can rerecord if we mess up or we don't like the way we sound. We are free to completely hide our insecurities behind this microphone and no one will be the wiser. And we have Julia to clean up any messes that we do manage to make. Apparently, I say "um" a lot. Who knew?

No, what I'm worried about is how people will take this podcast. And by take it, I mean, I hope they don't come after us…well, specifically me…with pitchforks. I mean, it's happened before, right?

After my daring rescue from the recording studio and the subsequent revelation that Paula and Elaina—mostly Paula—were behind Libby's murder, not only for revenge but to boost their podcast ratings and that I was completely innocent, well, let's just say, people owed me a lot of apologies. Not that I got many, but still, there was a contriteness in the air that I could taste when I walked into a room. Suddenly people were fascinated with my tale of woe and couldn't get enough of me. The spicy romance chapters of my book that had been leaked were also almost forgotten. *Almost.*

A woman named Fannie Franks (I kid you not), an agent for a small press that specializes in spicy romance, reached out to me and explained she had read the pages that had been leaked because a friend sent them to her and thought they had potential. The woman who sent her the pages? None other than Isabella. She emailed that night to let me know Fannie was a friend of hers, and that she had had been so impressed by my work she had asked Fannie to take a look at it.

Needless to say, I was flattered (and incredibly mortified), but after careful consideration (and quite a few visits to my therapist), I thanked Fannie and Isabella and explained that I decided writing in that genre was not for me, even if it had the potential to be quite lucrative. I have nothing against it, but the whole time I was writing I felt uncomfortable, and I'm think feeling uncomfortable in your career is a giant no-no for success.

Instead, Lexie and I decided that podcasting was something fun we could both do together, a second chance to reinvent my career. That is, after we completed the last book in the Lexie Maxwell, Girl Detective series. It's being released right before Thanksgiving, just in time for Christmas. The box set makes a great gift for kids. Wink, wink.

Even though Lexie will be going away to college in a few weeks, she'll be home for breaks, and we can record then. It'll be a great bonding experience for us, and when Lexie graduates, she can put the experience on her resume. Since she's planning on going into forensics psychology after she graduates, it's perfect.

The only thing I'm worried about, the thing that is making me nervous today as we get ready to record our first episode, is the specific subject we chose for our true crime podcast. It's a bit morbid.

It was Lexie's idea. She did a lot of research on the subject and was fascinated with the psychology of it.

I mean, at first, I was kind of insulted, like, did I somehow cause her keen interest in such a morbid subject?

Was I not nurturing enough? Did I not take enough interest in her school work? Did I not breastfeed long enough? Did she not feel safe with me?

Geez even when they're grown and flown you never stop worrying—not only about their health and safety and all that jazz, but whether it'll be your fault if they're permanently messed up.

Fortunately, my therapist assured me that this was all normal and not due to some character flaw on my part. That's when I decided we should go for it.

"Okay ladies," Julia says, "Ten, nine, eight, seven, six, five, four…" Julia holds up three fingers, then two and then she points at us.

I take another deep breath and begin.

"Hello and welcome to *Mommy Dearest*, a podcast about women who kill."

Other novels by Heather Balog:

Amy Maxwell & the Long 9 Months
The 8 Mistakes of Amy Maxwell
Amy Maxwell & the 7 Deadly Sins
Amy Maxwell's 6th Sense
Amy Maxwell's 5th Child
The 4 Dilemmas of Amy Maxwell
Amy Maxwell & the 3 Day Weekend
The Quiet Boy
The Dead of Summer
Friends From the Edge
In the Teachers' Lounge
All She Ever Wanted
Letters to My Sister's Shrink
Note to Self: Change the Locks
When the Bough Breaks
Lexie Maxwell & One Spooky House
Lexie Maxwell & the Two New Kids
Best Friends & Other Liars

Sign up for my newsletter at:

https://mailchi.mp/612a3e09b927/amy-maxwell-free

Or visit my website HeatherBalog.com

www.badmommyreads.com

Follow me on Facebook (Heather Balog Author)
On TikTok (badmommybooks)
Or Instagram (the_bad_mommy_books)

www.ingramcontent.com/pod-product-compliance
Lightning Source LLC
Chambersburg PA
CBHW060400260626
47160CB00006B/2382

* 9 7 9 8 9 8 9 9 3 8 2 0 9 *